Alison Littlewood is a writer of dark fantasy and horror fiction. Her short stories have appeared in numerous magazines, including *Black Static*, *Crimewave* and *Not One Of Us*, as well as the British Fantasy Society's *Dark Horizons* and the charity anthology *Never Again*. *A Cold Season* is her first novel. She lives near Wakefield, in West Yorkshire, with her partner Fergus.

Visit her at
www.alisonlittlewood.co.uk

A
COLD
SEASON

How far will one mother go to save her child?

ALISON LITTLEWOOD

Jo Fletcher
BOOKS

First published in Great Britain in 2012 by

Jo Fletcher Books
an imprint of Quercus
55 Baker Street
7th Floor, South Block
London
W1U 8EW

A CIP catalogue record for this book is available
from the British Library

ISBN 978 1 78087 136 3

10 9 8 7 6 5 4 3 2

Typeset by Ellipsis Digital Limited, Glasgow

Printed and bound in Great Britain by
Clays Ltd, St Ives plc

For Mum and Dad
and for Fergus

ONE

The fog swallowed everything: moorland, colour, sound. Even Ben was silent in the passenger seat. The road was little more than a narrow track winding across what Cass thought of as God's own country, which she knew to be wide and rolling and open where it lay hidden behind the fog.

Cass caught a glimpse of heather and bracken, everything sapped and rendered colourless. Ahead, the road dipped into a shallow bowl before winding upwards once more. She took her foot from the accelerator and allowed the car to slow.

'What's up?' Ben stirred, and she realised he had been asleep. 'Where are we?'

'Saddleworth Moor.' Cass braked to a halt and gestured down into the dip. 'Isn't it weird? You'd think the fog would gather here, but it's clear.' She turned to him. His face was closed, uninterested. 'You should take a look. You won't see much of the moor in this fog.'

He shrugged. *Don't care.*

Cass gripped the wheel once more and took her foot from the brake. As the car began to move, she slammed it down again.

Ben jerked forward and scowled. 'What's that for?'

Cass continued to stare down into the bowl.

Ben followed her gaze. 'There's nothing there.'

Her son was right, but Cass tightened her grip on the wheel anyway. 'Didn't you feel it?' She took her foot off the brake and the car rolled. 'It's going the wrong way.'

This time Ben saw. He straightened, looking back the way they had come.

Cass eased off the brake and the car rolled further, back. Up the slope. 'Damn,' she said, under her breath. She felt dizzy. 'It's a hill.'

'What are you on about?'

'I've heard about this. It's – I don't know, Ben – some kind of optical illusion. It looks like a dip but it's really a hill. We're on an upward slope, not downward.'

Ben's face lit and Cass felt a surge of something. Hope? Joy? She wasn't sure.

'Wow,' he said.

She reached out and rubbed his knee. 'Feel. I'll let it roll.'

'Go on, Mum.'

Cass grinned, easing off again. The car started to roll back, slowly at first, then picking up speed. A sound blared into the silence, cutting through the air and dopplering away as a dark shape shot past them. Headlights made everything brilliant; then it was gone. Cass stamped on the brake once more.

'Mu-*um*,' Ben complained. His face was closed again,

the way it had been when they started this journey. The way he had been since Cass had told him his father wasn't coming back.

'Sorry.' Cass checked the mirror, seeing only a solid grey wall. She eased down on the accelerator, going forward this time. Despite this, the car slowed again. Cass accelerated harder but the car stopped anyway and she let out her breath.

'Mum, stop messing about.'

The car rocked on its wheels and rolled back. Cass braked heavily, leaning forward, gripping the wheel and staring out at the road. It felt as though something was pushing them, but there was nothing: only that dip, a round, natural bowl as though a giant football had landed in soft earth.

She accelerated until the engine roared and suddenly the car was free and shot forward.

Ben made an exasperated sound and crossed his arms, turning to stare out of the window.

'Sorry,' Cass said. 'I don't know what that was.'

'You're doing it.'

'No – it must have been the wind or something.' Cass' heart raced. Her hands felt slippery on the wheel. It hadn't felt like the wind.

Her son remained silent.

The car navigated the dip – the *rise*, Cass reminded herself – and the fog closed in once more, swallowing sound, swallowing the road save for a grey strip in front of the car and the tufts of grass that marked the edge.

*   *   *

Cass tried to decide whether they were going uphill or down, but it took all her concentration to follow the curves of the road. The white wall of fog drew back as the car approached, permitting them a narrow space into which they could see, and closed again behind them. It deadened everything. Cass listened for the steady hum of the car, but it only seemed to be there when she tried to hear it. The fog was a visible silence.

She hadn't seen another car in a long time.

Ben wriggled in his seat. 'Are we still on the moor? I don't like it.'

'Yes,' Cass replied, and wondered how she knew that was true. 'It can't be much longer.'

She kept her eyes on the road. It was like floating. It reminded her of one of Ben's video games: she was driving a racing car and the road was nothing but two short lines in front of the stub of a bonnet. It had been impossible to stay between them.

'What's that?' asked Ben. He wriggled in his seat and turned to the window. Cass glanced over to see his breath spreading on the pane, fog coming out of his body and into the car.

'Don't,' she said, and then thought, *Why not?*

Ben raised a hand and spread it on the glass. Each finger left a dark smudge in the mist. He pressed his face to the window.

'What is it? Ben?'

'I thought . . . Nothing,' he said, slumping back into the seat. 'It's nothing.'

Cass turned back to the road. The fog retreated as the

car went onwards, headlights shining on its white wall, making it look solid. She was still shuffling in her seat as it seemed to dissolve, showing its true nature after all – nothing but droplets of water suspended in the air, a shifting translucent thing. The centre of it curled in on itself, revealing something dark in its heart.

Cass saw a figure standing in the road, its arms held out. There were no features, only shadow.

In that instant Cass remembered the murders that had happened thirty, forty years before. There were murdered children buried on these moors. Had they all been found? She couldn't remember. She also had no time to think. Even while the idea of lost children formed in her mind she slammed on the brakes and hauled on the wheel. The car slewed and rocked, and then the wheels gripped and she jolted to a stop. Ben jerked forward, was caught by his seatbelt and thrown back into his seat. He didn't complain this time.

Cass and Ben stared at each other. His face was white. Cass imagined her own was too.

She glanced in the rear-view mirror. The fog was lurid in her brake lights, pressing in close. If another car came along . . . She looked out to the side. It was impossible to tell how far across the road she'd finished up.

A rattle made her catch her breath. Ben cried out and Cass turned to see a face peering in at his window. Ben leaned away from it, his small arm pressing against Cass' body. She reached out and drew him in.

A tap on the glass. There was a flash of a hand curled up: not a fist, but the casual shape someone might make when knocking on a door, the knuckle of the index finger protruding. *Tap tap tap*. There was a large ring on the middle finger, something with leaves and flowers in brightly coloured stones.

Tap tap tap.

'Ben,' said Cass, 'wind the window down.' He pressed up against her and she remembered she could control the passenger window from her side. She put one arm more firmly around her son and felt for the button with the other. There was a loud *whirr* and tendrils of fog snaked in, bringing cold, damp air.

'Thank goodness,' a voice said. 'Thank you so much for stopping.' The figure bent and the face resolved into a woman's, her dark curls frizzed by the moist air. 'I'm Sally,' she said. 'Are you going to Darnshaw?'

'We'd better get moving,' Sally said. 'You don't want somebody running into the back of you. It's a bad place to stop.'

Cass prevented herself from shooting a hard glance at the woman. Sally was in the passenger seat. Cass had kissed the top of Ben's head and got him to jump into the back, where he was crammed in amid a pile of luggage. Now the woman's dark oilskin coat filled the space. When she'd climbed in, Cass saw she was wearing boots with fur around the top. One of them looked soaked, as though she had stepped into a bog. There was a smell too, which pervaded the car. Her hair was wet, and her face and voluminous coat were damp and shining.

'Sorry if I gave you a scare,' said Sally. 'I've broken down further back along the road.'

'Oh,' said Cass. 'I didn't see a car.'

'It's pulled into a lay-by.'

Cass hadn't seen a lay-by either, but she didn't say so. She could have passed within inches of the woman's car and not seen it. The lay-by could merely have been a break in the tufts of grass edging the road, maybe not even that.

'There's no mobile phone signal up here – I'm lucky you came along. It's a long walk home.' Sally laughed. 'Sharp left bend coming up.' She went on in this way, punctuating her conversation with directions, and Cass picked up speed. Was it so obvious she didn't know the road?

'You're into the S-bends soon,' Sally said. 'We'll be dropping down towards the village.' She twisted around. 'I've a son about your age,' she said to Ben.

He didn't reply. After a moment Cass said, 'Does he go to the Grange School?'

Sally smiled. 'You're the lady who's taken a place in Foxdene Mill, aren't you?'

'That's right.' *Small world.* Word had spread already.

'Yes, Damon goes to the Grange. All the kids in Darnshaw go there. It gets good results.'

'I heard. It's one of the reasons I came back.'

'Back?'

'I lived here for a while, when I was a child.'

'How lovely.'

'What's Mrs Cambrey like?'

'Sorry?'

'Mrs Cambrey. The head. She sounded really nice on the phone.'

'She is – yes, she is lovely.' There was something in Sally's voice.

Cass glanced at her. 'I have a meeting with her on Monday.'

'Of course.' Sally's voice brightened. 'Well, I'm sure she'll be delighted to see you both. I am. It's very quiet in Darnshaw. It's time we had some new blood.'

They fell silent as Cass negotiated the bends. The road had indeed begun to snake down, edged by a steep bank on one side and a high stone wall on the other. Anything else was lost in the fog – but then the car popped out of it and the view spread around them. It was like emerging from a doorway. Cass glanced in the rear-view mirror and saw the fog as a solid line across the road. Ben twisted in his seat to look at it.

'That's strange,' said Cass. 'It's stopped, just like that.'

Sally didn't look around. 'It happens like that sometimes. It gathers on the tops. When you drop down a bit it's as clear as day. Look!' She pointed. A pheasant stood on the wall. Beyond it was orange bracken, darkened by recent rain, and a few pines growing at a sharp angle. From the corner of her eye Cass thought she saw pale light flashing on water, but it was too late; it had already gone.

Cass remembered something. 'Sally,' she said, 'you know the road further back – it looks like it dips down, like a big bowl.'

Her passenger was silent.

'We stopped there. It looked like we were going down-hill, only we weren't. We were going uphill all the time. Do you know the place?'

Sally frowned. 'Can't say I do. I never heard of anything like that around here. It must have been the fog. It makes everything look different sometimes.'

'But it really looked like a dip – only, we rolled—'

'It's just the fog,' said Sally. 'I'd know if there was something like that. I know this road pretty well.'

It was Cass' turn to fall silent.

'Here we are,' said Sally. 'Welcome to Darnshaw.'

The first houses came into view, a row of terraces built of stone, blackened by passing traffic or smoke. Cass rounded the corner and found herself on a lane that followed the line of the valley. There were turn-offs to each side, where more houses nestled. She saw a general store, a small post office, a butcher, a greengrocer and a florist. To each side, steep hills rose to an opaque grey sky.

'You've gone past,' said Sally. 'That was your lane. Still, if you don't mind carrying on a bit, you could drop me at home.'

Cass nodded. She tried to glance down side roads as Sally pointed out a small park and the school. She told them where various walks began, mostly following the river. Then she indicated the road where she lived: Willowbank Crescent. It was ordinary-looking, the houses built from brick rather than the local stone. Sally gestured towards a small semi and Cass realised the woman was shivering.

'I suppose you won't want to come in,' Sally said, reaching for the door handle. 'You'll want to settle in and all that? Well, thanks again.' She smiled, got out and pushed the door shut behind her.

Cass turned round in a driveway and headed back down

the road. As she passed the house, she saw that Sally was still watching. Cass waved and turned onto the main road, only then realising she hadn't given Ben a chance to jump back into the front seat.

'We'll be there soon,' she said over her shoulder.

There was no answer. Cass slowed and turned, saw her son frowning.

'I don't like it,' he said. 'The lady smelled.'

'Ben, that's rude.'

'She smelled bad and I hate it here.'

'You need to give it a chance. I loved it when I was your age.' Even as she said the words, Cass found herself wondering if that was true. And yet when she had heard the name Darnshaw again, she had pictured Ben here, running about the hills and laughing. Enjoying an idyllic childhood, everything she wanted to give him.

'She smelled like a butcher's shop.'

'Oh, Ben.' She didn't know what to say. And there *had* been a smell, hadn't there? A musky smell, a little like wet wool. Something else, underneath the earthy moorland – a richer tang, more animal.

Like a butcher's shop.

Cass grinned at her over-active imagination. 'Let's go and see the new place, shall we?'

The mill glowed amid wintry skeletal woodland. From the top of the lane Cass could see a grey slate roof amid the reaching fingers of mature oaks. It would be beautiful in summer. Even now, early in the new year, the stone, sandblasted clean, was mellow and warm-looking.

The photographs hadn't done it justice. She grinned. 'What do you think?'

Ben shrugged.

The lane led steeply down to a wide gravelled area that crunched under the car's tyres. It stretched away to either side of the mill, but their eyes were drawn to the front. A central doorway was painted in deep crimson, an etched glass panel proclaiming 'Foxdene Mill'.

Ben stirred at last. 'Will there be other kids?' He slipped his seatbelt off and leaned over to get a better look. The building was four storeys high.

'Of course there will,' said Cass. According to the brochure, the mill had been converted into twenty-one apartments: six on each of the lower floors, with views towards either the valley or the millpond, and three penthouses on the top. 'There are bound to be lots of kids. You'll have a great time.'

Their apartment was at the back of the building on the left side, so they would have views over both the millpond and the river. Cass had snapped it up as soon as she saw the brochure, though she had opted to rent, not buy. She needed to build a home for Ben quickly, get him settled into something new. Renting meant everything would be provided – beds, wardrobes, tables and chairs. She needed all of those things. They had been hers only while she stayed in Army accommodation, and she couldn't do that for ever, not without Pete.

When the brochure landed at her door and she saw that the mill lay in Darnshaw, it had felt like fate. She hadn't even waited for a viewing.

Cass parked by the door. As soon as she stepped out she heard the river, rushing and burbling down the valley. The air smelled green and fresh: woodland after rain. She stared up at the building, spotted the clock tower she had seen in the pictures. The clock had a white face, as she remembered, but no hands. Time was standing still in the valley – that was appropriate. She remembered herself as a little girl, leaning over the garden gate and listening to the river rushing by.

Ben got out and stood by her side. She ruffled his hair and he squirmed, but she didn't care. 'Do you smell that?' she asked.

He wrinkled his nose.

'Come on. Let's have a look at the place before we unload.'

'Where is everybody?'

Cass tapped the entry code into the panel by the door. It beeped and she grabbed the brass handle. 'I could get used to this,' she said. The door was double-width and panelled. Probably not original, but it looked grand enough.

The hall was wide and a little cold. To their left a stairway led up, carpeted in red. Mailboxes, each bearing a brass number, were set into the right-hand wall and ahead was a door which must lead towards the ground-floor apartments. The lobby was flagged, the rough-surfaced stones showing the wear of many years.

Cass felt like she already knew the way: up the stairs, through the fire-doors and into the hall. Ben hung back as they went, stomping his feet behind her.

The upstairs hall was as grand as the entrance had been, red-carpeted, wide and lined with white-painted doors. Cass went down without looking to left or right until she stopped in front of one of them. It looked like all the others they had passed but somehow she knew it was theirs. Sure enough, the brass number set into it was a 12.

A delightful apartment with stunning views to the millpond and down the valley, the picture of peace and solitude . . .

Cass pulled the key from her pocket. It had a cardboard tag with the number 12 scrawled on it in biro, along with a dirty fingerprint, a builder's fingerprint. The mill had been freshly converted. Everything would be new; they were to be the first occupants. Cass felt a shiver of excitement as she pushed open the door. When she turned to smile at Ben, though, there was no expression on his face at all. Cass beckoned him inside.

The apartment's hall was also lined with white doors, all of them closed except the one directly ahead. Cass went through and found herself in a wide lounge with windows set into two of its walls. She went to the nearest, realising as she approached how large it was. She would be able to sit on the sill quite comfortably, reading a book maybe, or simply taking in the view. She looked out.

The millpond was a line of acid-green between the trees. Between the mill and the water were piles of gravel and sand, with a yellow digger standing desolate among them.

'Where is everybody?' said Ben, and Cass realised it wasn't the first time he'd asked.

'It's a Saturday,' she said. 'They won't be working on a

Saturday. They must still be fitting out some of the apartments.'

'So where are all the people?'

Cass frowned and went to the other window. This one looked over a wide gravel parking area with an outhouse at one end. What looked like bags of cement were piled against its wall and beyond it, a stile led into a field and a path wound towards the river. Behind everything, the hills rose steeply away.

'Look,' said Cass, 'we can walk along the riverbank. Won't that be nice?'

'But where are all the kids?' Ben scowled, his eyes narrowed. There was a gleam in them Cass didn't like. She turned back to the window and noticed an odd thing. The parking area was completely empty.

'I want Dad,' Ben said.

'Ben, *please*.'

'I want him back – how's he going to find us now? He won't know where to look.' His face crumpled.

Cass bent and put her arms around her son. Ben's whole body was hot to the touch and she felt his forehead. He didn't push her hand away. 'I want him,' he repeated.

'I know. I'm sorry, Ben. But you have to understand, he's not coming back.'

Ben struggled in her arms and she drew him in closer. Holding him. 'I want him too,' she whispered. 'Ben, I want him too. I do. But we'll be okay.' She drew back. 'It's you and me now,' she said, 'and everything will be all right.'

TWO

Cass opened her eyes. Everything was in shades of grey, and that wasn't right. There was no sound, and that was wrong too; she'd heard something. It had woken her.

For a second everything turned sepia, the colour of the desert. She rubbed her eyes. It had been Pete; she'd been dreaming of him.

She heard a sound. *Scritch, scritch.*

Pete had been holding her close. He held her while the building shook and crumbling plaster rained down on her head, settling in her hair like snowflakes.

Scritch, scritch.

Cass turned, put out a hand and touched the wall at her back. It was rough under her fingertips. The scratching stopped. She heard a different sound, like the pattering of little feet running away. She grimaced.

Cass turned back to face the empty room, and that was when she saw Pete standing in front of her.

She blinked, but he was still there, his blond hair pale-grey in the dark. He held out his arms and his lips moved.

She couldn't hear what he was saying. As she watched he opened his fists to reveal handfuls of blue stones. They were bright, the only colour in the room. The stones fell, one by one, to the ground, and the ground swallowed them. Everything was soundless, everything colourless, except the things he held.

Cass heard a noise and she jumped from her bed. When she turned back to face Pete, he had gone. She found herself looking for the blue stones on the carpet, but of course there was nothing.

She swallowed and took a deep breath. She had to keep it together. Of course she had just been dreaming of her husband. This thing she thought she'd seen – it was an after-image, nothing more, a clinging remnant of sleep.

There came a new sound. A dry scrape, as of heavy boots treading through sand.

She shook her head. The sound went on, but it resolved itself into something she could understand and Cass began to breathe once more. *Scritch, scritch.*

There were mice behind the walls. *Scritch, scritch.* It didn't sound like sand any more; it was more like the scratching of tiny claws. Of course an old building like this was bound to have mice. She should have thought of it. She'd have to get traps or poison. Cass had a sudden image of Ben coming across a trap, holding up a grey-furred body by its tail, and pulled a face.

Cass squinted and let her eyes adjust to the dark: ahead and to the right, where there was a darker patch, that's where the door was. She went towards it, felt her way into the hall without switching on the light. Ben's door was outlined by the pale glow that crept beneath it. She felt for the handle and went in.

Ben's nightlight glowed, a small plastic blue moon. It was one of the first things she'd unpacked. Her son didn't like to sleep without a light, not since Pete had left them for the last time.

He had the covers heaped up over his body, a snug bundle. Cass leaned over and looked into his face – then started back. His eyes were wide open, staring up at her. She took a deep breath, then waved her hands in front of his eyes, but he didn't move. His cheeks looked wan and sickly in the nightlight's steady glow.

He was sleeping with his eyes open.

Cass eased the covers away from his face, loosening them, careful not to wake him. Part of her wanted to see the expression restored to his eyes, but it must be better not to interfere. Better to let him sleep. She tucked the bundle of covers in around him. She felt the need to do these things but then remained standing there, looking at his face. She knew there was something else she needed to do for him, but couldn't think what it was.

Then she knew, and put out a hand before she could catch herself.

She pulled away at the last moment. The thing she'd wanted to do was reach out and put her hand to his eyes, smooth his eyelids down, like closing them on a corpse. Cass shuddered.

Quietly, she backed out of the room.

THREE

Ben stood in the lounge, looking out of the window. Cass stretched as she went to join him, still trying to shake off sleep, and put a hand on his shoulder.

'We're still here,' her son said in a small voice.

She bent and hugged him, feeling frail bones through his pyjamas. 'Why don't we set the telly up?' she said. 'And your video games.'

His eyes widened. 'Can we? I'd like that, Mummy.'

Mummy. It was as though he was a toddler again. Cass grinned, lifted him onto the windowsill, propped a cushion behind his back. 'Watch the world go by,' she said. 'Tell me if anything happens.' She glanced out of the window. There were no cars, no movement. It was overcast, the colours muted, not even a breeze stirring the branches. Nothing happening at all. *Good*, she thought. *Nothing was good.*

Soon Ben was glued to the TV and Cass set up her computer in the corner. The Web connection worked fine, just as the estate agent had promised. Still, it was a relief.

She'd known mobile phone reception would be poor here, but the Internet was her lifeline. She had a website to develop for her client – her only client so far – and she had to make this work. With Pete gone, she had to take care of Ben: build something for him, a new life for them both.

'I want to play a game, Mum,' Ben called out.

She set it up for him, and then returned to the computer screen: there was an email from her client, listing some changes needed for the website. She responded: 'Will upload site changes for checking ASAP.' Her client wouldn't even know she'd moved.

That done, she closed it down; it was Sunday, and work could wait. That was something her father had always insisted on, and she found the habit had stuck.

She looked at Ben, who was sitting on the floor, the controller loose in his lap, staring at the television, his mouth hanging open.

'Ben, what is it?' She went to him and saw that his favourite game was on the screen. It was a war game and the ground was littered with rubble and barbed wire. Everything was sepia, the colour of sand.

'Ben?'

The game had been a gift from his father. At the time Cass had thought it a little old for Ben, but Pete had liked it, and he'd played it with him: for a while the two of them had been soldiers together.

She reached out and smoothed her son's hair, then took the control pad from Ben's lap. His lip started to jut out, and she knelt down and hugged him, holding his head tight to her body.

'Come on, sweetie,' she said, 'it's a beautiful day. Let's go out and see it, shall we?'

Cass looked back at the mill as they walked up the lane towards the village. The mellow stone suited the dour weather, blending with the surrounding greens and browns. It was good to be outside, breathing in cold, clean air. On their way out of the building it had struck Cass that she didn't like the walk through the silent mill. She had strained her ears, but still she had heard no sound from any of the other apartments. The crimson carpets swallowed the sound of their footsteps too, so that it felt like no one was there at all.

All of the shops in the village were closed save one, the general store. Cass bought some sweets for Ben. The grey-haired woman at the till was stony-faced; she took Cass' money in silence and gave the change in silence, only nodding when Cass said goodbye. Outside, Cass exchanged a glance with Ben; they both burst out laughing and she felt a stab of gratitude for the unfriendly woman. Ben offered her a sweet and she took one.

They headed towards the park, which sloped down towards the river. The grass was short-cropped and scabbed with patches of bare earth and at the bottom there was a little playground with some swings, a roundabout and a slide. Empty crisp packets and sweetie wrappings had accumulated under the shrubbery hiding the chattering water, looking as though they were sheltering from rain.

Cass and Ben raced for the swings, and sat there side by side.

'How do.' A man's voice came from behind them.

Cass turned to see an old man emerging from the riverside path. A grizzled black dog followed him through a gap in the bushes. The man had patches of grey hair clinging to his scalp, as though just holding on. He was hunched over against the cold, hands shoved deep into his pockets. His cheeks were red and veined.

Ben jumped from the swing and ran to his side, bending to pet the dog. As Cass made a mental note to talk to him about strangers she was smiling at the same time.

'You'll be from t' mill,' the man said.

News spread fast. Did the whole village know about them?

'Bert Tanner,' he said, 'from t' flats.' He said this as though she should know where the flats were.

'I'm Cass,' she said, holding out her hand to shake his. 'This is Ben.' They turned and watched Ben stroking the dog, whispering something in its ear. The dog was a squat, stolid thing, greying around the chops. It huffed in Ben's face and he wrinkled his nose as he smelled its breath.

''e's an owd un,' the man said, 'like me. Been 'ere man and boy, I have.'

Cass didn't know what to say. 'That's nice.'

Ben jumped up and ran to the bushes. He thrust a hand underneath, among the litter.

'Ben, don't – that's dirty,' she started as he turned and held up a faded green tennis ball. It looked well chewed. He held it under the dog's nose.

'Captain dun't chase balls no more, lad.'

Ben threw it anyway and it flew up the slope and rolled

part of the way back. The dog looked up, sniffed, turned its head to Ben and then waddled, tail moving in a slow wag, up the slope. It picked up the ball and then turned as if to say, *Aren't you coming?*

'Well, I'll be,' said Bert. 'You've got the touch, lad.'

He turned to Cass and pointed towards the river. 'It's a nice walk, that,' he said. 'A long way, mind. It keeps me going. Not that I go out of Darnshaw much.' He started to tell her where the school was, and the shops, and Cass let him talk. No need to let on that Sally had already pointed them out. They walked together back towards the village. 'Up there's the post office. I'm above, if you ever need owt. Just say.'

She smiled, touched. 'That's really kind. Thank you, Bert.'

'And up there's t' church.'

He pronounced it 'chuch', without the r. Cass followed his gesture and froze.

The church stood almost at the top of the hill, its tower rising against the pale sky. From here it seemed to loom over them, a forbidding presence. But that wasn't what made her shudder.

'Tha's not a churchgoer, then,' Bert said.

She looked at him. He had very pale eyes, rheumy under their drooping lids.

'It's not that,' she said. 'We always went when I was a kid. It's just that it's the only part of Darnshaw that looks really familiar. Memories, I suppose.'

'Goose walked over your grave.'

'Something like that, yes.'

'Well, anytime you want to go, you're right welcome. Priest comes ower from Moorfoot every other Sunday. Next week's his turn.'

Cass started to tell him she didn't attend any longer, not now, but something in his gaze stopped her and she merely nodded. Ben came chasing up, the green ball in his hand, a sparkle in his eyes.

Bert nodded. 'We'll be off. Remember what I said. You ever need owt, come see me. Ower the post office.'

They watched him go, Ben still panting. Her son had been running about more than the dog. Cass glanced back across the quiet park. When they were gone, it would be empty. That was sad. She'd promised Ben children to play with, lots of children, and all they'd found was one old man and a dog.

Still, her son smiled at her, flashing his teeth. 'Can I keep it, Mum?' he asked, holding out the grubby spittle-covered tennis ball.

'Of course you can.' Cass smiled back at him. She looked up into the sky. It looked completely flat. As she watched, pinprick flakes floated out of it, drifting like tiny fragments of ash.

Ben held out his hand. 'It's snowing,' he said.

Cass craned her head back and let the snowflakes fall on her face. They were so fine she barely felt them land, just felt the chill spread slowly across her skin.

FOUR

The valley was clothed in swathes of mist, a half-erased picture. The snow hadn't settled, but Cass got Ben's warmest coat ready anyway. When she woke him he screwed up his face, a nasty-medicine expression, but he didn't say anything. Monday morning, and he was going to school.

The main road through the village was busier than Cass had yet seen it. Every car had a child in the passenger seat and she barely needed to think about the school's location, just followed the line. The car park was already full but she managed to fit into an end slot narrowed by an overhanging Land Rover.

'Sorry.' A young woman with sleek dark hair waved from the other side of the vehicle. 'In too much of a rush this morning. I'm Lucy.'

'I'm Cass. And it's no problem.' Cass spotted a young girl peering round the Land Rover's bonnet and smiled at her while encouraging Ben from the car. She introduced her son.

'This is Jessica,' said Lucy. 'You two will be good friends, I think. Jess, you could watch out for Ben, since he's new. Why don't you show him inside?'

'We have a meeting with Mrs Cambrey first,' said Cass. 'But you could play later, couldn't you?'

The little girl nodded. She was a couple of inches shorter than Ben, and a girl – he didn't often make friends with girls. Cass saw her son's lower lip jutting. Well, they'd tried, and who knew? The children might hit it off anyway.

'Mrs Cambrey's really nice,' Lucy said. 'Well, I'd better get off.' She watched Jessica walk towards the double doors, then waved before climbing into the Land Rover.

'Right,' said Cass, forcing a positive note into her voice. 'The head sounds great, doesn't she, Ben? Let's go.'

The hall was gloomy, even after the greyness of the morning. While Cass was getting her bearings she saw the walls were lined with pictures, bright splashes of colour emerging from the dim light, and she caught the faint smell of poster paint.

They walked past classrooms where children were chatting and removing their coats. The building was single-storey and Cass could see offices at the far end of the hall. One was marked 'Staff Room', another 'Head Teacher', and beneath that, 'Mrs Cambrey'.

Cass knocked, and knocked again when there was no response. She leaned closer to the door, trying to hear if there was someone inside.

'My apologies,' called out a voice behind her, a man's voice, smooth and cultured. 'I'm sorry to keep you. There's such a lot to organise.'

Cass turned to see a tall man with dark tousled hair and artfully shaved stubble which outlined his slightly hollowed face. He met Cass' eye, took her hand and squeezed it in his. 'It's a little chaotic this morning,' he said. 'Do come in.'

He led the way into the office and they sat on either side of a large wooden desk strewn with papers. Cass stared at a desktop sign that said MRS CAMBREY.

The man followed her gaze, picked up the sign and dropped it into a drawer. 'Unfortunately Mrs Cambrey has been called away,' he said. 'A family emergency. I'm Mr Remick – Theodore Remick – stepping into the breach.' He turned. 'And you must be Ben.' He stretched out his hand for Ben to shake. Ben stared at it, glanced at Cass, then shook hands and smiled up at Mr Remick.

They ran over a few details – Ben's progress in his last school, class times, after-school clubs – and Cass thought the teacher quick and efficient. Then he stood and she followed suit. As they left the room Mr Remick turned to Ben once more. 'You're going to be in my class,' he said. 'I'm sure we'll get along famously.'

A voice rang out along the hall. 'Cassandra. Yoo-hoo, Cassandra, come and meet everybody!'

Cass turned to see Sally heading towards her, pulling along a boy of about Ben's age. She was trailed by a group of women.

'This is my lady knight in shining armour from the other day,' Sally said as they drew near. 'She quite rescued me from the moor.' Then the woman noticed Mr Remick and something in her face changed. She took Cass' arm and pulled her away, her curly hair brushing Cass' shoulders. 'Ooh, you lucky thing,' she said. 'He's a fox, isn't he?'

Cass smothered a smile. She was sure Mr Remick must have heard.

'Come and meet the girls. This is Helen. Dot. Myra. Girls, this is Cassandra.'

'It's lovely to meet you. Actually, my name's just Cass – it's short for Cassidy.'

'Cassidy? Well, I never heard the like,' said Sally.

'It comes from—'

'Like David – David Cassidy.' Sally's laugh rang out.

'You've met the new teacher,' Myra said. She made it sound like an accusation. She was a stocky woman in a flowery dress, with long auburn hair.

'He's a dish, isn't he?' Sally laughed.

The corner of Myra's mouth twitched. 'He's a blessing.'

'Quite right,' said Sally. 'We've been praying for someone like him.'

Helen grinned at her. 'I'll bet you have. Lucky cow,' she said, and they all laughed.

Cass glanced from one to the other.

Sally laughed louder and longer than the others. 'You're right, I am. Don't I know it.' She grinned at Cass. 'Teaching assistant,' she said. 'And I used to help Mrs Cambrey, so . . .'

'So,' the others echoed.

'Of course, this one swooped on him first.' Sally nodded at Cass.

'I just had a meeting about Ben. It's his first day.' Cass

looked around for her son, but he had already been swallowed up by one of the classrooms. She wasn't sure which one.

'He'll be in Damon's class,' said Sally. 'Damien, more like.' She spluttered laughter and the others joined in. 'Well, I must be off – new acquaintances to make and all that. As long as he hasn't lost his heart to another.' She looked back at Cass as she went into one of the classrooms. 'Don't forget to call in on us some time.' Then she was gone and the hall fell silent. When Cass turned back to the other women, they were already moving away.

She looked back towards the classroom doors, closed now, and considered peering through the glass panels. But Ben might see her, and Sally might make something of it, maybe embarrass her son on his first day.

After a pause Cass turned, alone, and headed back towards the exit.

The shining door of the mill opened onto silence. Cass started up the stairway, then remembered her empty floor, all the closed doors, and she changed her mind and headed instead through the door that led from the lobby into the ground-floor hall. This hall looked just like the one on her floor, with its red carpet and rows of white doors. The apartments were numbered 1 to 6. Cass walked past each one, listening for any sound from inside, but she heard nothing.

She retraced her steps, and this time as she passed each door she knocked softly. Still nothing. When she reached the apartment below hers, she rested on the handle while listening and it moved under her hand.

She took hold and pressed. There was a click.

Cass peered back down the hall, but she was still alone. She stared at the brass 6, then pushed the door open with one hand while knocking with the other. Her lips formed a hello, but somehow she didn't make the sound; the mill's silence had swallowed her voice.

Cass saw at once she needn't have bothered knocking: the apartment was not just empty, but unfinished. The floor was nothing but bare wooden panels and she saw why it was so cold. There was no glass in the windows, nothing to stop the biting air flooding in, nor were the walls any hindrance; wooden studwork sketched out where the rooms would be, but no plasterboard covered them. Cass could see the bundled wires inside, and sockets hanging loose on the floor.

She crossed to the window, her feet echoing on the boards, and looked out. The digger was still parked outside. Its cab was empty. She glanced at her watch: almost ten o'clock on a Monday morning and the builders had not come.

She looked down and saw something on the floor: half-buried in a heap of dust and wood shavings was a child's doll. She picked it up and dusted it off. Two pieces of cloth had been cut into a roughly human shape and stitched together, but it was a sorry-looking thing, the fabric stained and mildewed. It reminded Cass of a ginger-bread man. Its hair was a few strands of wool and its face was drawn on. Scrawled lines suggested a top and a skirt.

Cass held it closer to her face; it had a peculiar smell. It could be years old, some mill-worker's doll, maybe, but it didn't quite look like that. The face appeared to have been drawn on using a felt-tip pen.

She looked down again, and saw another shape, smaller than the other. It looked a bit like a boy. It wore a T-shirt and shorts.

Cass grimaced and dropped the doll. Her fingertips felt tainted by the dust.

There was no sound from the apartments on the second floor, or from any of the penthouses. Cass tried the handles too, growing bolder and pushing at the doors, longing to see the views from the top floor of the mill, but she didn't find any that would open.

When she returned to her own floor Cass found a newspaper had been pushed partway under the door of Number 10. She stopped and looked at it. Odd that someone had come up here to deliver it when there were mailboxes on the ground floor. She went to the door and knocked.

She waited. No one came. Cass listened at that door too, and heard nothing; they must be out.

There was no answer from any of the other apartments on her floor either.

She thought back to the conversation she'd had with the estate agent. 'Number 12 is free,' he'd said as though this was a sudden discovery and she should snap it up before anyone else found out. As though the mill was full to bursting.

She remembered the scratching noise she'd heard in the night and shivered, pushed the thought away, opened her own door and went to fire up the computer, ignoring the sense of emptiness at her back.

There was another email from her client – more work Cass hadn't expected, but that was good; she could charge extra. She started on the website changes, moving pictures and changing set-ups, mentally ticking off the items as she sank into the work. Finally she uploaded the files and sent an email: 'All done. Hope you like it. Let me know if there's anything else I can do.'

She sat back and rubbed her eyes, then stood, banishing the stiffness from her joints, and turned.

The world outside the window was white.

Cass exclaimed and went for a closer look.

The car park was covered over, maybe an inch deep in snow. The hillsides were white, and so was the sky; the flakes that filled the air were fat and white and drifted lazily down, settling on everything. Snow had caught in the treetops, swelling each branch. Only a flash of yellow remained where the digger stood. The world had turned monochrome.

She thought of Ben and cursed under her breath. At least he had his thickest coat with him, the red one.

But the road. Cass traced the journey to school in her mind: the main road headed straight through the valley, running more or less flat through the village. The road down to the mill, though, that could be treacherous. She took a deep breath. She had never thought of it before, hadn't checked what access would be like. Still, it didn't matter, not really – she could work anywhere. And she could walk Ben to school if the roads got too difficult.

Cass looked out of the window. Whatever problems it brought, the snow was beautiful. A memory came to her, startling in its vividness. Cass and her mum and dad, walking together in the snow, back when such a thing was possible. Cass wore a frothy white dress under her coat and she twirled, laughing, partly because snow was dancing around her hair and partly because she knew the other children would be jealous. She opened her mouth and tasted snowflakes on her tongue.

Then she looked up and saw the church. Her father turned and—

Cass frowned. She didn't want to remember what followed, when things became stern and severe and joyless; only the fun of them being together, all of them laughing, still a family, before Cass went into the church.

Of course, she hadn't been called Cass back then.

FIVE

Fresh snow spread away from the mill's crimson door. It was pristine, innocent of footprints. No one could have been in or out of the mill in the last few hours, and Cass wondered once again about her mysterious neighbour in Apartment 10.

Her car was the only vehicle parked by the door. Cass brushed snow from its headlights, then the mirrors and windows. The snow darkened her sleeves and turned her hands red and tingling with cold. Her face too was stinging by the time she slipped behind the wheel and turned the key.

The engine made a rough sound, the geriatric cough of a lifelong smoker.

Cass swore, pumped the accelerator and tried again. More empty spluttering, then the engine fired. Cass ran the heater for a while, holding her fingers in front of the vents. She promised herself she'd wear gloves next time.

She put it in reverse. The car juddered, and the wheels spun. Cass eased off on the accelerator and it started to move, rocking over the snow, then it slid sideways. In the rear-view mirror Cass could see the lane heading steeply up the hill to the main road. Too steeply. She sighed, took the car out of reverse and eased forward, back into what she'd already come to think of as her space. Her watch read 3.15 p.m.

Cass jumped out of the car, slammed the door and hurried up the hill.

Her calf muscles ached by the time she reached the school, and her feet were soaked. A few kids were still in the yard, throwing snowballs and giggling. They were decked out in scarves and hats and boots. Cass' heart sank. Ben's boots were still packed away in a box somewhere.

Then Cass saw the stand-in headmaster, Mr Remick, by the door. Judging by the white patches on his coat, he'd been entering fully into the spirit of things. Either that or some of the children were bolder than she might have expected to find in a quiet part of the world like this. He waved at her.

'Sorry I'm—'

'No need, no need. We've been having a wonderful time. It's not altogether how I imagined my first day, of course.'

'I don't suppose Ben expected this either.' They smiled at each other and Cass saw that Mr Remick's eyes were blue, the colour strong and clear. 'Where is he?'

'He's waiting with Mrs Spencer.'

Cass raised her eyebrows.

'You met her earlier today, I believe. Sally Spencer.' He grinned. 'You can't miss her.'

'Oh. Of course.' Cass laughed in spite of herself.

'Sally's keeping him occupied with some drawing. I hope you don't mind, Mrs—'

'Cass.'

'I hope you don't mind, Cass, but I took the liberty of asking Mrs Spencer if she wouldn't mind running you both home. Just in case you had any difficulty. I imagine the lane to the old mill can be treacherous.'

'It is,' said Cass reluctantly. She didn't want to ask Sally for help, but the thought of Ben walking home without any boots . . . She should have been more prepared. And they had helped Sally get back from the moors, after all.

Then she thought of something. 'I think Sally's having car trouble.'

'Oh? She didn't mention it – it must be all fixed, I think. She said it was no problem.'

'I'll drop you off.'

They turned to see Lucy, the woman with the Land Rover, standing behind them. 'It's on my way.'

'It's fine, thank you,' said Mr Remick. 'We have everything under control.'

'But Sally lives in the other direction.' Lucy turned to Cass. 'You can jump in the Landy. Jess is all ready – I just popped back for her scarf.'

'That's really kind of you,' Cass said. As she spoke Ben appeared at the doorway, his face pale. He came to his mother's side and stood without speaking. Cass felt an urge to bend and hug him tight, but she resisted. Potential playmates might be watching; it was too easy for the new boy to become a victim. Instead she rested her hand on his shoulder and squeezed.

'Great,' said Mr Remick. 'Thank you, Lucy.' He leaned towards Cass and his expression became warm. 'I'll see you tomorrow,' he said, and she almost thought she could feel his breath on her cheek.

The kids sat in the back of the Land Rover without speaking while Lucy and Cass chatted. Lucy was from the next village, she said, a few miles along the valley.

Cass told Lucy to drop them at the top of the lane, but she insisted on taking them to the door. The Land Rover managed the slope effortlessly, sliding into the spot on the opposite side of the entrance to Cass' car.

'Busy car park,' Cass quipped. 'Watch out for the traffic.'

'Yes, it's a pity about this place,' said Lucy, peering up. 'It's an impressive building.'

'But still only half-finished. I wondered why the builders didn't show today – they must have known about the snow.'

Lucy gave her a sidelong glance. 'Sorry,' she said. 'I thought you knew – I mean, it might be nothing—'

'What is it?'

'Well, the rumour going round is the builders have run out of money. They stopped work a few weeks ago. Still, they'll probably find another investor. Did you . . . ?' Her voice tailed away.

Cass shook her head, her system flooding with relief. 'No,' she said, 'no, I didn't buy, thank God. I might have bought outright if I'd been able to visit first, but as it is, we're only renting.'

'That's good. You should be fine then. And the place might fill up a bit soon. They're still trying to let the finished apartments, I think.'

Cass barely caught the words. She was thinking about all those doors, closed and silent, and Ben's pinched face, watching from the window for playmates who might never arrive. And then she thought of the empty apartment with no windows, open to the elements. So that wouldn't be fixed any time soon.

'I'm sure you'll be fine.' Lucy looked concerned. 'Look, any time you want a friend, or a chat, or need anything . . . Here, I'll give you my phone number.' She pulled a scrap of paper from the glove box and scrawled on it.

Cass said her thanks and waved them off, Ben standing quietly at her side. They stood together in the cold for a while. 'Did you talk to Jessica?' Cass said at last.

'She's a girl.'

Cass hid a smile. 'So she is. Well, did you talk to her?'

Ben shook his head.

'Is she in your class?'

No answer.

'Who did you talk to?'

Her son looked up. 'Damon.'

Damon – it would have to be: the son of the loudest woman in Darnshaw.

'And you drew pictures with Mrs Spencer. Did you like that?'

Ben shot her a look and pulled a face. His lips pressed tight together.

Cass sighed. She should try to lighten his mood. They could do something fun together, build a snowman, maybe. But she looked around and realised that night was already drawing in. The sky was deep grey, like gunmetal, and as they stood there it began to snow again, white flecks filling the sky, coming down in a steady drift.

Cass sat bolt-upright, her hair in her face. Something had woken her – *Ben*. She jumped out of bed, rushed through the apartment and into his room. When she reached her son's side, though, he had fallen silent. Cass knelt by him, finding him hot and tangled in the sheets. She put out a hand. His cheeks were damp, but not with sweat; he had been crying. He screwed up his face and pulled away, muttering. His eyes were vacant.

He said the words again. 'He's still my daddy.'

'Shush, Ben. Of course he is.'

'He is. He is my daddy.'

Cass held him, trying not to think about Pete. If Ben cried, Pete would swing him up in the air, making fun of his tears, but in such a way as not to make Ben feel bad about crying. He'd do it in a way that would make him laugh.

Ben wriggled in her arms and Cass pulled back. Her son was fully awake now, his eyes wide open. 'If I got another daddy, he'd still be Dad, wouldn't he?'

'What?'

'Daddy. If someone else wanted to be my dad, he'd still love me, wouldn't he?'

'Of course he would.' Cass drew her son in tight, her

thoughts floundering. Where could he have got that idea? She thought of Sally's words in the hall, her loud foolish laughter. What had the woman said? *You are lucky.* Something like that. Ben must have heard.

Cass leaned back and met Ben's eyes. She chose her words carefully. 'Of course he's still your dad,' she said. 'He always will be.'

'So where is he?'

Cass' heart curled in on itself.

'Where is he?'

She took a deep breath. 'Your daddy . . . Pete' – she stumbled over his name – 'he died, Ben. He was a soldier, and he was very brave, and I'm sorry, but he's not coming back. Not ever. It doesn't mean he stopped loving you.' *Us*, she thought. He loved *us*. She felt her hands shake.

'It's not fair.'

'I know, Ben. I know it's not fair. Shh, shh.' She rocked him, holding him tight, his damp hair pressed against her chin.

'I don't want another daddy,' he whispered.

Cass silently cursed Sally Spencer. She opened her mouth to reassure her son and closed it again. What should she say? An image of Mr Remick came into her mind. The look in his eyes was vivid, as though he was in the room with her.

Cass couldn't see her son's face but she knew he was waiting for an answer.

'I know,' she said once more, holding him close. 'I know.' She sat in the dark, rocking him, but the tension in his body didn't fade for a long time.

SIX

Cass woke early, her mind dragged unwillingly from sleep. She was still tired, had not slept well after waking with Ben. She didn't remember dreaming about anything at all, but she could see Pete's face in her mind when she woke, and the thought of it stayed with her.

It was the idea of Ben going off to school without any boots that got her out of bed. This time she found his scarf, gloves and boots before she woke him. He rubbed his face and smiled at her as though nothing had happened. 'Is it snowing?' he asked.

'Let's go and see.'

Even before reaching the window, Cass could see that the sky was white. When Ben looked outside his mouth fell open and Cass tousled his hair. More snow had fallen overnight. It obscured the lane and coated the trees, lending them strange white foliage.

'We'll have to walk,' said Cass. Her gaze drifted to the white hills that blended into the sky. It was as though they were at the bottom of a huge bowl, hemmed in on all sides.

When they were ready they went out into the cold, huffing out clouds of breath, obscuring the crispness of the air. The car was under maybe six inches of snow and Ben ran to it, sticking in one finger and then drawing a face on the bonnet with his whole hand. He bunched a loose snowball together and threw it at Cass. It disintegrated before it reached her and she grinned. 'Later, soldier,' she said, instantly regretting the choice of word, but Ben didn't notice; he was running up the lane shuffling, leaving a single wide track.

'What am I?' he chanted. 'What am I?'

'A big dog,' Cass guessed, and he turned, wide-eyed, and nodded.

'I'm Captain,' he said. 'Woof! Woof!'

Despite the way their boots sank into the snow they reached the school in good time.

'Greetings,' called a familiar voice. 'You made it. Good! We're precious few this morning.'

Cass saw Mr Remick standing by the door, pressing his gloved hands together. His cheeks were pink, his eyes bright, and Cass found herself smiling. Ben reached up and caught her hand, tugging on it, but when she looked down he didn't say anything and didn't look at her.

'A lot won't make it in today,' said Mr Remick. 'Lucky I got here. I imagine some of the teachers will be snowed in too.'

Cass looked around. The car park was empty, and only a few pupils milled in the yard. 'Should I take Ben home?' she asked, and felt his grip tighten on her hand.

'No, no need for that. I think we'll only get enough for

one class, though. For my special pupils.' Mr Remick bent and winked at Ben. 'It's fine; I can take them.'

Behind them a loud shuffling and giggling told Cass more *special* pupils had arrived.

Mr Remick straightened and gestured, gathering everyone together. His voice carried over the chatter and the children fell silent. 'Since you've done so well to get here this morning while everyone else has stayed at home, I think we'll begin with an early break. Snowman competition, anyone?'

There was cheering all round. Ben's eyes lit up and he smiled too, flashing small white teeth. He pulled his hand away from Cass' as though he'd just become aware of it. Cass grinned at him. Mr Remick was watching them. 'I hope that meets with your approval,' he said. 'We'll have serious lessons too, of course.'

'It's perfect,' said Cass. 'A nice way for him to settle in.' Maybe the snow was a blessing after all. She cast her gaze around the hillsides that surrounded them, their pristine white marked only by the occasional line of a stone wall or a scarecrow tree.

Mr Remick spoke more softly. His voice was smooth, almost without accent. 'You could stay if you like.'

Cass looked at him and the sight of his clear eyes jarred through her. She caught her breath.

'I mean you could join in with the snowman part. It might be fun. You can be our guest of honour.' Mr Remick smiled.

Cass glanced down to see Ben staring at her. She looked

back at Mr Remick. 'That's all right,' she said. 'I don't want to cramp your style, eh, Ben?'

'Mum's rubbish at snowmen,' Ben said.

Cass caught Mr Remick's eye and they laughed.

'Well, we can't have that. Another time, maybe.' The teacher reached out and lifted Ben's rucksack from Cass' shoulder. He did it lightly, his fingers gentle, not lingering, though his gaze rested on hers while he did it.

Cass broke eye contact. She bent to Ben, using the pretext of straightening his coat to cover her confusion. She forced a neutral expression onto her face as she stood up straight again.

When she reached the road Cass turned to look down over the school playing field. There were maybe twenty children of different ages running about and squealing. They bent to their task, rolling the snow, revealing streaks of patchy green beneath. Cass made out Ben's red coat among the others. One of the boys beckoned and Ben went to help lift one snowball onto another to make a head.

A familiar voice rang out across the field. Even from here Cass could recognise Sally's bright tones. The woman stomped around, encouraging the children to build faster, and then she turned towards the road and shielded her eyes. Cass found herself stepping to the side so that she was hidden behind a tall gatepost.

'How do,' said a voice.

Cass turned to see Bert, hunched into his coat, with Captain waddling after. The dog's sides were heaving, red tongue lolling.

'Hi, Bert. Be careful. Captain might get roped into the snowman-building.'

Bert looked down at the dog, which had ambled to a stop. 'Aye,' he said, and turned to watch the children. 'All stocked up, then?'

'Sorry?'

'Aye. You got yersen stocked up?'

'Stocked up?'

He nodded. The dog stood there and panted. 'A snowflake falls in Darnshaw and the shops run out o' bread.' He rattled it off like a saying. 'An' milk. An' owt else you might want.' His shoulders shook in a silent laugh. He gestured towards the road. 'I doubt they're going to get stuff in for a bit. You'd best get to t' shop, if you 'ant got owt in.'

'Oh,' said Cass. 'Thank you.' Why hadn't it occurred to her there might be a problem getting food? It had been easier to get about in her old home, but here—

'They'll plough the roads soon, won't they, Bert? Or grit them, so they can supply the shops at least?'

He let out a long sigh. 'You never know. O' course, the council's short o' cash these days. They'll do the towns, but a blind eye falls on Darnshaw some o' these times.' He paused. 'Aye, you stock up, love.'

'All right, I will. Thank you, Bert. I appreciate it.'

He nodded. 'Post office,' he said. 'Flats. Don't forget: you need owt, you come to old Bert, an' he'll see what he can do.'

'You're a hero.'

The old man turned and stared at his dog. His cheeks

had begun to redden. 'How do,' he said suddenly. The words obviously passed for both greeting and farewell. He headed off towards the park, his back ramrod-straight. Captain shuffled along at his side.

Cass looked down the slope towards the children. A circle of snowmen was taking shape. It reminded her of some prehistoric site ringed by standing stones. Mr Remick stood in the centre, holding out his hands and laughing. The children pulled hats from their heads and scarves from their necks and used them to adorn their creations. Cass heard shouts, though she couldn't make out the words. As she watched, Mr Remick took off his own scarf, wrapped it around the neck of Ben's snowman and ruffled the boy's hair.

SEVEN

As Cass approached she saw that the shop was crammed. She could see this because the window was almost empty of the display it had previously held. The shelves behind the glass bore only an odd assortment of items – a small pink teddy bear, a box of rubber balls, skeins of wool that hadn't appealed to the local knitters.

Inside, bodies were pressed close together, fumbling past each other to pull free plastic shopping baskets. The till was by the window, and Cass could see the back of the dour woman who'd served her – was it only the day before yesterday? The woman's arms moved steadily, passing items through the barcode reader in an endless stream.

Cass pushed open the door and the sound hit her: the scraping of tins, footsteps, rustling as packets were pulled off shelves and added to baskets. The constant *beep – beep – beep* of the barcode reader, the rattle of the cash drawer. What was missing was conversation. The shop was full of people, mostly elderly, grey-haired, clothes bulky against the cold, and none of them were saying a word to each other.

Cass reached for a basket. The greengrocery display behind them was empty save for a wrinkled plum or two, a few stray mushrooms. Two days ago they had been stacked high. Cass glanced down the aisle. Many shelves were empty, the former contents marked only by plastic tabs showing meaningless prices.

Cass grabbed the remaining fruit and edged past an old man who was sniffing dubiously at a packet of dried noodles.

There was no bread. Cass managed to find cereal, tins of vegetables, dried pasta. It took an age to reach the till. She put the load down on the floor, shuffling it along at her feet. She couldn't carry more now, but she could get these things home and come back. She'd pick up some things for the freezer maybe, the soft drinks Ben loved – enough to keep them going for a few days, just in case.

She closed her eyes, picturing Bert. *Thank you*, she thought.

Arms aching, Cass set the bags down on the kitchen floor and threw a few items into the freezer, which was empty except for a tray of ice cubes. She went straight out again, heading back up the lane and into the village, walking with her head down, trying not to notice the burn in her calf muscles. She reached the shop, put out a hand and pushed the door, but it didn't budge. She looked up, tried to see through the hazy glass, but there were notices stuck to the back of it, mostly yellow and peeling at the edges: a lost cat. Band practise. She moved to the window and looked inside and now she could see the shop was empty, the lights switched off, a green cover pulled over the till. There didn't appear to be anything edible left on the shelves at all.

There was a small butcher's shop, Winthrop's, and not much available there either, but the butcher wrapped a few things for her and put them in a blue-and-white-striped carrier bag. Cass was hardly aware of what she'd bought.

The greengrocer was closed, as was the post office. The last shop, the florist's, was no use, and anyway, it too was closed. It looked like it hadn't been open in a long time. The plastic box trees in the window were coated in dust. Cass stared in for a while, then turned away. There was nothing to be done but go home to the apartment.

When Cass got back to the mill she reached for the keypad by the door and froze where she stood. She moved to the centre of the door and stared at it, put out her hands and touched the rough edges of the marks that had been scratched into the new paint.

A cross had been carved into the door, the lines scored over and over, deep into the wood. Fragments of paint and shards of wood marred the surface. Cass brushed her fingers against them, caught her skin on a splinter and put it to her mouth. The wood beneath the paint was black and damp.

A cross. Cass thought of her father. She wondered what he would have said.

She looked around. She hadn't been gone long; it had

been done recently. It must be kids, skipping school and playing stupid pranks. Anger flooded into her. If they were wandering around in the snow they surely could have walked to school.

But it didn't feel like kids. Why should they have chosen a cross?

Cass tapped her code into the keypad and went in, making sure the lock engaged behind her. She looked through the glass. Nothing moved outside. She could see a mess of tracks in the snow; impossible to tell who had made them. She could only make out her own footprints and the wide trail Ben had left as he'd walked up the hill.

She thought of the apartment beneath hers, the empty framework of a room, its windows gaping onto the hillside.

As she went up the stairs and along the quiet hall she saw that another newspaper had been delivered to her neighbour's door. Its pages were splayed where it had been pushed half under the first.

The bags were still lying in the kitchen where Cass had dumped them. She pulled out the butcher's parcel, which felt unpleasantly pliant, and put it in the fridge. She couldn't remember what was inside, and didn't want to examine it. Instead she left the rest of the shopping and went into her room, drew a box from under the bed.

She had promised herself she wouldn't do this, not now, not when she was alone in a new place. She was supposed to be starting again, building something new, and Ben was settling down, making friends. And yet, *He's still Daddy,* her son had said.

Her fingers wrapped around the box and pulled it closer. Pete was still Ben's Daddy, still her husband. *Was* her husband. Inside the box was a bundle of letters. Cass flicked through them, stopping when she came across a picture; saw the familiar face looking out, his sand-coloured hair blending with the uniform, the tent behind him and the ground upon which he stood. Everything was sepia. She ran a finger over the surface, half expecting to feel the grit of sand.

She shuffled through the thin papers, reading lines at random.

We're doing up the mess with silly drawings. Funny how we make them look like kids' drawings. I wish I could see him. I miss him so much.

Cass remembered when that letter came. She and Ben had drawn pictures of Pete and stuck them around the kitchen, doing up their own mess with silly drawings. But it hadn't brought him home.

She put the letters back in the box and kicked it until it was out of sight, back in its dark place under the bed.

EIGHT

Cass fired up the computer, her mind still on other things. An email was waiting for her. Her client needed a new product range adding to the website ahead of a launch next week. He was all apologies for the short notice, but made it clear the job was urgent.

'No problem,' Cass replied. 'It'll be done for tomorrow morning.' Then she sat and stared at the screen.

She couldn't think about work. Instead she remembered that day in Darnshaw when it had snowed and her family had walked, all together, she wearing her new white dress, dancing up the lane to the church.

She had stood with the other girls and waited while her father walked down the line. He had given Cass the same sort of look he gave everyone else: considering, appraising, assessing whether she was good enough.

Cass had a sick feeling in her stomach that she never would be.

She shook her head to clear it, grabbed the mouse and closed the screen down.

Cass had never been good enough, even in her white dress. She'd known that she would do something stupid, drop the wafer, spill the wine onto the snowy cloth. And now she was back here in Darnshaw – what did she think she was doing? And why had she thought this place would be good for Ben? If he had an accident now she couldn't get him to a hospital. Maybe soon she wouldn't even be able to feed him.

Cass jumped as the telephone rang. She pushed herself back from the computer and looked round, half expecting to see someone standing there.

Ben. She had been thinking of something happening to him and now the telephone was ringing. No, it couldn't be anything like that: it was probably just a wrong number, or someone from the Army base at Aldershot, calling to wish her well. Except it wasn't. She *knew* it wasn't. Those with husbands still living didn't want to be connected with the dead, not in any way at all.

'Hi. Sally,' a bright voice said, and Cass almost said, *No it's not; you have the wrong number*, when she recognised the voice.

'I was just calling to see if Ben could come to ours for tea tonight. We'd love to have him. Oh, and excuse me for getting your number – I was in Mr Remick's office, and I thought . . . Well, he wouldn't mind. So naughty of me!' The woman's laugh rang out, making Cass hold the phone away from her ear.

'Damon's got this new game, *Street Skirmish* or something like that, and they'd like to play. They're such friends already – isn't that nice?'

Cass licked her lips. 'It's very kind of you,' she started, 'but—'

'Wait a sec. I'll put him on.'

Cass' heart sank. A voice she almost didn't recognise spoke in her ear. 'Can I, Mum? We're going to eat Jelly Babies, and go on the games, and Mrs Spencer said we could walk back all together later, in the snow. And . . .'

Cass closed her eyes. There was something different about her son. He sounded *happy*, that was it. Carefree, as a child should, the way he used to sound. 'Of course you can,' she found herself saying. 'Of course. You go and enjoy yourself, love.'

'Super.' It was Sally again. 'We'll take good care of him, I promise. That's settled.'

'All right.'

'I'll give you a ring when we're setting off. No need for you to do a thing; we'll bring him back. Damon's looking forward to it.'

'Thank you very much,' Cass said automatically, and the line went dead. She stood there holding the phone to her chest. That sadness was back again, the feeling she'd woken with, that'd been hanging over her all day. *He's fine,* she told herself, *not hurt, not in need of hospital.* And he'd made a new friend. He sounded so happy. Ben settling in, having a real home in which he could estab-lish himself – hadn't that been the idea all along?

NINE

Cass was engrossed in her work when she heard knocking, so involved that she wasn't sure she'd heard anything at all. She raised her head, waiting; then the sound came again and Cass got up, wondering if she was about to meet her mysterious neighbour at last. She went to the door, remembered at the last moment that she was alone in a new place, and looked through the peephole to see a male figure in a dark coat. She only had time to register that his shoulders were flecked with snow when he knocked again, almost as if he knew she was standing there. She reached out automatically and pulled the door open.

It was Mr Remick. Cass blinked at him. *Ben.* 'Is there a problem?' she blurted. She must have got the days mixed up – Sally had meant she'd take Ben *tomorrow*, not today, and Cass should have collected him from school after all. But if that was the case, where was he? She peered around Mr Remick, half-expecting to see Ben standing behind him, lost and unhappy because his mother hadn't come to fetch him.

Instead she saw that Mr Remick had something under his arm. 'No problem,' he said. 'I just thought . . . Well, you only just moved in, and Sally mentioned Ben was going to their house after school, so . . .'

Was he blushing? His words tailed away and he held out the thing he had been carrying. Cass blinked at it. It was a loaf of bread.

'I thought you might be lonely. I also know what it's like around here when the snow starts to fall – fresh bread's the new currency.' He grinned.

Cass took it. 'That's so thoughtful of you. Thank you.' She led the way into the kitchen. 'You must have been quick. I tried the shop this morning; I was beginning to think we'd be living on tins of Spam.'

'It's a survival situation, all right. Although, truth be told, I wasn't that quick. Mrs Bentley at the shop has a soft spot for me, I think. She keeps things back for her special customers.'

'Lucky you.' Cass laughed. It made her feel lighter, just talking and laughing. It was almost like being back at Aldershot, surrounded by her friends, friends who weren't yet afraid of being tainted by her loss.

'I don't know about that. I'm a bit worried about what she wants in return.' He laughed too, his blue eyes flashing, and Cass had a sudden image of the surly Mrs Bentley pursing up her tight thin lips and closing her eyes.

She found himself suppressing a grin. 'Coffee?'

'If it's not rationed.'

'I think I can manage.'

'I need one after today. Those kids . . . So much energy.'

'I thought that was a nice touch this morning.' Cass remembered the way he'd donated his scarf to Ben's snowman. He wasn't wearing it now and she wondered if it was still there, soaked through and freezing in the playing field.

'Purely selfish.' He sipped his coffee. 'It's a good way of getting to know the kids. And for the new ones to settle in, of course.' His smile faded. 'Actually, I wonder if I might ask you something.'

'What is it?'

He sighed. 'I'm a little concerned. It's probably nothing, but . . . Well, you noticed we've been doing a lot of fun activities with the kids. It's only fair when half their classmates are out sledging. We had an art session today.' He took something from the inside pocket of his jacket, a piece of paper.

As he unfolded it Cass saw coloured scribbles, primary colours: sunshine yellow, blue, red. Something inside her froze. Was he saying Ben had a problem? The picture looked bright and colourful. She'd heard that unhappy kids, depressed kids, drew everything in black.

Mr Remick held the picture out. 'It's probably nothing,' he started, but Cass wasn't listening any more. The main colour was yellow. It was the desert, stretching on and on. In the foreground was a soldier with sandy hair and a sandy uniform. His face was scribbled out. Cass could see where the pencil had punched and ripped its way through the paper. A black pencil.

One of the figure's limbs was bent backwards, a

broken, puppet thing. Red spray spouted from his chest. The ground, though, was littered with specks of brilliant blue.

Cass closed her eyes and remembered the stones Pete had held out to her in her dream. The ones that fell to the ground and disappeared. She reached out and touched the edge of the paper, but she didn't take it from Mr Remick's hands. *So angry*, she thought. She'd never suspected her son was so angry.

'Forgive me,' he said. 'I thought you'd have seen similar things before. Obviously not.'

Cass shook her head, sucked in a deep breath. 'He lost his father.' It was the first time she'd managed those words without her voice breaking. 'He was in Afghanistan.'

'I'm sorry.'

Cass' lips formed the word *No*, but she didn't speak.

Blue stones. A yellow sky, the same colour as the earth. And red, all that red.

'Well, there's no wonder in that case. Expressing his feelings in some way is probably good for him under the circumstances.'

Cass nodded, remembering the way Ben had sat in front of his game the last time he'd tried to play, letting the controller slide from his hands. It had once been his favourite game, but really that had been because of Pete.

He might simply have drawn something he'd seen on the screen.

Cass wondered what her son was doing now. He'd gone to play Damon's games, hadn't he? She bit her lip, and felt Mr Remick's hand gently resting on her arm.

'He'll be fine. He's a great kid, a credit to you. He's finding his feet already.'

She turned, and found Mr Remick's face inches from her own, his eyes full of concern. She drew back. She hadn't sensed he was so close.

He straightened and Cass found herself wanting to apologise. She bit her lip instead. She didn't trust herself to say anything. *It was my loss too*, she thought.

As if he could read her, Mr Remick said, 'You'll both be fine. It'll be like you belong here in no time.'

Cass frowned.

'Hoarding bread, building a bunker, burying tins . . .'

She flashed him a startled look and they both burst into laughter. Cass' lasted longer than Mr Remick's. She felt that lightness again, something lifting from her shoulders.

'I'd better go,' he said.

'You could stay for something to eat, if you like.' Cass glanced at the clock. How had it got so late so quickly? 'I could do . . .' She paused.

'Toast?' He smiled, glanced at the loaf of bread.

'I think I can rustle up something better than that.'

'Really, I'd better get back. I have essays to mark.'

When Cass saw him out and closed the door behind him, the apartment felt too quiet. She stared around at the hallway. There were still boxes waiting to be unpacked, pushed under the stairs. Her eyes fell on the telephone that was fixed to the wall.

It was an entryphone – visitors would ring her apartment from the main doorway, and she would press a button to let them in. She frowned. Mr Remick had come straight to her door – she hadn't thought anything of it until now, but how had he done that?

She remembered the door down the hall with the papers pushed underneath. Maybe whoever lived there had let him in. Mr Remick was new in Darnshaw, wasn't he? There was no way he could have the code – unless he'd been and looked around the mill himself, considered moving here before finding somewhere else. The code was 1234Z, which wasn't difficult to remember.

Still, she wished she'd asked him if he knew who was living down the hall. And how long he'd been in Darnshaw, exactly, to be Mrs Bentley's special customer, even to know her name. Cass found herself wishing she'd asked him lots of things.

It was a shame he'd had to go so soon. Time had passed more quickly when Mr Remick was there. Now she was alone, and with no Ben filling the place with noise it was too quiet in Foxdene Mill. Cass remembered the empty windows in the apartment below hers and shivered. It was a pity more people hadn't moved in. Mr Remick might even have been a neighbour. She had a sudden picture of him climbing in through an empty window frame downstairs and smiled.

Cass went to her own window and saw the snow drifting silently down, smothering everything. The light was failing and the hilltops appeared paler than the sky. She felt anxious about Ben. He would have to walk back later, through the dark and the snow. Still, with a friend he'd enjoy it, kicking a new trail and throwing snowballs all the way.

She unpacked the last of their boxes, crushed them and sat looking at the pile of cardboard. It was good to have that finished – the place felt more like a home – but it also meant that she was staying. Before, she had been half-settled in, half-ready to walk out of the door again. She thought about the people she'd met: Mrs Bentley, with her surly glare, slamming Cass' shopping down on the counter. Loud, brassy Sally – and Mr Remick. When she thought of him he was smiling, and his blue eyes looked directly into her own. He saw into people, she thought. She imagined reaching out a hand and touching the teacher's slightly hollowed cheek, the stubble under her fingers. Him wrapping those arms, thin but sure, around her.

She pushed the thought away, remembered Pete. Her husband had been taller, stronger, nothing like Mr Remick, and yet she thought that she could find the teacher attractive. Mostly it was in the way he looked at her, those clear, appraising eyes.

Cass glanced at the clock. It was past six. Sally hadn't said how long they'd be, and she hadn't thought to ask. *We'll call when we're setting off.* Hadn't she said that? At least Cass knew where she lived. It was lucky they'd picked her up on the moor. She wondered if Ben would come home complaining about her smell again, and tried not to smile.

He'd be enjoying himself; they all would, Sally and Damon and Ben.

Cass noticed that Mr Remick had left Ben's drawing on the sofa. She picked it up, straightened it out and ran a finger over the paper where his pencil had punched through. She imagined his face while he was doing it, his head bent over the page, his eyes fixed in a glare while he scribbled, over and over, and then taking the most brilliant blue he could find and adding those stones, if that was what they were, across the yellow sand. She frowned, wondering what had made him think of it.

Cass looked at the clock again, wishing her son would come home. The night grew darker, the snow kept falling, and still Sally didn't call. Cass sat back on the sofa and closed her eyes, letting the picture fall to her side.

When Cass stirred and looked out of the window it was no longer dark. Mist had swallowed the hills and the sky and now it was shining back the moonlight, making it bright as morning. When she checked the clock, though, she found it was late – after nine o'clock – and Sally still hadn't called. She must have fallen asleep; now her head ached. She walked from window to telephone, wondering if it had rung after all and she had been too deeply asleep to hear it. She bunched her hands, fidgeted. How could Sally be so late? Why hadn't she been in touch? Tears surprised her, stinging her eyes. She could try to recover the last caller's number from her telephone and ring her. Failing that, she could walk to Sally's house, but what if Sally took the riverside path, or some other route? She could miss them.

There were voices in the hall.

Cass rushed to the door and pulled it open and found herself staring into an empty space. She looked up and down the hall, wondering if this was some game they were playing.

She heard the sound again. This time it came from behind her.

It was the voice of a child – it sounded like a little girl.

She waited, reluctant to turn round, then she heard the deeper tones of a man. She felt her grasp on the door slip and it banged shut in front of her.

A new sound began, low at first, then gathering in volume, a ratcheting and banging of wood on wood, wood on metal. It grew louder, became deafening.

Cass slowly turned round, half expecting to see a space full of machinery, but there was only her own hall, all the doors closed except the one dead ahead.

Cass went to it, outwardly calm but her heart hammering. She looked into the lounge and saw only a familiar room, its darkened windows reflecting back the vaulted ceiling. It was silent. The sound had stopped.

—but it had ceased only for a moment; as though called back by her thoughts it started up again, the rhythmic pulse of running machinery, reverberations echoing from the walls. The floor beneath her was full of the sound, vibrating under her feet. The noise came from the room below her own, Apartment 6.

Cass couldn't move. She couldn't breathe. She saw again the abandoned dolls, the empty windows, cold air snaking inside.

Then she heard a bang on her front door and every-thing fell silent.

Cass looked around at the floor, her jaws clenched. The

bang came again and she made a sound in the back of her throat.

Another bang. It was the sound of someone knocking.

Cass found she could breathe again, roused herself, hurried to answer. She yanked the door open, and saw Ben standing on the threshold, his arm outstretched in readiness to knock once more. He jumped back, his smile fading.

'Goodness,' said Sally, 'is everything all right? You look awful.'

Cass didn't turn away from Ben's face. He had looked so happy when she'd pulled the door open; now there was a trace of sadness in his eyes. It was her; she had called it back again.

'I'm sorry we're late,' said Sally chattily. 'We lost track of time, didn't we, boys? I tried to call, but the lines must be down. It always happens this weather. I should have known. And these two – you wouldn't believe how long it took them to walk down here. The snowballs I've been fighting off, you wouldn't believe—'

'Did you hear something?'

'What like? Has something happened?'

Cass looked at her. Sally's face was full of confusion, and something else – annoyance perhaps. It occurred to Cass that she didn't look sorry for being late at all. There was no sense of urgency about her. 'It's quite all right,' she said stiffly. 'He's back now, aren't you, Ben?'

Ben's eyes were fixed on his mother. He shrugged, and somehow this made Cass angry, really deeply angry, but she swallowed it down. She couldn't turn Sally straight back out onto the street after they'd walked all this way, and that look on Ben's face – he had been enjoying himself, at least until he got home.

She noticed Damon standing behind his mother. The boy glared up at her through his black fringe.

'Hi, Damon,' she said pointedly. 'Have you had a good night?'

It was as though she hadn't spoken.

Sally answered for him. 'We've had a lovely time. They played for hours on the computer. I swear my hands would be claws if I did that.'

'It was *Street Skirmish*, Mum!' Ben's smile had returned. 'I was the baddie, and then Damon was, and we had a tournament, and he won, but I got loads of rounds, didn't I, Day?'

Damon swung his head round to look at Ben and he grinned, his eyes clear and smiling.

Cass shook her head. What was she thinking? 'Thank you for having him, Sally,' she said. 'Will you have a drink before you go? Something to warm you up?'

They bustled in, and as they took off their wet coats, discarded gloves and scarves and boots, something Sally had said finally registered. 'Sally,' said Cass, 'did you say the phone lines are down?' Her voice was sharp and Sally looked up with surprise.

'I did. It often happens with the snow. It'll take a few days to fix, I shouldn't wonder.'

But Cass was already striding into the lounge, snatching up the telephone. There was no buzzing on the line, nothing but a faint silvery noise like snowfall.

'They'll be back up before long. I'm sure people will realise. Was there someone you wanted to call?'

'Not really.' Cass slowly replaced the phone. 'Just some files I should have sent off for work.' *It'll be done for tomorrow morning*, she'd said. Now she'd have no email, and she couldn't even ring her client to tell them the job would be late. She couldn't get a signal on her mobile either. Why hadn't she done the work today? She could have finished it this afternoon, sent it off at once. But surely the telephones would be fixed tomorrow. Maybe everything would be: the road cleared, the car running smoothly, everything working the way it should. She glanced at the window. She could just make out the steep hillside, mocking in its beauty.

'Oh dear,' said Sally. 'Well, they'll understand, won't they? It's not as if it's your fault, after all.'

We launch in a week.

Cass bit her lip. She had a week – no, not so long. They would want it all in place before that.

Sally's right, they'll fix the phones tomorrow, she told herself. It'll be fine. Even Mr Remick had said so. That hand on her arm. Those eyes. *It'll all be fine.*

Ben and Damon sat on the floor, drinking hot chocolate. Damon had asked for Coke, but Cass didn't have any and Damon had looked his contempt at her. Ben didn't seem to notice the older boy's surliness. He showed Damon his games, chattering away about each one, and they both groaned when Sally declared it was time to go. She clapped her hands and Damon scowled as he dragged himself to his feet.

'Say thank you.'

'What for?'

'Don't be rude. Say thank you for the drink and hurry up.'

Damon turned those eyes on Cass. The irises were dark, almost as dark as his pupils, and they held a pale gleam. 'Thank you for the *chocolate*,' he said.

Cass chose to ignore the emphasis in his words. 'You're very welcome.' She took the cup from his outstretched hand and saw an ugly mark crossing his palm. 'Oh, what happened? Are you all right?'

She felt Sally's gaze on her, but she bent and took Damon's hand anyway, turning it so she could see the wound. It wasn't fresh, nor was it as livid as she'd thought. He'd cut it some time in the past, and the skin was a deeper pink where it had healed. Damon left his hand in hers for a second, a cold, limp thing, then whipped it away.

Cass expected his mother to say something, tell him off again, maybe, but she did not. When Cass looked round she saw that Sally's mouth was pressed into a thin line. They said their goodbyes and Cass closed the door on them, leaning her head on it in relief.

Then she thought of the entryphone. Sally hadn't used it either; she'd come straight up the stairs to the apartment door. So either she knew the code too or the main entrance hadn't been locked. Cass didn't think that Ben had memorised the code yet – he hadn't come in alone before, had never needed to.

She turned to Ben. 'How did you get in? Did Mrs Spencer have the code?

He shrugged and turned back to his games, stacking them in a neat pile, lining up the edges.

'Ben, I asked you a question.'

He looked up, shrugged again, stuck out his bottom lip.

Cass sighed. 'I'm popping downstairs for a minute,' she said. 'Be ready to let me in, okay? I might ring the entry-phone. You know where it is, right?'

He nodded without looking up.

Cass slipped out of the door and down the stairs, wall lights flickering on in response to her movement. The newspapers outside Number 10 hadn't moved. They looked forlorn, abandoned.

The mill grew cooler as she went down the empty stair-case to the front door. She turned the inside handle a few times, listening to the clicks, trying to work out if it was locking. Then she pulled the door open and stepped outside.

She began shivering at once. There was a single light outside the mill, a wrought-iron lamp designed to look like an old-fashioned streetlight. Snow flurried around it as though attracted by its brightness. Everything else was dark. When Cass looked up, pale flakes danced out of the blackness and into her face.

She looked about and let the door shut behind her. When she turned back she found herself face to face with that nasty knife-work in the door. She had forgotten the cross. What must Mr Remick have thought? He'd not mentioned it. She put her hand to the cold brass handle and tried turning it, but it wouldn't budge; the lock was obviously working.

Cass flicked snow from her hair, brushed more from the keypad. She began to tap in the entry code, then cancelled it and put in the apartment number instead. The entryphone was an internal system, so it shouldn't be affected by the snow. She could hear it ringing: three, four, five. *Come on, Ben.*

The ringing stopped and Cass put her face to the grille. 'Ben, it's me.'

There was only the almost imperceptible sound of snow settling around her. She tapped in the apartment number again and waited. Maybe it was wired wrongly and wasn't connecting with Number 12 at all. She imagined the phone ringing in an empty apartment – the one on the ground floor maybe. She had a sudden image of someone in there, a dark shape turning and hearing the sound. Rising to its feet and going to answer.

Cass cut it off. She punched in the entry code instead, the metal slick and cold against her fingers, and heard the buzz as the lock disengaged. She stepped inside and slammed the door behind her, hurried up the stairs and rapped at the apartment door for Ben.

She waited. After a while she knocked again.

No response. She couldn't hear any sound from inside. 'Ben, do you hear me?' she called out. She knocked again, louder this time. Stared at the brass 12 screwed into the wood. 'Ben!'

He didn't answer. Cass waited, then banged louder,

angling her fist to make it resonate on the wood. She felt the pain in her knuckles as a distant thing. 'Ben!' She tried again, knocking seven, eight, nine times. Then she opened her hand and slapped it against the door. At last she subsided, leaning against it.

She glanced down the silent hall, and for a second she imagined neighbours, lots of them, opening their doors and leaning out to stare. She squeezed her eyes shut and turned back to her own door. Her breath came heavily, as though she'd been running up the stairs and up and down the hallways, all over the mill, in search of her son. But he wasn't lost; Ben was safe at home; it was she, Cass, who was stuck outside.

She knocked again, harder, so that her knuckles sang out, and when she put them to her lips she saw they were red. 'Ben, please! Let me in.'

She tried to steady her breathing. What if he wasn't inside at all? What if he'd already gone? *Already?* Why had she thought that? It wasn't going to happen, would never happen. They would always be together; she would look after him—

That's why you're out here yelling yourself hoarse.

Cass slid down the door and rested her back against it. Then she turned, rising to her knees as though pleading with the door to open. She reached up and caught the handle, twisted it, rattling the door on its hinges. 'Ben, it's me. Let me in, now!'

She got to her feet and pressed her ear to the wood, but there was no sound, not even the burble of the TV or the flush of a toilet to explain why he hadn't let her in.

'Oh God,' she whispered, 'Ben, *please*.' She banged again, then pushed at the door with her whole body, and she felt it give a fraction before it met the jamb.

'Ben—' She wailed, not a mother's voice, a capable in-control voice, but a little-girl-lost voice, the same voice that had been threatening and pushing at her insides ever since Pete had left and they said he wasn't coming back, not this time, not ever again. *Her* voice.

She knocked. This time, when she took her hand away, there was blood on the knuckles. She sank back onto the floor and closed her eyes. There was no sound from inside, and none from the rest of the mill. Cass thought again of that apartment downstairs, the one with the empty windows. They would be like black eyes now, the snow swirling in and covering the floor, the dust, those dolls.

If anyone got inside she would be trapped in the hallways with them. Cass' throat went dry.

Ben might be ill – he could have collapsed in there, might need help.

Cass looked down the hall to Number 10. The newspapers were still there. She pushed herself up and went to the door. She hesitated before she tried it, but even so she knew there would be no answer. She had been banging so loudly, there was no way anyone inside wouldn't have heard her.

The door of Number 12 opened and Ben stuck his head out. His hair was tousled, in need of a cut, and he had brushed it down over his eyes like Damon's. He looked up and down and saw her. 'Are you coming?' he asked and closed the door.

Cass walked down the hall as though sleepwalking, her legs unsteady. She pushed on the door with its brass 12, half expecting it to have locked again behind her son, but he had put it on the latch. Why hadn't she thought of that?

She went in, slowly, and locked the door behind her.

Ben was in the lounge, starting up his game. His back was turned to Cass. He sat quite still, only his hands moving on the controls, small and capable.

'Where were you?'

There was no answer. Nor did he stop.

'Ben, why didn't you let me in? You must have heard me knocking.' There was a plaintive note to Cass' voice she couldn't banish. *Little girl lost.* She looked down at her hand, spreading the bloody knuckles.

There was a pause before Ben answered, as though he wasn't really listening: 'I did,' he said.

Cass stormed over and pulled him to his feet, turned him to face her. 'You didn't,' she said, 'not for *ages*. Look.' She held her hand out to him, showing him the blood.

His face was blank and he looked at her with half-closed eyes. 'I didn't hear anything,' he said. 'Only the rats.'

Then his eyes came into focus and he looked at her hand. It was shaking. Ben took hold of it in both of his and leaned forward. Cass expected him to kiss it better, but he did not; he stuck out his smooth pink tongue and licked her bloody knuckle.

Cass snatched it away. 'What are you doing?'

When he met her gaze there was a light in his eyes she didn't like: an appraising look, a knowing look. 'Ben?'

The expression in his eyes vanished as though it had never been there. He grinned, showing his white teeth. 'Are you going to play with me, Mum?'

Cass straightened.

'We can have a competition. We did that at Damon's. He's my best friend.' His expression was genuine, the transparent smile of a child, but Cass still heard the words with dismay. *He's my best friend.* She remembered Damon's surly glare, the way Ben had looked at her just a moment ago. Is that where he'd learned it?

'He's got *Street Skirmish*. Did I say? It was a present – for Christmas. No, not Christmas. Something else.'

'Something else?'

'Yeah. And it was really, really good. Can I get it, Mum?'

'We'll have to wait and see.' The words came automatically, but while she was speaking Cass noticed something. She bent and took hold of Ben's top, twisting it. A dark stain was splashed onto the fabric. It had crusted over, a deep rust-brown. 'What's that?'

Ben pulled away. 'Ribena,' he said. 'Have we got any Ribena, Mum? Damon's mum has. She's got everything.'

'Has she?' Cass muttered, but Ben didn't hear, he had already dropped to the floor, the controls ready in his hand, and started up a new game.

Ben slept peacefully that night. Cass knew this because she kept waking in the dark, wondering where she was, feeling uncomfortable and unsettled. She imagined Ben the same way, hot and feverish, but when she went in she found him lying on his back, resting his head on one hand, his face tilted to one side. The nightlight illuminated the pale curve of his cheek. He breathed steadily, as a sleeping child should.

Cass stood over him for a while, not wanting to go back to bed. She knew she had been dreaming, and though she couldn't recall any of the details, the feeling of it stayed with her.

Eventually Ben sighed and turned over, and Cass tiptoed from the room. She lay awake a long time, and then, as though on cue, as she began to close her eyes the scratching in the walls began.

When the dream came, Cass sensed someone leaning over her. She couldn't see a face, but she knew the tall, broad figure, the black folds that fell from it. She could feel the way he looked at her.

Her father leaned in closer, hair gleaming as candlelight shone through it. He held something out, a small white disc.

Cass opened her mouth, and he placed it on her tongue. It was dry and papery and tasted of nothing. 'This is love,' he said, and Cass woke again, cold to the bone, sitting up and staring into the dark.

TEN

The world was hidden by a mist that drifted in sheets across the hillside, masking everything, turning the trees into veiled figures with their arms outstretched. Cass stood at the window, drinking coffee that failed to clear her head.

Ben munched on Weetabix from his football bowl, stuffing in great mouthfuls and swallowing as quickly as he could. He poured more milk with one hand, still scooping up spoonfuls with the other. He saw her watching. 'We're playing football in the gym today,' he said. 'Damon's going to show me how to do keepie-uppie on my neck.'

Cass stirred. Her neck was stiff, her limbs sluggish. When she'd looked in the mirror there were dark circles under her eyes. She'd spent half the night thinking about Ben, and now she was awake it was her client she was worried about, pacing up and down his office, waiting for his missing files.

'Come on, Mum.' Ben's spoon clattered into the bowl, scattering droplets of milk. 'Have you got my kit?'

Cass checked the clock, swore under her breath and gathered it together, grabbed his bag and lunch and the keys. They pulled on their coats as they went down the stairs. Last night's lockout already felt unreal, like something she'd dreamed.

They waded through the snow, which squeaked under their boots. The lane was solid white, the top layer hardened like pastry crust. Ben picked some up, karate-chopping it into pieces.

'Hurry up, Ben,' she called.

He jumped up and ran ahead, waving his arms, and Cass saw Bert standing at the top of the hill, a now-familiar figure. Captain was, as usual, at his master's side, chest heaving between squat wide-set legs, breath puffing out rhythmic plumes.

Cass waved and hurried on, but she wasn't as quick as Ben, who ran straight for the dog, arm outstretched to stroke Captain's black muzzle.

Cass was still yards away when she heard Captain's jaws snap together. She blinked. Everything was still, so that she thought she must have imagined it: the lunge forward, the heavy chest straining, the neck stretching forward as grizzled lips drew back over old yellowed teeth.

Then everything started to move: Ben pulling his arm away, cradling it in the other, shrieking; Bert holding Captain back; Cass calling her son's name.

She reached Ben's side and took his arm. His eyes narrowed and he fought, hitting out with his other hand. His splayed fingers caught in her hair and Cass felt strands of it rip from her skull, but she didn't care; she was too busy running her fingers over his arm, checking for blood, for the holes Captain's teeth must have made.

There was nothing, only a string of drool that had dribbled across his coat, darkening the red cloth so that it looked like blood.

Ben twisted, dragging his arm away. 'Get off me. Get *off.*'

'I'm sorry,' Bert said, over and over, a monotone background to everything. 'I'm sorry. I never— I never—'

'Ben, are you all right?'

'I don't think 'e got 'im; 'e just tried it on, that's all. He were 'appen messin' about, weren't you, Captain?'

Ben stepped back, glaring at the dog. That gleam in his eyes, the cold look of the evening before, was back.

Something inside Cass clenched and she turned to Bert in a fury. 'Get that dog away from my son! He's dangerous. He ought to have a muzzle.'

Even as she saw Bert's shocked face she pictured them together, Ben and the dog, playing with the old green ball in the park, the dog waddling after the ball, slow but game, tail wagging furiously.

'Sorry,' Bert said again. The old man stared down at his dog, his face pale, lost in disbelief. 'Captain,' he said. '*Captain.*'

Cass felt for Ben's hand. He pulled away but she caught and held it. She skirted Bert and the dog, keeping her son behind her.

'Miss,' said Bert.

She turned and saw that his eyes were pale and more watery than ever. Brim full. 'I'm so sorry—'

'I'm sure . . .' she began, but she didn't know how to continue, and anyway, how could she tell him it was all right? It could have been far from all right. Cass closed her mouth and walked away, leading Ben towards the road.

When she had put some distance between them, she stopped and squatted down in front of Ben. 'Are you all right, love?'

Ben nodded. His lips were pressed together, almost vanished into his face.

'We can go home again if you want. Did the dog hurt you?'

He shook his head.

'Just your feelings?'

Ben's eyes narrowed, and that light was back in them. He screwed up his face and shook his head. There was hatred in his look.

'I'm sure he didn't mean it. He's an old dog, he must have been startled. We'll have to be careful, won't we, if we see him again.'

Ben blew out his breath with a *tch*. Cass felt the warmth of it on her face.

'All right,' she whispered. 'You're the boss.'

This would normally draw a smile, but Ben didn't even look at her. He stared into the distance until Cass straightened and they began walking towards the school once more.

As they approached the gates, Ben pulled away and bounded off towards a group of children. He tapped on someone's back and they put their heads together, gossiping with their hands cupped around their words. The other boy looked up, and Cass saw without surprise that it was Damon. She smiled at him, but he just stared at her.

Ben waved, ran with Damon to the entrance and was gone. Cass stopped. She could not see anyone she knew except one of the mothers Sally had introduced her to. Moira? Myra? She had long hair that hung loose, very straight down her back. Cass caught her eye and smiled. The other woman's eyes slid away and she bent to kiss her child on the cheek. Cass pursed her lips. She was sure Myra had seen her.

Mr Remick appeared in the doorway and walked towards her, his arms spread in a welcoming gesture. 'Nice to see you,' he called out.

'You too,' said Cass, and found she meant it. She looked up at him. It struck her that his face shouldn't be attractive: the hollowed cheeks, the nose with its slight hook. His skin was dry, a little uneven, almost pockmarked, but his eyes – they were beautiful.

Cass shook her head and tried to look as though she hadn't been staring. She couldn't think of anything to say.

'You look well, Cass. Darnshaw agrees with you,' Mr Remick said in a low, confidential voice. 'It's a beautiful day.'

She followed his gaze to see the sun shining on the hillside. It picked out the brilliant snow against the sharp-blue sky.

'Really,' he said, 'you'll love it here.' He touched her arm, so lightly she wasn't sure she'd felt it, and walked off, already calling out to another parent.

Cass turned to see Myra watching her, and this time the woman was openly glaring. So that's how it was: she was jealous; all of the mothers besotted with the new teacher, and Sally no doubt starting rumours with her silly jokes. Well, Cass wouldn't let it bother her. She gave Myra a friendly smile, turned to go and saw Lucy's Land Rover pulling into the car park. She waved and Lucy grinned as she jumped down and helped Jessica from her seat. Lucy noticed Mr Remick too and waved, but her eyes were distant. It looked like she at least was immune to his charms.

'Funny about Mrs Cambrey,' she called out as Cass approached.

Cass had almost forgotten about the teacher she'd spoken to before Ben joined the school. 'She had a family problem, didn't she? I wonder how she's doing.' It occurred to her that Mr Remick's tenure at the school might be short-lived.

'I haven't heard anything. I suppose it might be a while before we do, with the phones being down in Darnshaw. She might be ready to come back, but with this snow she'll be stuck on the other side of the hills.'

Cass nodded, but her thoughts were on the files, the work that was waiting to be sent to her client. It had been at the back of her mind all morning.

'Is everything okay?'

'Oh yes, I'm fine.'

'Sorry. It's just you look a bit tired.'

Cass knew that Lucy was right, despite Mr Remick's earlier compliment. 'I didn't sleep so well. I suppose I'm still getting used to the place. It's nothing really. It's nice of you to ask.'

'Well, come on,' said Lucy, and took Cass' arm. 'I'll give you a lift home. No, I insist. You're on the way anyway. You can thank me with a cup of tea, and show me Foxdene Mill. I'd love to see it. I'm something of a history buff, but I've never been inside – silly really, when I drive past it all the time.'

'I can even manage biscuits – despite the rationing.'

'Oh heavens, has the shop closed already? Ridiculous. You'd think we were in the Arctic, not Saddleworth. Honestly, a bit of snow in this country and everything comes to a grinding halt.'

Cass climbed into the Land Rover. 'Some people are better equipped than others. I wish I had one of these.'

The car climbed easily up the slope and onto the road. 'They haven't even gritted down here yet,' Lucy observed, 'or sent the plough. It gets worse every year. Too expensive, I suppose.'

'I can't even get my car up the hill.'

'Have you got plenty of food in?'

'Yes.' They might have to skimp for a while, but it would do.

'Our nearest shop's the size of a postage stamp, but we go straight to the farms in times like this. If you need anything, let me know. I keep the shelves well-stocked.'

'I don't suppose . . . ?'

'What is it? Anything I can do.'

'Well, it's just— You said before that the phone lines are down in Darnshaw. I don't suppose they're still working where you live? I really need to send some files to someone and if you had email . . .'

'No problem at all. Our phones were still on last night. Stick them on a disk for me.'

Cass' face lit up. 'Are you serious?'

'Of course.' Lucy turned to her and laughed. 'It's no problem, honestly. Happy to help out an almost-neighbour. Most people will, around here. We're not all in the Mothers' Club. I saw that Myra woman glaring at you. That'll teach you to chat up the new bloke.'

Cass turned, her mouth falling open, and they burst into laughter.

Lucy turned the car onto the lane and braked at the top of it. The mill was golden against its black and white backdrop. The sun had gained a little height and its rays struck the stone, turning it the colour of the desert. It was silent and still and peaceful. There was barely another house to be seen looking down the valley. Lucy caught her breath. 'It really is beautiful. You lucky thing.'

Cass found herself smiling. 'I suppose I am,' she said. How many people lived in a building like this, in countryside like this? Not many.

Then she remembered the silent halls, the sense of emptiness pressing in. 'It's very quiet,' she said. 'I think there's only us living there – except that someone's been getting the papers delivered. I don't suppose you know who else might have taken an apartment?'

'I'm afraid I don't. You're the first I've heard of. I dare say a few more will be snapped up once the roads clear. Then the builders will finish it, I suppose.'

'I hope so. That might clear the mice.' *Rats*, Ben had said.

'Mice? Oh no! Well, I suppose it is a big empty building.'

'As long as they don't nick the bread.' They were laughing again as they jumped out of the car and ploughed their way to the front door. Cass' own car was buried in the snow, only a band of metal visible along the side. Everything was colourless except the stone of the mill and the scarred red door.

'Look at that,' Lucy exclaimed as they drew near. She went to the door and put out her hand towards the thing scratched into the wood, but drew back without touching it.

'I know,' said Cass, 'it's such a mess. I don't suppose it'll be painted over in a hurry either.'

Lucy bit her lip. 'Vandals, I suppose.' She was leaning in, staring at the mark.

'What is it?'

Finally Lucy did touch it, slipping her glove from her hand and running her fingertips along the length of the cross. 'It's strange,' she said. 'Who would use a cross in graffiti? If it was a cross of confusion, or inverted . . . but a normal cross? It doesn't exactly spell rebellion.'

Cass nodded. 'I thought it must be random, or . . . I don't know, part of a band logo or something.' She paused. 'What's a cross of confusion?'

'It's a cross that curves – here – into a question mark.

A sign of rebellion against authority – any authority, earthly or heavenly, or so it's believed.' She grinned at Cass. 'I really do like history. Well, the cross of confusion was used as a symbol in Darnshaw to gather witches together – under its banner, so to speak. Darnshaw was something of a centre for it.'

'Witchcraft?' Cass was incredulous. She had heard no such stories when she'd lived here as a child – but perhaps they weren't the kind of stories to tell children.

'I'm afraid so. They say the mill-workers were among the most dedicated followers. It's a bit nasty, actually: not just black candles and dancing-round-the-campfire sort of stuff, but blood rituals and sacrifice – even children.'

'They sacrificed *children*?'

Lucy looked away. 'I did hear of one case . . . But it was more a matter of the children doing the sacrificing.' She paused. 'It was adults who planned it all, of course. They believed that the loss of innocence, by a child committing some terrible act – well, they thought it gave them power. Nasty stuff. Of course it was years ago.' She turned back to the cross. 'I'm sure this is just kids messing about.'

'It was here? In the mill?'

'God, no – I'm sorry, Cass, I didn't mean to scare you. There was nothing in the mill itself, at least, not that I know of.' She frowned. 'It was all down by the river, I think, or out on the moor. And in the church.'

'The church?' Cass' eyes widened.

'Apparently so. Christianity took over all sorts of old signs and symbols. You can still see pagan symbols in the building if you look. But it was used for worse things too, unfortunately.'

All Cass could see was her father, bending towards her in his black robes, pressing dry bread onto her tongue. *This is love.* The commitment he'd shown, the zeal of a convert – had he known about the church's history here?

'It'll be kids,' Lucy said, 'messing about. Like you said, it's probably random.'

'Just kids,' Cass repeated under her breath. *Children, doing the sacrificing.* She shivered, and looked up at the mill once more. It would be easy to let her imagination run wild, being out here alone. Too easy.

'Teenagers with nothing to do.' Lucy tossed her hair back. 'They're too cool for sledging these days, aren't they?'

Cass tapped the entry code into the keypad, showed Lucy inside and made coffee, trying not to think about witches hiding around every corner.

While they chatted Cass fired up her computer, already composing the message to her client in her mind. She transferred the files onto a disk and explained to Lucy what she'd done.

'I'll let you know later if he answers,' Lucy said. She sat back, taking in the high vaulted ceiling, the tall windows. 'This is a great building. However did you find it? Where did you say you were from?'

'All over, really.' Cass paused. 'My husband was in the Army. We moved around a lot – it was hard on Ben.'

'That's rough.'

'This was meant to be a permanent base, somewhere nice for him to grow up.'

'It is a lovely place.'

'That's what I thought. A good school too.'

'You said it *was* meant to be a permanent base. Aren't you sure any more?'

Cass hadn't been aware she'd said it. 'I don't know. It's not like I remembered.'

'You're from Darnshaw then?' Lucy sounded surprised.

'Not originally. I lived here for a while when I was young.'

'Well, you've not had the best welcome, with the snow and all. But it is a good place to raise a family. It's lovely, really.'

Cass looked out of the window again and saw that yes, it was. The hillside blazed with light, glowing against the crisp blue sky, which deepened in colour at its zenith. She had a sudden image of Pete. In his hands he held the blue stones. They were the colour of sky, and his lips were moving, but she couldn't hear the words.

'Cass, are you okay?'

'I'm sorry. I was woolgathering.' Cass brushed it off, but felt tears pricking at her eyes anyway. 'You're right: Darnshaw's exactly what we need – what *Ben* needs. It's just . . . I miss Pete so much. We both do.' She paused. 'He was lost in Afghanistan.'

'God, Cass, I'm so sorry.'

'No, no, it's not your fault. I shouldn't have said anything. We both need to move on. I shouldn't even keep saying he's lost. They said he's never coming back. *Lost,* I keep saying, and then I expect Ben to understand that he's not coming home.'

Lucy was silent.

'I'm sorry, going on like that. I didn't know that was coming.'

They sat for a while, not saying anything. Then Lucy straightened up and rose, and Cass thought she would probably never come back, but at the bottom of the stairs she turned and looked at Cass. 'Listen,' she said, 'if you ever want to talk, it's fine. It's nice to meet someone who doesn't want to go on about the best recipe for strawberry jam, or play the "my-kid's-better-than-yours" game.'

Cass thought, *You'd rather talk about dead husbands?* But she smiled.

'Any time,' Lucy said. 'I'll see you later. I'll let you know how I get on with the email.'

She means it, thought Cass. *She's not just trying to get away.* 'I'll look forward to it. And no tears, I promise.' They laughed once more, and Cass waved her off. The Land Rover went steadily up the hill, leaving Cass alone at the scarred red door.

She started to go inside, then stopped and ran her fingers over the splintered wood. When she turned and looked towards the village, she could see the church spire rising blackly over the valley. Pagan signs, Lucy had said. Had her father ever mentioned such things? Cass couldn't remember.

A short while later she walked up the hill towards the church. This was where her father had spent so many days when she was a child, almost as though the church had been his home and Cass and her mother the distractions.

He had been drawn to it, circling it first, then drawing closer and closer, until he became that black creature, the one who put a dry wafer into her mouth and called it love. She closed her eyes. *Dad*, she thought.

And then, *Ben*. Oh God, Ben.

How had she not seen it before? Ben, crying for his dad, and Cass trying to show her son how to move on, trying to convince him that Pete wasn't coming back, to give up his father. And all the time in some way she'd been searching for her own father; following his traces to Darnshaw, the last place her own family had been complete, back when she was a child.

She shook her head, forcing herself to remember the good school, the healthy rural life, the way Ben was already fitting in. He would be happy here; she had done the right thing.

The church seemed to grow taller as she approached, and its stone looked blacker than ever as it rose against the sky. The promise of more snow was in the bitter air. Cass put her hand to the door and was surprised to find it wasn't locked. It swung in until it caught on the flags beneath and when she looked down she could see the stone bore deep scratches, etched by years of scraping. She tried to remember if it had been that way when she was a child and found she could not. She stepped inside, and it was as though she could smell the past, the tang of ancient stone and cold earth. It was tasteless. *This is love.*

At first everything inside the church was colourless. There were dark pews and a dark altar, and grey passages of light fell between them, thick with dust. Then Cass looked up and saw the splendour of the windows, almost dazzling: red, yellow, brilliant blue.

Cass walked across the stone floor. As she trailed a hand across the back of the pews she remembered the feel of them digging into her spine, the way she had kicked her feet, watching them bob in front of her, up, down, in buckled leather sandals. *White socks. The foamy froth of her dress.* She had looked up at her father, standing in front of everyone, so important. She hadn't known this place would take him away from them, that this was his family now, this dark church with its dry old smell. That he belonged to God.

She hadn't understood why God would want to take him from them – he didn't have to leave them behind; surely he could have kept them with him? She remembered her mother screaming that at him while Cass listened from her hiding place on the stairs. But her father was adamant once he had decided something, and in the end it was her mother and Cass who'd been the ones to leave.

Her mother had said *It was never a battle I could win.* At the time Cass hadn't understood what her mother had meant, but here, now, she almost thought she did.

Cass had been jealous, and the feeling flooded back into her mouth like bile. She was jealous of the God who had taken her father from them. And isn't that what they called him? A jealous God. She had imagined them, Cass and God on opposite sides of the room, being jealous of each other over this man.

He was mine first, she thought, closing her eyes. When she opened them, the colours mocked her.

All this time she had seen Darnshaw as a place for family, somewhere to build a home, and she had forgotten it was in Darnshaw that she had lost her own family – lost her father.

Cass sank into a pew, looking up through the layers of light. The high vaulted ceiling was studded with wooden bosses. A face peered down at her through a spray of leaves: a green man. A pagan emblem, just as Lucy had said. This one had its tongue sticking out in mockery.

The next boss looked like a mermaid, its long tail twisted around a young man she had saved or stolen, it wasn't clear which; then there was a reptile with its tongue lolling from its mouth. Cass leaned back. Next was a hairless man with a snake writhing about his head and caught between his teeth. Then a stag with human arms, and a sheep biting into the head of a wolf.

There are signs. Even in the church.

It wasn't so unusual; Lucy was right: lots of churches had been built on the holy sites of older religions and subsumed or fed upon them, taking their signs and symbols and making them into something new. Some even had ancient dolmen set into the walls or turned into gravestones, stone altars torn from their original places of worship.

Cass stood and walked to the front of the church, not liking the way the colours from the windows fell over her feet, her clothes; she could almost feel them on her skin.

The altar was heavy, a single stone slab, irregular and worn.

Cass reached out and put her hand on it, wondering what she had expected to find. The surface was partly covered by a narrow white cloth running down the centre. A silver crucifix stood upon that. A tiny Jesus stared back at Cass, his face twisted in agony.

Cass ran her hand over the cold stone. It was uneven, possibly still bearing the marks of ancient tools. As she ran her palms across the surface, her fingers found a neat groove nestled into it. She stroked the smooth runnel. Then she looked down and saw that the groove ran the length of the altar. *For drainage*, she thought, and pulled her hand away.

Rituals. Blood rituals, right from ancient times.

It didn't mean anything. The church had taken these old things long ago, made them part of the new religion. And this stone had been the right size and shape for its altar, that was all.

It was interesting, but it didn't mean anything.

ELEVEN

Cass walked back through the village. Everything was quiet. She saw a woman in the distance, brushing snow from her step with a dustpan and brush, but she straightened and went inside before Cass got close enough to say hello. The school was silent, although Cass thought she saw a figure pacing back and forth behind one of the windows. The next road down the hill ended in the park, and Cass turned that way. By the motionless swings was the gap in the bushes that led to the riverside path, where she'd first seen Bert and his dog.

Cass peered through, seeing no one, and stepped onto the narrow path, which was choked with snow-covered brambles.

The river chortled down the valley, splashing over black rocks. Snow overhung the banks, the edges fringed with transparent ice. Trees lined the river, their glossy black roots reaching into the water. Above them everything was white. Fields, moorland, sky. The air was potent with snow.

A rook stirred in a tree, stretching out a wing and one curled claw together. The branch he sat upon was edged with lace icing. Each small thing was beautiful.

There was a row of cottages that backed onto the river in a place where the path broadened out. Cass glanced at them curiously and had almost gone past when she stopped and turned.

The gate should be green, she thought, *not white.* She could see it in her mind: a small child hanging over it, swinging back and forth, listening to the river, dreaming of white dresses, perhaps, or buckled sandals, or simply of having her father come home.

Cass walked back and looked at the row of cottages, trying to decide if she really did remember it. Her mind felt emptied. She looked up and saw that the windows were blank, reflecting back the featureless white sky.

Her gaze fell to the riverbank and she saw grey down flecking the snow: a bird had died there. There was no blood, but there were bones, each one of them picked clean. Cass saw the socket where two bones had once joined. She frowned. The bones looked *arranged.* She leaned over and saw that they formed an almost perfect circle. She looked up once more at the cottages with their blank windows.

Rituals, Lucy had said – but in the past, before the mill became apartments and Cass came back to Darnshaw, probably long before even her father came here.

But stories like that: it was something that bored kids might seize on. They might have heard of Darnshaw's history, been excited by the thought of witchcraft and bones. They could have found the dead bird and amused themselves by arranging the bones that way.

Cass turned her back on them and followed the path, putting the bones out of her mind. Before long she could see the school playing fields. The snowmen were still there. She saw they had been built in a ring, and they now had faces. Stones had been thrust into them for noses or mouths – stones that were inexpressive, that couldn't smile, and yet each one looked startled, or sombre, or horrified.

Cass tore her gaze from them and saw that Bert was heading towards her on the path. His eyes were fixed on the ground so intently she was sure he was avoiding looking at her. She glanced about for a different track leading back up to the village that she might take, but there was none.

As he came closer Bert raised his watery eyes and tipped an imaginary hat. ''ow do, love. I'm right sorry about before. Glad to see yer, like.'

Cass cast a wary eye towards the dog, which stumbled to a halt behind Bert, his sides heaving. He looked docile, little inclined to move, let alone bite anyone.

'Hi, Bert,' she said. 'I'm sorry it happened too, but if he can't be trusted around children, maybe you should have him on a lead.'

Bert's face twitched. ''e's never been no trouble.'

'I know, but—'

'All right, love. I'll put 'im on a lead, if it makes yer feel better. It's no trouble. No trouble. I'd hate it if owt 'appened.'

'Me too. Thank you, Bert. I do appreciate it.'

''ow is 'e?'

'Ben? He's fine. He'd forgotten all about it by the time he got to school, so no harm done.'

'Good, good. Nice little feller— I mean . . .' Bert paused. 'You should watch 'im.'

'What?'

'You should watch 'im, in case he does owt. Make sure—'

'Ben's fine. He hasn't done anything wrong.' Even as she spoke, Cass remembered the look in her son's eyes, the way he had locked her out. *I thought it was just the rats.*

'I know, but—'

'Bert, he didn't *do* anything to Captain. You should watch your dog, never mind my son.'

'I din't mean that—'

Cass stared at Bert, and he stared down at the ground. After a long moment he gave the dog a nudge with his leg, edging him onto the verge so that Cass could get past.

'Thanks,' she said, walking away.

Bert turned. 'I meant it,' he said. 'If you ever need owt, you come and see me.'

Cass stopped and looked back at him. 'I know,' she said. 'It's very kind. Bye, Bert.' She said this last more firmly than she intended to, and instantly regretted it. Whatever the old man's words, he meant well. Though what did he mean – she should watch her son? He had a nerve.

Cass headed for home, pausing when she saw the back of the mill. Ice was spreading its fingers across the green surface of the millpond. Snow began to fall, feather-light flakes she couldn't feel as they settled in her hair. She didn't look at the cross carved into the door as she let herself in.

She checked her mailbox on the way, putting her hand inside, but she could already see there was nothing.

TWELVE

Cass stood outside the school waiting for Ben. She was early. Snow swirled around her, landing on her coat and gloves, the flakes remaining there, cool and perfect, before sinking into the fabric. Now that she'd stopped walking it was bitterly cold.

At last the doors flew open and the children poured out. Some whooped and grabbed handfuls of snow, shoving it in each other's faces, and others walked off, bored with it already. There weren't many children; more roads must be impassable now.

Ben was towards the back, his pale head bowed close to another boy's dark mop. Cass knew it was Damon, even without seeing his face. Then the boy looked up, his skin winter-pale, and smirked. He nudged Ben, whispered to him. They laughed together, and when Ben looked at her Cass barely knew him; there was an expression in his eyes she hadn't seen before.

Sally came out of the doorway with files under her arm, wearing a bulky purple coat. Right behind her was

Mr Remick, looking taller and thinner than ever by contrast. Then Lucy was at Cass' shoulder, her face pinched, holding something out. 'You got a reply,' she said, thrusting a sheet of paper into Cass' hand. 'I've got to run, Jess is waiting. Sorry.' And she was gone.

Cass stared after her. What had possessed her to tell Lucy about Pete this morning? The first friend she had made in Darnshaw, and Cass had obviously driven her away.

The paper crackled in her hand as she curled her fingers. Cass smoothed it out. It took her a moment to make out the words, though the message was short: 'What the hell? I've overwritten the files as instructed. Is this some sort of joke? Whole site now pulled. Need a fix ASAP.'

Cass stared at the printout. The ink shifted before her eyes but resolved into the same message.

Lucy. What had she done? She couldn't have sent the files properly. Or perhaps something else had been sent along with them, some virus perhaps. No wonder she had left so quickly. Cass turned, but the Land Rover was already pulling onto the road. It was too late to catch her.

She turned back to the note.

'Cass?'

She blinked. Mr Remick was standing at her shoulder, his eyes full of concern. 'I said, how are you doing? Everything all right, I hope.'

She looked at him. Ben was in front of her, his face blank.

'I – I don't understand.' Cass' voice wouldn't seem to come.

'Step inside a minute,' said Mr Remick. 'You look a bit faint.'

Sally's voice cut in. 'I'd run her back, but I didn't want to try the car down the lane this morning. It's too icy.'

'It's fine, Sally. You head off. I'll see she's okay.'

Cass breathed in deeply, the cold air shocking her lungs and bringing her back. 'I'm fine.' She managed a smile. She crumpled the note in her hand and stuffed it into her pocket; for some reason she didn't want Mr Remick to see it. 'Really, I just felt a bit dizzy. I'm okay. We'd best be off, hadn't we, Ben?'

Ben shrugged. He looked up at the teacher.

'I insist. Anyway, I owe you a coffee.' That dimple in his cheek, the slightly uneven skin made Cass want to reach out and touch his face. Mr Remick's voice was warm, comforting, and she allowed him to lead them both towards the school, down the corridor and into his office. He settled her into a seat and came back with coffee and biscuits on a tray. Ben grabbed one of the biscuits and started munching.

Everything on the desk was ruler-straight. A sign in the middle said MR T. REMICK.

'How's Mrs Cambrey?' asked Cass. It came out sounding blunt, and he just looked at her. She hesitated. 'I wondered how her family was doing.'

'I'm afraid I haven't heard – although I must admit I haven't enquired yet either. There's been so much to sort out, and classes to run since the other teachers haven't made it in. The road to Gillaholme is blocked altogether now.'

'It is?'

'There's a tree across the road – I dare say the snow brought it down.' He gave a sudden smile, flashing white teeth. 'Heaven knows when they'll clear it.'

Cass sipped her coffee.

'Of course some of the children live out that way too. We're running reduced classes – mixed-age groups, but it can't be helped. Ben seems to be enjoying it though – you are, aren't you?'

Ben grinned, swinging his legs under his chair.

'He's settling in really well.' It sounded almost like he was waiting for a response.

'Good. Good.' Cass looked up. 'And you – you seem to have settled in really well too.'

'Oh goodness, it's just like old times. A pea in a pod – it's like I've never been away.'

'You've been here before?'

'I'm a local.' Mr Remick grinned, picking up his own drink. 'My family's been here for generations – I own the old rectory. I'd already decided to come back so when Mrs Cambrey left shortly afterwards, I offered to fill in for a while.'

'That was lucky for the school. I wondered how you ended up here.'

'Oh, I always find my way back to Darnshaw. It's like you never quite get away.' He winked.

Cass shot a glance at Ben, but he hadn't seen. 'I wondered how you'd wangled the bread. Mrs Bentley didn't appear to be the friendly type.'

'She's a lamb – they all are, really. You'll find out.'

Cass tried to imagine having a friendly discussion with Mrs Bentley, and couldn't. 'We'd better get going,' she said.

Ben jumped up at once, though he still didn't look at her. He was staring at the door. 'Can't we go in the car?' he asked. His voice wasn't whiny, wasn't soft; it was hard, demanding. Cass stared at him.

'Don't be rude, Ben.'

Mr Remick gave a wry grin. 'I'd offer you a lift, but I don't often drive,' he said. 'No need, on the whole.'

'We wouldn't dream of putting you out. Come on, Ben. It'll do us good.'

They walked out into the snow and the darkening evening. Cass turned and waved, but Mr Remick had already gone inside. Ben hurried on ahead, ignoring her when Cass told him to wait.

'Ben, what's got into you?'

He stopped dead and stood with his back to her.

She hurried and caught his hand in hers. It was cold, limp in her fingers. 'Where are your gloves? Aren't you cold?'

Ben didn't even show he'd heard, just looked straight ahead into the snow, his face hidden under his hood.

'Ben? Did you hear me?'

Nothing.

'*Ben.*'

'You're crap at your job.' His voice was expressionless.

'What?'

Ben whipped his hand from hers and stomped away, his arms flapping noisily at his sides.

Cass watched him go. She put a hand to the pocket where she'd stuffed Lucy's printout and a sour taste flooded her mouth. Ben was already fading into the distance, swinging those loose arms at his side. She couldn't shake the thought that it was nothing but empty clothes walking away from her, heading into the greyness, inhabited by no one she could recognise.

Ben threw down his rucksack, went straight to the television and slumped down in front of it. When Cass finished taking off her coat he was sitting close to the screen with his back to her, a game already running.

Cass looked over his shoulder. The stub of a machine-gun jutted from the bottom of the screen, scanning left and right across a landscape of sand dunes. A helmet appeared over a rise and Ben fired, the helmet disintegrating in a spray of red.

'I thought you didn't like that game any more?'

Ben didn't answer. His character strode up the rise, scanning once more. This was the game he had played with his father. Pete had liked to give instructions, tell his son things he knew about, the kind of things he should watch for: *covering the angles*. Ben would listen, rapt, and then pretend he was defending his dad, getting the bad guys before the bad guys could get him.

Too late.

Ben threw a grenade into a wooden shed and it exploded in a whoosh of yellow flame.

'Are you winning?'

Another soldier, this one with a scarf covering his face,

exploded into red fragments. A hand landed on the ground, twitching, bleeding red pixels.

Cass opened her mouth and formed her son's name, but no sound came out.

She walked around the television and looked at his face. It was small and pale, his eyes gleaming. He didn't blink. His fingers were the only things that moved, dancing across the buttons, delivering death. He didn't whoop in triumph as he used to; instead, his face was cold. There was no excitement and no pain, no connection with his father in his eyes at all, or with anything else.

Cass turned from him and went to switch on her computer with fingers that felt numb. She touched her hand to her pocket and felt the crumpled paper.

She needed to check her files, then she could meet Lucy in the morning and ask her to re-send them. Or maybe Lucy would know someone whose computer would be clean who could do it for her.

You're crap at your job. Had her son really said that?

Cass stared at the screen, her frustration rising. Not long ago she had been able to send files herself at the press of a key. Now everything around her was breaking down: the telephones, the roads – if just one of those things functioned, even her mobile phone, it wouldn't be so bad. She could drive to her client, hand-deliver the files, explain – if she could – or at least speak to him. But this–? It was as though everything had stopped.

All the files were there, listed neatly in the client folder. Cass clicked it open and the page unfurled. The client's logo was still there at the top of the screen, and the header was the same, but the rest—

For a long moment, Cass didn't draw breath.

The headline product had been replaced by a swastika, and underneath it said FUCK YOU in large red letters. Incongruously, some of the product images had survived, sharing space with more signs of hate. The product copy had been replaced everywhere: 'He lives', it said, and 'He rules. He will triumph. He is coming'. At the bottom was a cross turned on its side and ending in a curve. It looked a little like a sickle, a little like a rotated question mark. Below that: 'He is your father'.

Cass stared at it: a cross of confusion, just as Lucy had described.

She turned to check on Ben. He was staring at the television screen, light playing across his face. There was cold water in the pit of her stomach. She turned back, opened some other files. Some had been changed, some had not. She took the note from her pocket. 'What the hell? I've overwritten the files as instructed. Is this some sort of joke? Whole site now pulled. Need a fix ASAP.'

'Christ,' Cass said, and covered her eyes with her hands.

'No,' said a voice at her shoulder. 'No, not him. I don't think so. He's coming, Mummy.'

Cass turned to see Ben was staring straight up at the ceiling, his eyes rolled back in his head. They gleamed in the light from the computer screen.

Cass opened her mouth; nothing came out but a gagging sound. She grabbed her son's arm, pulling him towards her, and found her voice. 'Ben?' She shook him, put one hand on the side of his face and turned him towards her.

His eyes spun back, meeting hers. 'I want my tea,' he said.

Cass watched her son eat, never moving her gaze from him. She didn't want to look away in case his eyes did that trick again. The thought of those gleaming orbs made her shudder. *It wasn't him,* she thought. He stuffed huge forkfuls of beans into his mouth, chewing mechanically, staring into the distance. When he had finished he pushed away his plate and started to get down from his chair.

'Ben?'

He froze, one hand on the table.

'Are you all right?'

He shrugged.

'Something happened to my work on the computer – some really important files got corrupted. Have you touched it? Were you playing with it?'

A single emphatic shake of his head.

'Do you know what might have happened to it?'

Ben turned to her at last, his eyes shining. He opened his mouth, but not in a smile; he just opened it wider and wider, so that she could see his teeth, his pink tongue, pooling saliva. He made a sound that was almost like laughter.

'Ben?'

'*Agh – agh – agh–*' He closed his mouth with a gulp and pulled his lips back over his teeth in a snarl.

Cass roused herself and went over to him, but as she

reached out, Ben knocked her hand away and hissed. His saliva flecked her face.

'What are—?'

'That tea was *shit*,' Ben said. 'I'd rather be at Sally's.'

Cass' eyes widened and she drew back as though he'd slapped her. She was dismayed to find tears welling at her eyes. She blinked furiously, and Ben saw.

He smiled.

'Go to your room, Ben,' she said, trying not to choke. '*Now.*'

Her son pushed the chair away and walked from the room. He didn't hurry and he didn't slam the door, just did as he had been told and went into his bedroom. He closed the door carefully behind him.

Then Cass heard something bang against it.

She padded into the hall and listened, thought she heard the rustling of sheets. She tried the handle and the door jammed against something on the other side.

'Ben, open this door.'

Silence. She took a deep breath. 'Ben, I am telling you to open this door, right now.' Her hands shook. If Pete had been here he'd have known what to do. If Pete had been here, this would never have happened.

The next instant she heard something being moved away from the door and when she tried it again the handle turned easily and the door swung open. Ben was climbing into bed, pulling the covers over himself, turning to face the wall.

'What's got into you, sweetheart?'

He did not reply.

Cass went to his side and touched her fingertips to the heap of duvet. 'What's wrong, Ben? Do you want to talk about it?'

No response.

'If something's upsetting you, I can help.' Cass waited. She reached out and stroked his hair. It felt damp under her fingers. She sighed, straightened up. Perhaps it was best to leave him alone for a while, let him calm down. She bent and switched on the nightlight. It cast a pallid glow over the room.

Ben shuffled around. His hand snaked from under the covers and snapped off the light. 'I don't need it any more,' he said, snuggling back under the duvet.

Cass drew a deep breath, then turned and closed the door behind her, leaving her son in darkness.

THIRTEEN

Ben was up first the next morning, grabbing his rucksack and throwing it against the front door. Cass heard him in the shower. When she emerged from her room, bleary-eyed, her skin taut and dry, he was already dressed for school: grey trousers, white polo shirt.

'I'm ready,' Ben almost shouted, but Cass shook her head. He scowled.

'Ben, I've been thinking. I'm sorry you're all ready, but you won't be going to school today.'

'I *will*. I have drawing with Mrs Spencer. She says I'm really good.'

'Well, that's nice, but I think we need to get away from here for a little while. We're going to have a nice walk over the moors – it'll do us both good. Do you remember them? They're so pretty.' She thought back; were they pretty? All she remembered was a stretch of road walled in by fog.

'You're a liar.'

Probably, Cass thought. She took a deep breath. 'You've

been very naughty lately, Ben. We need to spend some time together. We'll walk over to Moorfoot and stay in a hotel there for a few days. We can see the sights, eat in cafés – won't that be nice?'

He didn't exactly frown, but he didn't look pleased either.

'It's an adventure,' Cass said. And of course it would give her the chance to try and keep the one client she had. She'd spent half the night redoing her work, checking every bit of copy on the website and amending the master files offline. But she still couldn't upload them. She could at least call her client from town, find a computer that worked and email the files. Failing that she could post them.

She rubbed at her eyes. She should have slept well, she'd been so tired after the work, and yet she didn't feel refreshed at all.

Ben was still standing there. 'You'd better put some clothes and things in a bag. Come on, hurry. And put some warm clothes on. It'll be cold up there, colder than down here in the valley.'

She had packed some things late last night but hadn't wanted to disturb Ben; not after the way he'd been, turning that face to her, his eyes nothing but a blank.

It would be a relief to be away from this place. She might even take Ben to see a doctor.

'It's the *law*,' he said at last. 'I *have* to go to school.'

Cass tossed her head. 'Half the children in Saddleworth aren't in school right now – what are they going to do? Hurry up, please.'

He scowled again and sulked off into his bedroom. This time he did slam the door behind him.

The sun was already high as they walked up the mill lane. Cass glanced back to see the sand-coloured stone warm and mellow behind her. Then her eyes went to Ben. He normally ran ahead when they walked, tramping down the snow, but today he was lagging behind, his mouth turned down, head drooping. His rucksack was slung over his back, his thumbs hitched in the straps. Cass bit her lip. She wanted to tell him to hurry up, but after last night she thought it might even have the opposite effect. Instead she walked more quickly, swinging her arms, hoping he would follow suit, but when she reached the top of the lane Ben was still halfway down, dragging his feet.

''appen he's going to be late,' a gruff voice called, and Cass turned to see Bert walking down the road.

She cursed under her breath. Was the old man *everywhere*?

Ben was still shuffling through the snow, creating a new trail. There was no question that Bert would reach them before they escaped. She felt a prickle of alarm. How would the dog behave? Ben might be scared after last time and she didn't want that, didn't want him to be afraid of animals for the rest of his life. She looked at Captain. The grizzled dog was following close at Bert's heels, and now she could see he was on a lead. It hung loosely from Bert's hand, tucked into his pocket to keep warm.

Cass swallowed her anxiety, reminding herself that children could learn fear from their parents. 'We're not going to school today.' She moved aside so that Ben could see her as she stroked Captain's head. The fur was oily, and gave off a warm animal smell.

Ben continued to shuffle up the lane; he hadn't even looked at her. Cass resisted the urge to wipe her hand on her coat.

'You're not?' Bert's eyes flicked to Ben. 'Nowt wrong, I hope.'

'Not at all. We felt the need for a break, that's all. There's been a lot going on, with the move and everything, and I want to spend some time with Ben. We're going to stay in Moorfoot for a few days, see the area a bit.'

'Aye.' Bert nodded as though he had expected this all along, as though that was what the locals did. His head swivelled towards the road. 'It's a fair old walk.'

'I know – but we're well prepared. I've got a flask of soup and some food, and we're not carrying much. We'll be fine.'

''appen the moor path'd be quicker.'

'A path?'

He pointed up the road. 'Watch for the stile into Farmer Broath's field. There's a path goes through their yard, up across t' next field, then t' moor. You'll see yon standing stones from there. Keep to the right-hand side of 'em, if you can't see the path for snow. Then head straight up onto t' road. It'll save a mile at least, winding round the bends.'

'Thanks, Bert, that's a big help.' As Cass spoke, Ben drew level. He kept his distance, though, looking over at Bert without speaking. He didn't show any fear; he didn't look at the dog at all. Captain raised his head and sniffed, and his sides heaved in a deep sigh.

Cass looked at Ben with surprise; reminded herself that she shouldn't make him feel afraid.

'Well, nice to see you, Bert.' Cass nodded at him and he nodded back. *I'm getting the hang of this*, she thought. The local lingo: a nod of the head for everything.

'Hang on,' said Bert, and Cass turned as she felt his hand snag her sleeve. 'Just a thought, but watch out fer t' lake. It'll be iced ower. Up by the stones. You might not see it.'

'Sure. Thanks.' How could she not see a lake? Still, she smiled, giving him a wave as they walked off.

'Bye, young man,' Bert called after them. 'You watch out for your mum, like.'

Despite the sun the air was biting cold. Cass kept up a strong pace, stomping her feet to drive warmth into them. She hadn't yet passed the stone terraces at the edge of Darnshaw and Ben was lagging further and further behind. 'Hurry up, Ben,' she called, 'we need to keep moving so that we stay warm.'

He looked up and his face twisted. 'The school won't know,' he said.

'What?'

'How will they know? You haven't told them I'm not coming.'

'Ben, the phones aren't working, and I'm not walking

all the way to the school just to tell them I'm taking you away for a while. There's no way to let them know, but they'll understand. They'll have to.'

Cass went on, walking more slowly. She drew level with the last row of houses. Ahead the road twisted around them and rose towards the moor. 'Ben, do I have to hold your hand?'

He gave her a dirty look and thrust his hands into his pockets.

'Well hurry up, then.'

He put his head down and stamped on the snow in a semblance of effort, but he didn't walk any faster. Cass turned and went on ahead. The road wound upwards, edged by a dark stone wall. On the other side was a pristine expanse broken only by a stand of trees. It was beautiful. It struck Cass she could turn this into an adventure: they could picnic high on the moors, away from anyone, alone with the spread of the land and the view. By Bert's standing stones, maybe.

Her gaze followed the line of the valley and it occurred to Cass she could have gone that way, following the river along its course. It would have been an easier walk, but then what? She'd get to another village like Darnshaw. No, she felt the need to get away, right away. The moors felt like a border, civilisation on one side, Darnshaw and all its strangeness on the other.

Mr Remick's smiling face rose before her, his clear honest eyes. She swallowed and blinked it away.

Ben reached her side. She tousled his hair. 'This is great, isn't it?' she said. 'It's a long time since we had a day out.'

Ben screwed up his nose and looked around. He didn't comment, but the look said everything.

'You'll see. And I'll buy you chips later.'

'I want to go on my game.'

'You can do that another time.'

Cass gestured him onwards and led the way up the hill. Soon she could see the stile set into the wall ahead of them. 'Come on, Ben. There's the farm.' They would be able to cut across the countryside, leaving the road behind. Beyond the stile a rough track led away towards a low house built from the now-familiar blackened stone.

When Cass reached the stile she pulled herself up, then stopped and looked out over Darnshaw. She saw snow-covered rooftops and the tall black tower of the church, and no other colour anywhere at all except the long blue arch of sky.

She fumbled in her bag for her mobile. There was still no signal.

Cass helped Ben over the stile and led the way, her feet slipping into unseen ruts beneath the snow. Her bag was starting to hang heavily on her back. She was carrying her own spare clothes and half of Ben's, plus the flask, some sandwiches and a disk with the client files.

Maybe they would have been better sticking to the road. It would have been smooth underfoot, not like this. But if she said they had to turn back now . . . Cass sighed at the thought of Ben's reaction. He was already lagging behind again, shuffling his feet. Better to go on and see what it was like past the farm.

'Ben, walk properly,' Cass said as they turned into the

farmyard. There was a faint rank odour, and somewhere a dog barked. The yard was enclosed by low wooden sheds, their doors all closed.

Ben stopped and pulled a face. 'It stinks.'

'It does not. Come on, Ben, I can see the path. Race you.'

Cass walked past the blank dark windows set into the back of the house. Steam rose from a vent on the side of the building, but other than that there was no sign that anyone lived there.

The path led away from the house and into a broad white field, following the line of the wall. It felt like they were really leaving the village now, escaping its pull, and Cass' spirits rose, though she could hear Ben behind her, kicking up flurries of snow. She took long strides, feeling her calf muscles pull as the slope grew steeper. The air felt cleaner, colder, stinging her ears and nose, and her eyes began watering, the moisture causing an irritating sting. She wiped at them, sniffed and kept going.

When Cass turned round, Ben was a small figure, sunk knee-deep into the snow. He had stopped swishing.

The road would have been so much easier.

Cass waited, leaning on the wall, rummaging in her pack, and when Ben reached her she put a bar of chocolate into his hand. He stared at it. His nose and cheeks were pink. Cass pulled his hat down over his ears and he sucked in his breath when she touched them. 'Sorry, Ben. Are you okay? This is hard going, eh?'

He ripped the chocolate wrapper open with his teeth, spitting out the fragment he'd torn off.

'Ben, pick that up.'

He kicked out, flicking snow high into the air and it spattered against Cass' coat, marbling the ground, covering the wrapper.

'You know you can't leave it like that. What about when the snow melts? It'll look nasty.'

'It'll never melt. It'll always be here, and so will you, and so will we.'

She forced a laugh. 'Whatever do you mean? Of course it will. And we'll go where we like, won't we? We're going now.' Cass stopped short. Her voice sounded hollow to her own ears.

She must be going mad. It was the effect of the last few days, that was all; being snowed in. It had started to feel like she'd never get out of that deep bowl of a village, back over the hills to where the telephones worked and the roads were passable.

Ben took a bite and chewed, swallowed, took another.

Cass sighed and scraped in the snow, picking up the wrapper herself. 'Come on. It won't take long to get up to the top. Then it'll be downhill.'

She remembered that strange experience in the car on the way here: the car heading downhill, but rolling backwards, as though something was pushing her away. It felt so long ago.

She lowered her voice. 'Come on, love. Let's shake a leg.'

Ben sighed. He balanced on one foot, raised the other and shook clumps of snow from it. Cass laughed, too hard. 'That's my boy. Now let's see if we can find these standing stones.'

Cass needn't have been concerned about missing their way. She saw the stones as soon as she reached the wall marking the top edge of the field. They were tall and black, jutting from their white surroundings like sentinels standing on the hillside.

'Do you see tha—'

Cass turned but Ben wasn't there. He was far back down the hillside, barely covering any ground at all. Cass cupped her hands around her mouth and cried, 'Ben, come *on*.' She leaned against the wall and waited until he caught up with her.

When he finally drew level he let out a huge sigh.

'If you stopped messing about, it wouldn't be so difficult.'

'It wouldn't be so difficult if I wasn't here.'

'Don't be a smart-aleck.' Cass put a hand on his back, steering him forwards, but he flapped his arms and shook her off. 'Well, walk by yourself then. I'm getting tired of this. Walk in front of me.'

Ben stomped along, hands pulled into his coat sleeves, flapping them at his sides, but Cass didn't care as long as he kept moving. The air was growing even colder, and snowflakes drifted, tiny particles like mist moving wraith-like across the hillside. Ben walked into it, towards the stones, his red coat fading from view.

Cass hurried after him. *How can he be moving so quickly now?* She caught sight of his short legs plunging into the snow up to his knees, and yet he was pulling away from her. A wind was rising, hissing across the slope and in and out of the stones. It carried the snow with it, hiding everything from view. It felt to her like Ben was being swallowed up.

Cass started to hurry, trying to catch up, but her feet slipped. She tried to keep from falling and her outstretched hand sank deep into a snowdrift, dragging her in up to the shoulder. She spluttered, fought her way clear. Ahead the path was a smooth blanket, Ben's footprints already covered over.

He appeared for a moment between the stones, a small figure, and was gone.

Cass shouted his name. The wind was picking up, and rough particles stung her skin. She held her scarf across her face with one hand, holding out the other for balance. 'Ben!'

He did not come back, nor did she hear him call. She put her head down against the wind and started after her son, and when she next looked up, she found herself standing among the stones.

Now she could see them clearly, they reminded her of gravestones, flattened and broad, the surfaces pitted. Snow dusted them, picking out whorls and other half-seen patterns. Some were almost worn through, eaten by the elements, and one had thinned so much that an irregular hole had opened in its centre.

Another lay flat on the ground, one edge just visible under the snow. It reminded Cass of the church altar, dressed in its white cloth. She blinked. On top of the cloth – no, the *snow* – lay her son.

She ran to him, pulled him up and slid an arm under his shoulders. She shook him; he was dead weight. Snow had blotted his cheeks, settled on his fine eyelashes, and she brushed it away. 'Ben, are you all right?'

His eyes opened. Above his ruddy cheeks his eyes glowed, and she felt heat rising off him.

'Fuck you,' he said. '*Fuck* you.'

Cass started, her arm jerking under him.

Ben pursed up his lips and ejected thin, cold spittle into her face. 'He won't let you,' he said, pulling back his lips so she could see his pink gums as he spoke. 'I'm not going. I'm *not*.'

'Ben, what is it?' Cass' voice broke. It was a sign of weakness, but she didn't care, she didn't know this fierce, angry person. *He's only a child*, she thought. How could he say such things? And how could she recoil from him, her flesh, her blood? She remembered when he was a baby, the way she had rocked him in her arms, and she rocked him now. 'Don't, Ben. It's all right. We'll sit here a while and have our picnic, and then we'll be gone from here and we'll never come back. We'll go far, far away—'

His head whipped around. What had she said? She had only intended to calm him; was only half aware of what she'd been saying.

'No,' he shouted, flailing and kicking. '*Nonononono*—'

Cass tried to hold on, but it was like gripping a storm. She gathered him in her arms, folding herself over him, their breath mingling in a single cloud. Eventually the storm subsided.

'Shh, shh, it's okay.'

'It's not – it's not. We're always moving. Daddy wouldn't make me move. I hate you. I *hate* you.'

'It's okay. I didn't mean it, Ben.' But as soon as she'd said the words, Cass realised she had – she *had* meant it, she had felt herself repelled by Darnshaw and its ways and the people in it, the church and the mill, almost as soon as they'd arrived. It felt *wrong*. She couldn't isolate it, couldn't think of one thing that made it wrong; it just wasn't her home. She couldn't imagine Ben growing up here, catching a bus to the big school, going out with a local girl. She couldn't see any of it.

Ben became still in her arms.

'We'll talk about it later,' Cass said. 'We're not going for ever, Ben, it's a little trip, that's all, just for a few days.' She leaned against the edge of the stone and slipped off her rucksack. She pulled out the flask and poured some soup, smelling the rich sweet scent of tomatoes before it was whipped away on the breeze. 'Here. This'll warm you up.' She offered it to Ben.

He hit out, knocking the cup from her grip, and soup splashed bright orange across the snow.

'What's got into you? Ben, you need to have something. It'll give you some energy. Stop being so naughty.'

He muttered under his breath.

'What's that?'

He said it again, his voice still low. 'I'm not going anywhere.'

'Please yourself.' Cass had some of the soup, closed the flask, clipped the cup onto it and stowed it away. She stood, slinging the rucksack over her shoulder. 'Come on. We're going.'

'I'm not.'

Cass grabbed his shoulders and pulled him to his feet. His body felt loose, like a puppet, and he slumped to his knees.

'Stand up, Ben. We're going on.'

'You can.'

'We're both going.' She pulled at him. 'Ben, please.' All the strength rushed from her legs and she sank down beside him. 'Ben, I can't do this on my own. Will you please help me?' She smoothed his fringe back, feeling the heat from his forehead through her gloves. She frowned as it occurred to her that he could be ill. What if there was something really wrong with him, and here she was, dragging him over the moors without a thought for his safety.

His safety. But wasn't that the reason she was doing this, really? She remembered Sally's bright, tripping words. Mr Remick's smile, his clear eyes. They looked accusing. 'Shit,' she muttered under her breath. Ben didn't move, didn't show any sign that he'd heard.

'It's not far to go now. We just have to get to the top of the hill. Then we'll be back on the road and it'll be easier. See?' She pointed, though she couldn't even see past the stones now. Everything was lost in white mist.

'Come on, sweetheart.'

Ben threw her off and curled in on himself, pressing his face down into his knees, wrapping his arms beneath his legs. 'I want to go home.' His voice was muffled. 'I want to go home. *I want to go home.*'

'Oh God, Ben, we're only going for a few days, just till I can get things sorted out.' Cass heard herself and squeezed her eyes shut. *Me*, she thought. *Is this all about me? About what I want?*

'I want to go home.'

'Soon,' said Cass. 'Soon.' She tried to pick him up, but he was so heavy and he pulled against her. His coat was speckled in white and she realised it was snowing again; the air, the sky, everywhere was white. Ben's trousers were already soaked where he had knelt on the ground and now snowflakes settled on his hood, melting into dark shapes. Cass' own legs burned with cold. Her toes were numb, pain spreading through her feet, and suddenly it was too much. All of it, too much. It was true: she couldn't do it alone.

'All right,' she said, leaning back against the stone. 'All right, Ben. You win. We'll go home.'

He didn't speak, just unfolded from the ground as if he'd woken up, reached out his arms and stretched. A smile spread across his face but as he brushed the snow from his body, Cass saw that the cold glow never left his eyes.

FOURTEEN

She should be glad, Cass told herself as they trudged back down the hillside: glad that Ben saw Darnshaw as home, that he already liked it so much he wanted to stay. That was good, wasn't it? It was what she'd wanted all along.

Still she found her irritation increasing. Progress was quicker now, the landmarks coming upon them in quick succession: the wall at the top of the field; the path by the wall; the scuffed area of snow where they'd argued over the wrapper; the opening into the farmyard. Even the rough bark of the dog sounded just the same, and there was the same smell of manure. But it wasn't just that they were going downhill, that the going was easier; Ben was standing up straight now, striding out, swinging his arms, all boundless energy. His movement was almost jaunty.

It didn't marry with that cold look in his eyes.

Cass pursed her lips. 'Wait,' she said, some part of her wanting to stem his enthusiasm. When he turned to her, though, the cold look had gone. His eyes were clear.

'Well, Ben, it looks like we're staying put for a while. We'd better try and get some more food, hmm?'

Ben shrugged.

'Let's see if they've got any eggs for sale at the farm.'

She expected him to grumble at the prospect of a delay, but his expression remained blank.

Cass walked around the farmhouse. From the front, it had a view of the whole valley. White mist curled over the village like a bird covering its brood, or its prey.

Cass peered in through the window. She could see a clutter of old wooden furniture, and an overcoat thrown over a chair. When she knocked, a machine-gun rattle of barks rang out and there was the squeal of wooden chair legs scraping a stone floor. Cass waited for what felt like an age. She couldn't resist turning and pulling a face and when Ben returned it she grinned; her heart felt lighter.

The door screeched open and a woman's solid body stood in the gap. She wore a flowered skirt and flesh-coloured tights and layers of faded cardigans. A sheepdog tried to push its way past her, letting out short barks. Its claws skittered at the flagstones.

'In, Jesse, *in*.' The woman's face was deeply lined. She wore a scarf around her head, secured in a tight knot. She tried to block the dog with her leg, but its lithe body curled past her and it got its head out of the door. Cass felt Ben's hands on her back.

The dog jumped up at her, snarling; then it looked as if it was trying to stop itself in mid-air. Its legs flailed and the snarl became a high, piercing sound that hurt Cass' ears. It turned and fled back into the house.

The woman stared after the dog. Then she turned to Cass, raising her eyebrows in query.

Cass said, 'I'm sorry to disturb you, but I wondered if you sold eggs and things? I thought—'

'Jack,' the woman called, looking over her shoulder. 'Jack!' She shot a suspicious glance at Cass before pushing the door to and walking away. Cass heard murmuring from inside, then a man's wrinkled face appeared in the doorway.

He nodded at Cass, so she nodded back. 'I wondered if you had any eggs for sale. The shop in the village is closed, and—'

'We've nowt,' he said. 'Only for t' locals.'

'But we are local. We just moved in to the old mill and we're snowed in. We could really do with—'

Cass' words faded as the old man swung the door closed in her face. It jolted against the jamb, catching on something. She heard him pushing on it, and a bolt snicked into place.

'Great,' Cass muttered, staring at the door. So much for thinking of Darnshaw as their home.

Ten minutes later Cass and Ben were within sight of the mill. When they reached the road Ben practically skipped ahead.

'Ben, wait,' Cass called, 'there's something I need to do.'

'I'm tired.'

'It's not far, and it'll save us coming out again later.'

'I can stay inside.'

'No, you can't, not on your own.'

A loud sigh.

'Come on. We're going into the village.'

Cass expected the post office to be closed like the shop, but when she pushed the door, it opened with a loud jingle of chimes.

A woman with slate-grey hair stood behind a plastic screen. 'The new lady,' she said when she saw them, 'from the mill.'

The woman's cheerful manner made Cass brighten. 'Call me Cass. "Lady" makes me feel old.'

'I'm Irene. And who's this young man?'

Cass nudged her son. 'Ben,' he said. 'I should be in school.'

'Goodness.' Irene pulled a face. 'Keen, isn't he? I couldn't wait to get out of school at his age.' She let out a squeal of laughter. 'Hope you enjoyed the papers.'

'Sorry?'

'Didn't you get them? That lad.' She tutted. 'He was supposed to put them under your door. We've got the code to get in, you know, so we can get to the mailboxes.'

'I don't follow.'

'You were supposed to get some free papers. We do it for anyone new to the village, for a week anyway. Of course we hope they'll order more after that. Not that there are many new arrivals round here. A quiet set, we are.'

The mysterious neighbour and his newspaper delivery. Cass' heart sank. She was the only one, after all, the only resident of Foxdene Mill. She licked her lips. 'I think they were sent to Number 10. I saw them; I just didn't realise they were for me.'

'Oh now. I thought you was at Number 10. I'm sure we had a letter for you there.'

'You did?'

'Aye. Now, it might have been put in the mailbox, or under the door. I'm sure . . .' Her voice tailed away. 'By the way, we haven't had any more deliveries, not after the first couple of days, what with the snow an' all. Or you'd have had more. Papers, I mean.'

'No problem. Thank you for the ones you sent.'

'We've not had any post in or out for the last couple of days. It stopped just after you got here, I reckon.' Irene laughed.

No post, in or out. 'I was hoping to send something,' Cass said, 'a disk with some files on it. I thought I might be able to buy a Jiffy Bag and send it off today.'

Irene pursed her lips. 'Sorry, love. The post's collected from Gillaholme, and the van can't get here.'

'No,' said Cass under her breath, 'no, of course it can't.'

'You must think you're in the back of beyond, what with no phones and no post. Hope it's not causing any problems for you.' Irene rummaged on a shelf. When she turned she had a Mars Bar in her hand. She flapped it at Ben.

'Here you are, young man. Welcome to Darnshaw.'

She winked at Cass as they said their goodbyes. ''appen he can take it to school.'

*   *   *

Cass let Ben in at the apartment door. He slipped under her arm, pressing against the opening until it was wide enough to get through, reminding her of the farmer's dog. 'Be good for a minute,' she said, putting on the latch. Ben turned, but he didn't ask where Cass was going. He shrugged off his coat and she saw him drop it on the hall floor.

There was one more thing to do before she had to resign herself to being in her new flat, the door closed on the world. *Home.*

The newspapers were still there at Number 10, crumpled where they'd been pushed up against the door. Cass picked them up. Old news, and yet she hadn't seen any of it, hadn't even watched the news on television. She must be getting insular, now she was – how had Irene put it? – in the back of beyond.

She shook out the pages of the newspapers one by one. A few fliers fell out, for florists, cheap trousers and carpet cleaning services. No letter.

She dropped to her knees and put her face almost to the floor. Under the door she could see the edge of an envelope, a thin line against the carpet. She poked a finger into the gap and tried to grip it, scraping her skin against the rough wood. She tried again, touching the edge of the letter, and it moved a little. The corner of a white envelope appeared and she pulled it free. It was addressed to her at 10 Foxdene Mill.

Cass recognised the handwriting at once. She pulled a face, folded the letter and shoved it deep into her back pocket.

Inside the apartment Ben was playing his game, shooting soldiers in the sepia desert where red flowers bloomed and died. He didn't look round.

Cass went into her room and pushed the door closed. The envelope was thick and white with an embossed crest. She ran her fingers along it.

The note was brief, and yet it took her a long time to read it. The words blurred and shifted under her eyes.

Sweetheart,

I know you may not want to believe this, but I do love you. I heard what happened to Peter. I'm sorry. If there's anything I can do, please know you can always call me.

I heard you're going back to Darnshaw. I don't know what to think about that. I'll pray for you both. Always thinking of you – as a priest and your father. Will write again soon.

Cass crumpled up the letter and held it to her face. *As a priest and your father.* That was the problem, wasn't it? He could never really be both. And why now? He only ever surfaced when anything changed in her life, as though he wanted to be privy to her every decision. She remembered the letter he had written when she'd got engaged to Pete. She had smiled when she opened it, expecting good wishes, or at most some thinly veiled request that she have a church ceremony. Certainly not what she received:

He's not good for you. I feel it. He will bring harm upon you and yours that will follow you all your days. You should turn to the Lord. He loves you.

She had crumpled up that letter too, crumpled it and torn it to shreds. She had never replied to any of her father's letters after that.

He's not good for you.

Well, her father had been right about that, hadn't he? Look at her now: alone in an empty building with a son who wouldn't look at her. Even her one and only client thought she was going mad. Would her father be pleased to know he had been right all along? Cass felt the thought worm its way inside her; knew it was wrong, that she shouldn't indulge it. She was too old for self-pity, had too much responsibility. Tears sprang to her eyes anyway. *Pete.* Oh God, to have him back, if only for a little while.

A sound broke into her thoughts. At first she didn't know what it was, then it came again and she realised someone was knocking at the front door. Cass wiped her eyes, hoping they didn't look red. When she saw Mr Remick standing in the doorway guilt turned in her stomach.

'I'm so sorry Ben didn't come to school today,' she began.

He held up a hand. 'It's all right,' he said. 'I'm not in the habit of making home visits when pupils don't turn up. If I did that I'd be at it all day at the moment. I'm sure you had a good reason. He's not ill, is he?'

Cass shook her head then looked away.

'It's purely a social call. Hey, tiger,' said Mr Remick. Cass felt Ben at her side. His face brightened as he grinned up at his teacher.

'I didn't go to school.'

'No, you didn't. Well, I won't tell if you don't.' Mr Remick winked at Cass. He had a way of making everything less grim, of clearing the air.

'I'm playing the game.'

Not *a* game. *The* game.

'Great, Ben. Why don't you show me? If it's okay with your mum, naturally.'

Cass nodded. 'Of course. I'll get us a drink.'

She could hear them from the kitchen: Ben prattling away about how many soldiers he'd shot, and how he'd been for a walk, only he didn't want to go. His words spilled over themselves as though he couldn't get them out quickly enough. Not like before, when he was with her. How could he have so much to say now? He sounded fine, a normal child.

It was her fault he'd been the way he had, trying to make him leave just when he'd started to feel at home. She'd dragged him out into the cold, made him walk all that way – and for what? Cass closed her eyes. The kettle started to boil, the hiss drowning out everything else.

'Are you all right?'

The voice was at her ear and Cass jumped.

'Sorry. I didn't mean to startle you.' Mr Remick gestured towards the lounge. 'He's engrossed in there.'

'I . . .' *I'm fine*, Cass was going to say.

Mr Remick put a hand on her arm. 'I had a feeling something was wrong.'

Cass shook her head, found she couldn't speak.

'You're not alone, you know. You don't have to be, anyway. You don't have to do everything yourself.'

Cass drew back, wiping her eyes. 'I'm sorry.' God, she

was always apologising to him. 'I didn't mean to— Of course I'm fine. I only just met you. You must think I'm—'

'I don't think anything. I like you, Cass. That's all right, isn't it? I don't want to make you feel uncomfortable.'

Cass shook her head. He didn't make her uncomfortable. His presence was like being with an old friend in a familiar place.

'You're welcome here. I mean it.'

She raised her eyebrows.

'Oh, I know I can't speak for everybody. But Sally really likes you. She was just saying so today.' He paused. 'Of course, having Sally on your side is a bit like being stuck in the china shop with the bull.'

She smiled.

'But I'm glad you came. I haven't been back for long, but Darnshaw can be a little insular, especially when it's so cut off. It's nice to have someone I can talk to.'

Cass found her heart was beating faster, as though something was about to happen.

'Ben told me you wanted to leave.'

She stirred. 'I—'

'You don't have to explain to me.'

'No, it's okay. I was just feeling trapped here – with the snow and no phones and everything. I thought a few days away would do us good.'

'It's easier for me, I suppose. There's no one outside I really want to call.'

Cass laughed. 'Me neither.' A tug at her heart. *Not any more.* 'It was for work.'

'Is that all? In that case you should definitely stay. There's more to life than work, you know.'

'Is there?' Cass hadn't really meant to say it, didn't mean the question, but when she met his eye, his look was serious.

'You know, Cass, next time Ben is out – at Sally's or whatever – I think I should cook you dinner.'

She didn't know what to say.

'It's not Cassandra, is it?'

'What?'

'Your name. Sally calls you Cassandra, but I don't think that's it.'

'No— No, it's not.'

'I think— Hmm, now . . .'

She pushed back her hair. 'You won't guess.'

'So it isn't Rumpelstiltskin.' He grinned.

'My name was Cassidy.'

'Cassidy. Yes, it suits you.' He paused. 'Was?'

'It was my maiden name. Before—'

'Ah. Sorry. So, Cassidy, what's your real name?'

She bit her lip.

'Come on, it can't be that bad.'

'I should make those drinks.'

'Something traditional, I think. Rebecca? No – Verity. Faith. Hope.'

She swallowed. 'It's Gloria.'

'Gloria.' He savoured the word, like a taste.

'How did you know?'

'What?'

'That it would be something traditional. My father was religious.'

'Well, it would have to be, wouldn't it?'

'Why?' She still didn't understand.

'Darnshaw's a pretty traditional place. And you came back. It's in your blood.'

Cass laughed. She went to the cupboard, lifting down mugs. Still she felt exposed, like a child caught in some secret. *Gloria.* She doubted even Ben would have remembered that.

Gloria. Because you will bring glory to God. Hosanna in the highest.

'I hope I can still call you Cass.'

She turned. 'You'd better,' she said. 'And if you tell anyone—'

He waved his hands in mock terror. 'I wouldn't dare,' he said. 'It'll be our little secret.' He headed for the door. 'In return for that dinner,' he said, and slipped out of sight.

Later Cass peeped in and saw them side by side, laughing and cheering at the screen. She made them pasta, not asking Mr Remick if he wanted to stay. He looked so comfortable – and when she brought in the food Ben turned to her. His eyes were sparkling, and this time they didn't fade when he looked at her.

The pasta was tasteless, the sauce bland, and Cass apologised for it, though Mr Remick ate with gusto. She told him about her visit to the farm and the result.

'The locals aren't all as friendly as me, are they, Ben?'

He winked. 'What you eat can depend on who you know around here. There's plenty of food about – a lot of farming land, you know. But they're a shy lot.'

Cass thought of the farmer closing the door in her face. 'Something like that.'

'They'll take to you soon enough. Then you won't be able to shake them off. It'll be apple pies at dawn, stewed mutton all day – as long as you don't mind taking half a sheep. Or the odd live chicken.'

Cass pulled a face.

'You can't be squeamish with this lot.' Mr Remick's eyes flashed. 'Can she, Ben?'

Ben nodded enthusiastically, spooning red sauce into his mouth.

'Anyway, you took your life in your hands trying the Broath place. Even I have trouble getting anything out of them.'

'We were going away,' said Ben.

'So you were. Well, I'm glad you came back. Who else would I play soldiers with?'

'We saw some stones,' said Ben.

'Ah,' said Mr Remick, 'you did, did you?'

'He means the standing stones on the moor,' said Cass. 'You could see them for miles against the snow.'

'I thought as much. Yes, I imagine they're quite a sight just now. They're called witch stones, you know.'

'They're what?'

'Witch stones. The one with the hole in the middle was meant to be especially efficacious, I believe. They were placed on the village boundary to keep witches and bad spirits out, supposedly. Of course, they could just as well keep them in. You have met the locals?'

He raised his eyebrows at Cass, mock serious, and she laughed. 'They make a good place for a picnic, anyway.'

'A picnic in the snow? Ah, an adventurous eater. I'll have to remember that.'

'Oh, no . . .'

'Hmm. I'm not sure I'll be able to rustle up anything too exotic.' He stopped short when he saw Cass' expression.

She turned to Ben, who was looking from one to the other, his eyebrows raised. Then he grinned at the teacher. 'I'm going to Mrs Spencer's,' he said.

After a moment, Cass and Mr Remick burst out laughing.

Cass went to sleep thinking of Mr Remick, the easy way in which he'd slipped into their household, wondering whether, some day, she might want him to stay. It was a new kind of thought. In the time since Pete had disappeared, Cass had considered many things: where they would live; how Ben would grow up, never again knowing his father; how to keep Pete's memory alive for him, making sure they never forgot. It hadn't occurred to her that she might some day think about moving on. It made her heart beat faster. Life, sneaking in the door before she had even recognised it, making all the colours seem brighter.

She remembered Pete offering up those fragments of blue, letting them fall to the ground. She closed her eyes.

When she dreamed, though, it wasn't Pete who came to her but her father.

They were standing in the church. Cass looked down and saw the frothy white dress. It was splashed with something dark, but the light was so dim she couldn't see what it was. She thought of blood, but no, it was raining outside – she could hear it pattering on the roof and the windows and the walls, knocking to come in. It was muddy out there and she had fallen, clumsy as usual, spoiling her dress. Spoiling everything.

The window behind her father suddenly blazed. There was no colour in it, just brilliant white light. Her father didn't notice. He caught hold of her dress, smoothing it, the dark stuff getting on his fingertips. He brushed it away with an expression of distaste.

The man, Daddy, Cass wanted to say, but she couldn't. Her mouth fell open. Someone dark was behind her father. He came out of the light and wrapped one arm around her father's shoulders. Her father didn't seem to feel it.

The dark shape was taking her father from her. Cass couldn't see its face but she knew that was what it was doing. She also knew the shape was *wrong*, too thin somehow. Although she couldn't see its expression, she knew it was smiling. The smile was wrong too, a twisted, diseased thing.

Cass sat upright, gasping for breath, a whisper still echoing around her ears.

Gloria. Because you will bring glory to God. Hosanna in the highest.

She pushed the covers away and swung her feet out of

bed. For a moment she thought she heard a faint *scritch* in the walls, then it was gone. Cass stood, the night air cool on her skin, and went to check on her son.

She had only got as far as the hall when she heard Ben moan, a long drawn-out sound that made her heart contract. She pushed open his door and went in.

Ben was on his side, his face relaxed, the image of peaceful sleep. His hand was tucked under his chin.

Cass bent over him, waiting to see if he would make that sound again. He did not. His breathing was steady and deep and she listened to it for a while. She wondered what he was dreaming of. Maybe he too had gone to sleep thinking about Mr Remick.

Cass straightened and turned to go, but as she did, Ben let out another sound. This time it wasn't a moan but a single word, spoken quite clearly: *Daddy*. Cass waited, but there was nothing more.

FIFTEEN

The first person Cass saw outside the school was Mr Remick. He grinned and waved, and Ben ran to him. Whatever his dream, it must have faded with the daylight, but it had stayed with Cass. She could still hear him saying that word: *Daddy*.

'A penny for your thoughts.' Mr Remick was at her side, the plume of his breath masking his face. It was colder than ever: winter, tightening its grip.

'I was looking out for Lucy,' she replied.

'I'm afraid you missed her.' Had the gleam faded a little from his eyes? 'She dropped Jess off early today.'

Cass frowned. She couldn't help suspecting that this might have something to do with the odd email Lucy had received from Cass' client. Maybe it had even prompted Lucy to look at the files she'd been given to email. Cass winced inwardly at the thought. She rested her hand on Ben's head, as much for her comfort as her son's. Then she pulled it away. Had it been Ben who had done that to her work? She wouldn't have thought him capable. But that drawing . . .

'Ben, why don't you go inside? I want a quick word with Mr Remick.'

'Mu-*um*.'

'Go on. I'll see you later.' Cass bent to kiss him and he squirmed away.

'They grow up so fast, don't they?' Mr Remick said. 'Is there something I can help with?'

'No. I mean, not really. I just wanted to ask about Ben. I was a bit worried, after the drawing you showed me. I wondered if you'd noticed anything else unusual.'

'Not at all. He's a fine boy, Cass. Nothing to worry about there.'

'Has he drawn anything else like that?'

'I don't think so. I'll check with Sally, but I'm sure she'd have mentioned it. Ah, speak of the devil.' He waved, and a shrill voice answered.

'Cass, glad I've seen you.' Sally barged over. Damon had been following in her wake but now he peeled away and headed inside. 'I wondered if Ben could come for tea tonight. We'd love to have him, wouldn't we, Damon? Now, where's that boy gone? *Honestly.* Anyway, he'd like to show Ben more games, and maybe have some of the others over so that Ben can make friends. Actually, that was my suggestion, but—'

Cass opened her mouth to answer and saw Mr Remick's eyes fixed on her, shining with amusement. She took a deep breath and made up her mind. 'It's really kind of you, Sally. I appreciate it. It's good of you to help him fit in like this – he likes it here. So, yes, thanks. But I'll walk over to yours and collect him this time.'

Sally took in a huge gulp of air. 'Oh, delightful! I'm really pleased. Thank you so much. One of these days we'll all get together, shall we? You, me and the kids.'

'I'd like that. I mean it; it's kind of you to be so welcoming. Ben and Damon really get on, don't they?'

'Of course, of course. Well, I must—'

'Actually,' said Mr Remick, 'we meant to ask you about Ben's pictures. Has he been drawing anything that might be of concern to you, Sally?'

'Like what?'

'Anything overly gruesome, maybe, or depressive. Anything you might not approve of?'

'Not at all. He's a good little boy. He fits right in.'

'Well, that's fine then,' he said.

Sally smiled and hurried towards the doors as Mr Remick turned back to Cass. 'Even better,' he said, 'it looks like you're free for dinner this evening.'

She paused. The way Ben had cried out in his dream echoed in her mind.

'No cold feet, I hope, Ms Cassidy?'

She took a deep breath. 'No, you're right. It looks like I am.'

He leaned towards her as if he were going to plant a kiss on her cheek, then straightened at the last moment and waved at a group of women walking down the hill towards them, their children in tow.

As Cass left two things sprang into her mind: the first, that she had forgotten about her client's files in the space of the last five minutes. The second was that if she didn't collect Ben from school that afternoon, she wouldn't see Lucy again before the weekend.

At three o'clock Cass set out up the lane. She was already irritated by the idea of another walk to the school, particularly as she'd have to get back again to get changed for dinner, and then walk into the village a second time. But she had to see Lucy.

At least thinking about Lucy saved her from worrying about dinner with Mr Remick. Her stomach rolled over whenever it entered her mind; it had been a long time since she had done anything like that.

She had been intimidated by Pete too at first, but he had been so full of colour, laughter, life – the things that had drawn her to him. Pete had drifted through the world, moving from one place to the next without ever putting down roots; it was something that never troubled him. It didn't touch him. And when Cass was with him, it hadn't touched her either.

When she looked up she was surprised to find herself already opposite the post office. Irene was just closing up. When she saw Cass she gestured towards the post box and shook her head.

Cass hadn't expected the roads to be clear today. Winter was really setting in. She looked up at the hills rising all around her and thought of the standing stones, keeping watch, keeping the witches out.

Soon Cass heard distant voices on the cold, sharp air: it sounded as if the children were outside. A shrill voice rose over the others, squealing. It didn't sound like a squeal of joy. Then came the lower, imperative shout of a man. Cass hurried to the corner and looked down. The children were huddled together, a mass of brightly coloured coats. Someone was on the ground.

She hurried down the hill, slipping on the ice, regaining her balance and pressing on. A red coat was among the rest, a flash of pale hair above it. *Ben.* He wasn't the one on the ground then. Cass drew a deep breath. The child on the ground was a little girl, long dark hair lank on her face. As she drew close, Cass could see that the child's cheek was streaked with red.

There was a shriek, and Cass saw Lucy rushing towards the huddle, pushing past a young boy to get to the fallen child. Cass realised the girl on the ground was Jessica.

When Lucy reached her daughter, Jessica had started to cry, and Cass felt a rush of relief. It wasn't crying that concerned a parent most when their child was hurt; it was silence.

Mr Remick was suddenly in the heart of the group and calm spread from him. The children subsided and the teacher glanced around and said something in a low voice that Cass couldn't catch. Some of the children moved back and now she could see Myra was there, holding a child by the shoulder and guiding him towards the car park. Cass caught Myra's eye, but the woman looked pointedly away.

There was one child still standing with Mr Remick, Lucy and Jess and Cass' heart sank. It was Ben. As she watched, Sally went to him and rested her hands on his shoulders. Then Ben saw his mother coming and he too looked away from her, down at the ground.

Lucy pulled Jessica into a sitting position and held her while she sobbed. Mr Remick bent and brushed the hair out of Jessica's eyes, examining the child's face. He straightened, noticed Cass standing there. 'No harm done,' he said. 'Just a scratch.' He said this to Cass, and she couldn't work out why. Then she did.

Ben was staring straight ahead. His face was flushed, but his eyes were steely.

Lucy half-straightened and looked at Ben and her eyes narrowed. Then she looked at Cass.

Cass found herself in the centre of a circle, all eyes fixed upon her, and she had no idea what she was supposed to say.

Mr Remick straightened. 'All right,' he said. His voice was quiet, the voice of a man who expects to be obeyed. 'Thank you, everybody. It's all in hand.'

Instead of retreating, a group of boys drew closer. They stared at Cass too, their eyes hard white glitters. Damon was among them.

Mr Remick bent to Jessica and helped her up. He spoke to her mother, quietly, and Lucy took Jessica's arm, wiped her eyes and guided her towards the car park.

Cass looked after her. She closed a hand over the disk in her pocket.

Mr Remick turned to Cass. 'Why don't you come inside?' he said. 'We'll have a quick chat about this.'

Cass nodded. Lucy had almost reached the Land Rover.

Sally was leading Ben inside, one hand on his back. The other boys followed at a distance.

One of the Land Rover's doors opened and closed, the *thunk* carrying in the clear air. 'I'll be there in just a second,' Cass said, and ignored Mr Remick's look of surprise as she hurried after Lucy. She called out as Lucy was walking round to the driver's side and she stopped, her expression guarded, as she waited for Cass to speak.

'I'm sorry if Ben . . . if he's done something,' said Cass. 'And I hope Jessica is okay. I'm sure it'll turn out to be nothing.'

'He cut her cheek.' Lucy's voice was cold. 'If you'll excuse me, I want to get her home.'

'Of course you do. I'm so sorry. It's just . . . I was hoping to ask for your help.'

Lucy's eyes widened.

'I know all this . . . Well, we need to sort it out. But I really need to send some new files to my client. I don't know what happened to the old ones; they must have been corrupted somehow.'

'You want *me* to send them.'

'If you don't mind. And if there's anything I can do, for you or Jessica—'

Lucy held out her hand without speaking and Cass went round the car and put the disk into it. She started to thank the woman she had begun to think of as a friend, but Lucy said nothing as she put the disk into her pocket, climbed into her seat and drove away.

*   *   *

The corridors were silent when Cass entered the school. The lights were dimmed for the evening, only a green haze glowing from the emergency exit signs. As she approached Mr Remick's office she heard a low buzz of voices. She stopped outside the door and knocked, and as she did so she sensed movement at her side. She turned to see a group of boys standing in the darkened corridor, staring at her. Their eyes were pale in the dim light. She saw the shine of teeth as one of them smirked; it was Damon.

Cass heard Mr Remick call out from inside the office. She pushed the door open and went inside. He smiled at her from behind his desk and Sally nodded from her seat. Cass smiled back, the warmth of their gaze a sudden, grateful release. Only Ben hadn't looked up. He was sitting on Sally's knee.

'We've been having a chat with Ben,' said Mr Remick. 'It seems Jessica said something to upset him, and it all got a little out of hand. Isn't that right?'

Ben nodded.

'What happened?' asked Cass.

'Jessica said something about someone that Ben didn't like, and he asked her to take it back. She wouldn't, and there was a bit of pushing, and the other kids started egging them on, I believe. She cut her face on the ice when he knocked her down.'

'Ben, you didn't *hit* her? How could you do that?' Cass remembered Jessica's face; it had been deathly pale, the blood a bright, awful stain. The child was younger than Ben by a year, maybe two.

Her son didn't meet her eye. That hardness was still in his gaze.

'What did she say?' Cass looked around. 'Does anyone know?'

Sally cleared her throat but didn't speak, only looked to Mr Remick. Cass was surprised to see him look flustered.

'Apparently she said something about me,' he said. 'Ben didn't like it.'

Ben did look up now, staring at Mr Remick with a fierce gaze.

'Ben, you shouldn't hit girls. You shouldn't hit anyone,' said Cass. 'We'll talk about this later. But you have to apologise to Jessica and her mum.'

Ben whirled to face her. 'I'm *not*. And we *won't*, because I'm not coming home with you, I'm going to Sally's!'

Sally's. Since when did he call his teachers by their first names? Cass took a deep breath. 'You're not going, Ben.' She looked at the others. 'I'm sorry, but we have to make our apologies. Ben and I need to talk.'

Ben opened his mouth to protest but Mr Remick stilled him with a look. 'Wait outside a moment, Ben,' he said, and the boy slipped off Sally's lap, glared at his mother and left the room.

Mr Remick took a deep breath. 'I'm sorry about this,' he said, 'but I don't think we've heard the full story. What I said was true – Jess apparently said something about me. But one of the other boys said that Jess was also talking about Ben's father.'

'Why on earth would she do that? She doesn't know anything about us.'

'I'm not sure, but children can be cruel, and he was understandably upset. That doesn't excuse his behaviour, and we'll speak to him about it, of course. And he will apologise. But may I recommend that you continue as normal for now? It's your decision, of course, but I'm not sure it would be good for him to have further upset today, when he's already so emotional.'

'I'm still happy to take him,' said Sally. 'As you say, sometimes it's best to let everything calm down in its own time. Then we can see everything a bit more clearly.' She paused. 'Poor boy. He was very upset.'

Upset? Is that what it was? The gleam in Ben's eyes had looked like anger to Cass. Did she no longer know her own son? She looked down, the black and white chequered flooring a blur. She rubbed her face. Then she remembered the way Ben had cried out in the night for his father. He was just a little boy, alone in a new place, and he was hurting. Perhaps she shouldn't be surprised; perhaps this was what was normal.

Slowly she nodded her head.

'That's great,' said Mr Remick. 'I'm sure it'll all work out for the best. And I benefit too, of course.' He gave a warm smile. 'Really, I don't think there's anything wrong with Ben that settling in and making some new friends won't sort out. Tonight should help enormously, I think. And we'll have a word with Jessica's mother tomorrow, won't we, Sally?'

Sally nodded. The bright smile was back. 'Well, I'd better round up the troops. I'll walk Ben back later if you like, Cass. You look a bit pale.'

'No, I wouldn't dream of it. I'll fetch him.' Cass forced a smile. 'Thanks, Sally. I appreciate it.'

Sally nodded and opened the door, already calling out names. Cass realised that the sullen children in the corridor were the ones Ben was going to have tea with, and misgivings fluttered in her stomach. No, this was a nice school, a good place. Sally wouldn't have them round if they weren't good kids.

Mr Remick was watching her. 'I'm sorry. I ought to have been there. It's difficult, with the mixed classes we have now.'

'No, of course not. It's not your fault.'

'Just one of those things.'

'Yes.'

'Cass, why don't you get your bag, and we'll head straight to my place? You can relax while I cook. It'll give you a break. There's no point in going all the way back to the mill and then out again.'

He held out his hand and smiled. After a moment she reached out and took it.

'Walk with me,' he said.

When they went outside, the car park was empty and light was draining from the sky. Cass looked up and the moon was already visible, a cool, pale disc.

Mr Remick set the building alarm and locked the doors, tucking the keys into his jacket. 'I love evenings like this,' he said. 'Everything's so still. What say we forget our troubles for tonight?' He offered her his arm and they headed up the slope together.

Cass was conscious of her arm in his. She peered down the road, looking for any sign of Sally and the boys, but they had already gone. She found herself missing Ben's hand in her own.

'Cass, are you all right?'

His voice was so warm. Cass closed her eyes. It was strange, having someone ask after her, look after her. It hadn't been that way since—

Tears sprang to her eyes and she found she couldn't catch her breath.

'Here, sit down.' He guided her, pushed snow from a wall and sat her down. When Cass opened her eyes he was rubbing her hands as though she was a child with cold fingers.

'It's all right. It's fine. He's a good boy, Cass. You've got nothing to worry about. Let me do that for tonight, hmm? Just for one night.' His voice was little more than a whisper. His fingers were warm on hers.

'Do you feel dizzy? I could take you back inside.'

Those dim halls, that green haze. Cass shook her head. 'I'm fine. I don't know what came over me.'

'I do.'

'You do?'

'It's the lack of a Theo Remick steak. That's what's causing the problem.'

'Oh?' She laughed.

'Better?' He took her hand, held it a moment before pulling her up. There was strength in his arms, despite his slight build. 'Your carriage awaits, ma'am. Actually, it doesn't. But you can't have everything, and I promise the steak will be pretty good.'

Cass smiled, brushed hair from her face. Down the road she thought she heard a distant shout – the boys maybe: Ben enjoying himself already. Mr Remick had been right. The trip to Sally's would do Ben good, help him settle in. She shouldn't be worrying about her son.

The rectory was a squat black building with narrow windows and a triangular pediment over the door. It was ugly, but once inside Cass found the kitchen cosy, with copper pans dangling from the ceiling and off-white paint peeling here and there in a homely fashion. She thought of the mill kitchen, spartan in its newness, the space too large to feel quite comfortable. Everything was too clean and neat there. Here, pupils' work was spread over the table as though he was midway through marking. He gathered it into a pile and shoved it onto a shelf already crammed with books.

He opened a bottle of wine and handed her a glass. 'A toast,' he said, 'to settling in.' He clinked his glass against hers. Cass smelled the wine before it reached her lips, spicy and sweet. It tasted that way too, and the heat of it slipped into her, radiating comfortingly.

Mr Remick pulled a face.

'I like it,' said Cass. 'It's different.'

'Good, well, let's see what I can mess up next.'

'You're not messing it up.' The words were out before she thought about them. The wine taking effect already? His blue eyes, looking at her. 'What did Jessica say about you?' she blurted.

He grimaced and Cass cursed herself. Why had she said

that? She hadn't even been aware of thinking it. She turned the wineglass in her hand, letting the light glow through the liquid.

'I didn't ask for details,' he said. 'Sometimes it isn't pleasant to see yourself through the eyes of your pupils.'

Cass thought of the way Ben's eyes lit up whenever he was there. 'Oh, I don't believe that.'

'They're fantastic kids. I'll be sad to leave them.'

'Leave?'

'When Mrs Cambrey comes back.'

'But won't you be staying on?'

'Maybe – they may need a class teacher. I might stay around for a while anyway, of course. This is my home.'

'But you make such a good head.'

'That's nice of you to say. It helps to know the area, of course. Even some of the children.'

'And the mothers?' Again Cass hadn't known she was going to say it.

'Some of them.' He met her eyes and she looked away.

'We should eat,' he said. 'Why don't you make yourself comfortable?'

Cass sat and watched while he tenderised steaks and made pepper sauce. After frying the meat he set it on plates with a green salad. 'Where on earth did you get all that?' Her words came out too fast, the wine rushing to her head.

He grinned. 'I have my secrets. Although I will tell you this: the steak came courtesy of the Broaths. They sent some eggs for you too, by the way.'

'You're joking. I thought you had to be a local.'

'Of course. But you are a local, aren't you, Cass? They know that now. Don't bother with the local butchers – the Winthrops are a waste of time. The Broaths will look after you.'

She didn't know what to say, but he gestured at the plates, and suddenly she was famished.

They ate in the kitchen, Mr Remick pouring more wine. He lit candles, dimmed the overhead lights. Cass felt a stab of anxiety about the candles, but it was all right; the room was so domestic, she still felt comfortable. She couldn't help but talk and laugh and joke with him, like old friends. Old times. Then he touched her knee, lightly, so that she wasn't sure he had made contact at all.

'Let's go through,' he said. 'I'll clean this up later.'

Cass was surprised to see the plates empty. 'That was really good – the best meal I've had in ages,' she said. She stopped short of saying, *and the best company*.

Mr Remick held out his hand, mock-genteel; she took it, and he led her into a small lounge – more of a nook, really, with barely room for the green sofa. He turned to a shelf and music started up, low and gentle.

Cass sat, suddenly shy, pressing her hands between her knees. When he turned, though, his expression made her smile. How did he do that, put her at ease with a look?

'You're thinking I might try and kiss you,' he said. There was a slight line of purple at the very edge of his lip.

'Maybe.'

'I was thinking I might kiss you too. But I won't.'

'You won't?'

'Not unless you want me to, of course.' He bowed. 'I hate to disappoint a guest.'

She spluttered into laughter. 'Is that what you say to all your visitors?'

'Yes. Absolutely. That's why I don't invite many people round.' He smiled. 'Seriously. I like you, Cass. I enjoy your company.'

She swallowed, shifted in her seat.

'I hope you'll come again. Humour an old man.'

'You're not old.'

He met her eyes. 'I'm older than I look.' He paused. 'But there's life in me yet.' His lip twitched, making him seem suddenly vulnerable, and he sat down next to her. Cass didn't move. 'May I kiss you, Cass?'

May I. Cass didn't take her eyes from his. She nodded.

He reached out a hand, and when he touched her cheek she caught her breath. His finger stroked her skin. He kept his eyes on her, as though she were some rare, perfect thing. Then he leaned in, again so slowly she thought he would never touch her at all, that this moment would stretch out until one or the other of them pulled away. His face was a dark shape against the candlelight, features merged in shadow. Then his breath was warm on her face, scented with sweet red wine, and his lips touched hers as lightly as was possible; almost a touch, almost nothing at all. He drew away, smiling, ran a wine-dark tongue across his lips. His hand was still on her cheek.

'Mm,' he said.

She could still feel the faint contact on her lips. 'Theo,' she said, trying out the word, conscious that she hadn't called him by his first name before. He had always been 'Mr Remick'.

'Theo it is.'

'I'd like you to kiss me.'

They leaned in to each other this time and paused only a second before their lips touched. This time the contact was firm, his lips fitting hers, easing them apart, the kiss widening, growing, the touch spreading its warmth down Cass' spine. She felt the tip of his tongue. She opened her mouth, meeting it with her own, drawing him close. He eased himself over her, his hand slipping under her back.

He lifted his head. He didn't speak, just looked down at her, his face almost lost in darkness. 'You are a very special lady, Cass,' he said.

She shook her head, looked away.

'And you don't even know it.' He pushed himself up, his heat fading, the cool air something like disappointment on Cass' skin.

She sat up too, glanced at the clock. 'Oh Lord, I should go and get Ben.'

'Of course. Listen, why don't I come with you to fetch him?

She smiled and stood.

'A very special lady indeed,' Mr Remick said, and pushed himself to his feet.

Cass felt the cold air envelop her body, and yet the warmth of the wine and Theo Remick's touch stayed with her as she stepped into the road. Their breath mingled. She found it was good to walk with someone's arm in hers, to not be alone. They turned together into Sally's driveway. Mr Remick knocked and they exchanged glances when they heard a welcoming bellow.

Mr Remick went in first. The boys were sitting in a circle, teeth and eyes glimmering in the lamplight.

'We were just having supper.' Sally bustled through with a tray loaded with cheese and biscuits. 'Care to join us?'

'Perfect.' He squatted in the circle and as Cass squeezed between him and Ben she noted that her son looked calm now. The children sat close together, their legs crossed. Sally set down the tray and they dived in, stuffing biscuits into their mouths.

'So, how are my boys?' Mr Remick asked.

They stared up at him.

'We shared,' said Ben.

'You did? That's great. It's good to share.'

'We played games,' Damon cut in.

'It's good to play games,' he said, grinning sidelong at Cass. His thigh was warm against hers. 'Did you have a good night, Ben?'

Ben bobbed his head, pushed a cracker into his mouth with his palm.

'James, why don't you pass the cheese around?' Mr Remick said to the boy sitting opposite, and he jumped to attention, grabbed the plate and held it out.

'Oh,' said Cass, 'you hurt your hand.' She could see a red line on his palm, half-hidden by the plate. It looked like the mark she'd seen on Damon's hand.

He whipped his head round and glared at her, and Cass

thought suddenly of the darkened corridor at school, the bright eyes shining. Then James looked at Mr Remick. 'I slipped playing football,' he said.

The teacher turned to Sally. 'A fine spread. You're a wonder, as ever.'

Cass said, 'Thanks, Sally – I should be getting Ben home now.'

'You're very welcome. It's a pleasure to have you all here. Any time.'

Mr Remick stood and helped Cass up, then pulled Ben to his feet. He didn't complain about leaving this time, just waited quietly with his hand in Mr Remick's. 'Are you coming too?' he asked. There was no resentment in his voice, only curiosity.

'Not this time. I'm just walking with you for a while.'

They said their goodbyes, and again the ring of cold eyes turned on Cass and she shuddered, but when they shifted to Mr Remick and Ben they only looked like young boys saying goodbye to their friend and their teacher. It was Cass who didn't fit, not Mr Remick, not Ben.

When Mr Remick took her arm again she felt it as a stranger's. She drifted along, only half-listening to her son and his teacher as they talked. But Mr Remick's voice was warm when they parted at the foot of the rectory lane. The church stood above them, a black shape against a curiously pale night. The sky was pregnant with snow. Cass didn't know what she said to him, some automatic thing, but she smiled when he said something about doing this again.

Ben fumbled for her hand and she let him lead her. They didn't speak again until they reached the mill and

Cass tapped the code into the door. It buzzed and she turned the handle, opening it onto the dark hall.

She turned back for Ben and saw that his eyes were cold, reflecting back the light from the entry panel, gleaming in the dark like the eyes of the boys in the school corridor. Cass remembered Jess, the streak of red on her cheek. Then Ben came inside.

He stomped on ahead, up the stairs.

'What is it? Didn't you enjoy yourself?' she asked.

He turned and leaned over the balustrade. 'I *hate* you,' he said.

'*What?* Ben, what's got into you?'

'You sent him away. You send *everyone* away.'

'I didn't send anyone away – Ben, what do you mean?'

'You made my teacher go away. You shouldn't have done that.' Ben's face collapsed and she realised he was holding back tears. 'You sent Daddy away.'

'Ben.' Cass went up and put her arms around him. He was trembling. 'Sweetheart, I didn't send Daddy away – I loved him, you know that. Is that what this is about? Did Jessica say something about him?' *Past tense*, she thought, *I loved* him *– no wonder he's confused.*

Ben twisted away from her and said forcefully, 'He's coming back.'

'What?'

'Daddy's coming back.'

Cass stroked his hair. She tried to look into his eyes, but his face was obscured by shadow. 'I'm sorry, Ben, but you can't go on thinking that. I wish it was true, but it's not going to happen. Daddy died.'

Ben shook her off, and as Cass started back he lashed out and struck her face.

She put a hand to her cheek, not sure if the blow had been an accident or something else.

'He's coming,' said Ben, 'and you can't stop him.' He ran along the hall, turning the corner before Cass could bring herself to move.

Above her, a door banged and she raced up the stairs, slamming through to the first-floor hall. Where was he? But Ben was there, sitting with his back to their door. She still couldn't see his face, but as she went to him she realised he was crying.

'Theodore's going to be my daddy now,' he gulped.

'Oh Ben. No, sweetheart— Shh. Look, it's okay. No one will ever replace your daddy.' She looked at him helplessly. 'Ben, if it upsets you so much, I won't see Mr Remick again.' How had he known his name was Theodore?

Ben looked up and brushed tears from his eyes. 'You have to,' he wailed, 'you *have* to.'

Cass gathered him in her arms and sat with him. Eventually she spoke. 'I know this is hard, Ben. So many things have changed. But you know your daddy loved you very much, and no one can ever take that away. No one's trying to replace your daddy.' He shifted in her arms. 'You're my Number One, you know that? No one will ever take that away from you either.' She tightened her grip. 'Come on, let's go inside.'

'But Sally says that Theodore—'

So that was it. Cass bit her lip. 'Sally shouldn't be saying anything at all.'

Ben scowled, his eyes going distant, and she bent and kissed his head again. When she unlocked the door he pushed past, knocking her into the frame. 'Ben. Maybe you shouldn't go to Mrs Spencer's any more, if it upsets you so much.'

He went straight to his room, slamming the door in her face, and Cass rubbed her elbow where she'd banged it.

When she went into the bathroom and flicked on the light, Cass flinched at the sight of her face in the mirror. She was deathly pale, save for a red mark where her son had hit her.

Cass pulled the box from under her bed. She ran her palm over the top, heard the dry rustle of ageing paper. Pete was in there somewhere, in among the old bills and papers and pictures. His voice.

She found the bundle by touch, slipped off the smooth ribbon and held the letters against her cheek.

Pete had always said he wasn't good at writing letters, that it didn't come naturally to him, but once he started, he could describe a scene exactly – she could almost see it through his eyes.

We saw a wedding party today. Life going on as normal, at least for some, or as normal as they can make it. They do what they can. The bride wore the local dress and had ribbons in her hair. They all danced in the street, kicking up a big cloud of dust, and they never stopped smiling. Everyone danced, the grandmothers and grandfathers and everyone right down to the little kids. It was so loud, but good loud, you know? Not like the shelling. It was strange, hearing something so loud that wasn't trying to kill me.

I thought about our wedding, and wondered if your family would have come if you'd asked. Isn't it time you made up, Cassie? Life is short. Too short, sometimes.

Cass started and almost dropped the letter. She had forgotten that – how strange that she should choose that one to read out of them all, the dry, desert-smelling letters, when she had so recently received one from her father.

It must be her father Pete had meant. The rest of her family had been at the wedding – her mother and an uncle she'd almost forgotten she had. Neither of them had danced.

Life is too short, sometimes.

He got that right.

She stuffed the letter back into the pile. There was no point thinking about it now; with no post going in or out of the village she couldn't write to her father anyway.

And yet . . . just why had Cass chosen to come back to Darnshaw?

She shoved the bundle back into the box and pushed it out of sight, lay down and closed her eyes. After a while she heard a sound and she half-sat, turning towards the wall at her back. It was sharp and loud and deliberate: *scritch, scritch, scritch*, like fingernails scraping on wood. Cass put her hand against the cool plaster. Now it sounded as though the noise was coming from her hand. She tapped it against the wall.

The scratching stopped and instead there came a skittering, heading away.

Cass wondered if Ben had heard it too. It had been louder than before. Maybe he was right: it could be rats, not mice. She shuddered, pushed herself up from the bed and went to check on her son.

She switched on the hall light, blinking in the sudden glare, cracked open Ben's door, then pushed it wider: his bed was rumpled, the sheets pushed back, but it was empty. She stepped in, looking about. There was no sign of him.

'Ben?' she whispered. She switched on his nightlight. There were his clothes, in a pile, his books all heaped on the shelf, but no Ben. And then Cass did a double-take. It was his pyjamas lying on the floor: Ben had never changed out of his daytime clothes.

She stood stock-still, then rushed into the lounge, flicking on the lights, checking behind the sofa in case he was hiding. She kept expecting to hear him giggle, but never heard a sound except her own ragged breathing.

The bathroom was empty too. She swept back the shower curtain, hurried into the kitchen—

—and stopped in the doorway.

The cupboard doors gaped, their contents strewn across the worktop. It looked as though everything had just been thrown out, cereal boxes and tins and packets, but she had never heard a thing. It had been done quietly.

There was nowhere left to look in the flat.

Cass caught her breath, putting a hand to her chest. The blood rushed in her ears and she leaned over the counter, feeling sick. *No Ben.* She pushed herself up and went back into the hall. He could have sneaked from one room to the next while her back was turned, could even be hiding in his own room, or in hers – in the wardrobe, or under the bed. He could be lying in the dark, grinning, one hand resting on the bundle of letters.

But no, she knew he wasn't. And as if in answer to that thought she saw that the front door was ajar.

Cass pulled on her shoes, grabbed her dressing gown from the bathroom and went out.

The hall was quiet, but the lights were flickering: someone had come this way a short time ago, the movement triggering the lights. Cass hurried along the hall. If she was quick, the lights might show her where Ben had gone.

A yellow glow shone through the glass panel of the door to the stairwell. She ran to it, trying to keep quiet, and reached for the handle just as the light on the other side went out.

'No! Damn.' Cass banged through the door, the lights coming back on in response. Downstairs it was brighter, as though the entrance hall lights were on too.

She swallowed her panic, trying not to think of worst-case scenarios: if Ben had gone outside she might never find him. She brushed away the image of the millpond that came into her mind, inky-black water beneath an acid-green coating.

No.

Cass jumped down the last few steps and her ankle gave, but she recovered and kept going. She went to the entrance and pressed up against the glass. Light spilled onto the snow outside, turning footprints into deep black arcs. Cass grabbed the handle and had started to turn it when the light behind her went out.

She stopped. *Think.*

She waved a hand, triggering the lights. The footprints reappeared. She recognised Ben's, but her own prints were there too, facing in both directions, criss-crossing. Ben's could have been from this morning, earlier today, even yesterday. But the lights – the lights at her back had already been on when she came down the stairs.

The lights went out again. She turned. The ground-floor hall was dark now, but it felt *present* somehow. Had the lights really been on when she came down? She wasn't sure, but she thought they probably had been. It *felt* as though they had.

She mouthed his name as she headed away from the front door. The hall lights came on with a low buzz, but just before they did, she saw a pale moonlit glow coming through one of the doorways: the empty apartment. Apartment 6. That must be where Ben had gone.

Cass took a deep breath and padded softly along the hall to the apartment that lay beneath her own. The door was open, and when she looked in she saw Ben at once. He was sitting motionless on the floor, muttering something over and over. It made her think of an elderly person trying to remember something long forgotten.

Ben didn't turn round as she stepped towards him. The

light was dim, the air granular, and Cass' ears rang. She couldn't make out what he was saying.

'Ben,' she said, but her voice cracked. She cleared her throat, took a step closer. And then she froze.

The floor around her son was moving: shadows flowed around his legs and across the floor, always moving, darker grey against the grey boards.

Cass took another step forward and everything clicked into focus. A boiling mass of rats covered the floor around her son. They flowed into and out of the window frames, down the walls and across the space between, throwing up clouds of dust. She heard them now too, the faint scratching of their claws.

Cass' voice dried in her throat.

They crawled into her son's lap, piling up, fighting to get close. Ben sat with his eyes closed, hands in his lap curled like dead things. Rats pushed their heads between his fingers, lapped at his palms.

'Suffer the—' he said, his voice distant, like a child speaking in his sleep. 'Suffer the little—'

'Ben!'

His shoulders jumped.

'Suffer them to come.'

The rats ate out of his hands, lapped at his fingers. His palms shone with their saliva. They thrust forward and stole the crumbs he held. Around him the rats crawled over empty packets and boxes, their contents carried away like trophies, and streamed away out of the empty windows. The pale night shone down on their slick, smooth fur.

One rat turned to stare at Cass, its eyes a sudden white glow, like the boys in the hall, the ones she hadn't seen until they turned to glare at her. Like Ben's eyes earlier, when he turned on her.

Cass made a choking sound. Then she was moving, grabbing her son by an arm and pulling him clear, rats falling from his lap.

Ben cried out at last, a sound without words, but he didn't fight her as she dragged him along at her side, his feet streaking the dust.

Cass pulled him into the hall and tears came as she bent over him, crying into his hair, feeling it against her skin. She knelt and pulled him against her. 'What were you doing, Ben?' she asked. 'What are you doing down here?'

His eyes were glazed, looking blankly over her shoulder. She squeezed his arm. 'Ben, look at me.'

And he did: he turned his eyes on her so that the empty white of them took her in.

Cass wanted to scream – and then his head moved, just a little, and the reflected light passed on, restoring his eyes to their own soft grey.

'Ben, do you hear me?'

He looked at her and blinked, like a child waking from a dream.

'What were you doing?'

'I heard them,' he said in a small voice. 'They were hungry, Mummy. Very hungry.'

'Oh Ben.' Her head sank onto his shoulder.

'I thought I heard them talking.'

'I heard them too, Ben. They've been getting into the walls somehow. But you mustn't go off like that. Never, ever do that again, do you understand?'

His eyes clouded. 'I'm tired, Mummy.'

'I know. So am I. Come on, let's go back.' But first Cass took his hands in hers and turned them, wiping the sticky dampness on her clothes, checking for marks or bites. She found they were whole, not a scratch to be seen.

He pulled away; she was gripping too tight.

'Time for bed.'

She led her son back down the hall, pulling the door to Apartment 6 firmly closed behind them. His hand was clammy, and she imagined long yellow teeth nestled into his palm, whiskers snuffling against the skin, and shuddered. She half-carried him up the stairs, glancing back and half-expecting to see a trail of rats following them like the Pied Piper. Then they were inside their own apartment. Cass leaned on the door with relief.

'They were hungry,' Ben said again. 'They only wanted a daddy to look after them.'

'Oh sweetheart.' Cass picked him up and carried him into the bathroom. She rinsed a flannel and then soaped him with it. Halfway through cleaning his hands, she paused. Apartment 6. Her own, the one above it, was Apartment 12. Two sixes. She shook her head.

'Mummy?'

Cass looked down at her son. She ran her hands through his hair, pulling bits of plaster and dirt from it, letting them patter onto the linoleum. She wanted to shower him, but Ben's eyes were closing. Better that he should sleep.

As she put him to bed and tucked him in she could already hear sounds in the wall. She pulled a face.

'Suffer them to come,' Ben murmured, his eyes closed, already half-asleep.

'What did you say?'

He turned, burying himself in the covers.

Cass watched him a while longer, then went to the front door and double-locked it, pushing the bolt home with a snap. At least she would hear something if Ben chose to go wandering in the night again.

She sat on her bed for a long time, watching her hands shake.

'Suffer them to come,' she said at last. 'Suffer the little children.'

She slipped her legs under the covers, laid down her head and tried, pointlessly, to sleep.

SIXTEEN

Loud banging roused Cass from sleep. The quality of the light told her it was late morning, much later than she usually stayed in bed. She rushed into the hall in time to see Ben, fully dressed, pulling back the bolt and opening the door.

Mr Remick stood there, waving bread and the carton of eggs from the night before. 'I'm too early. Sorry.'

Cass ran a hand through her hair, fingers catching in the tangle. 'No, it's me. I'm so late.' She was still wearing her nightdress. 'Ben, take Mr Remick through to the kitchen. I'll be with you in a second.'

She backed into her room, threw on jeans and a jumper, tried to pat her hair down in the mirror. As she went back out she heard the kettle boiling.

Mr Remick and Ben were sitting at the kitchen table, chatting companionably. Mr Remick looked up and smiled. 'Here's your mum,' he said.

Ben looked up without speaking. His mouth twitched; he still looked pale.

'We slept in,' said Cass. 'Well, I did.'

'And why not? I shouldn't have disturbed you on a Saturday. It's just I forgot to give you these.'

Cass looked at the bread and eggs. 'Why don't I make us something?' She looked around and saw the tins and empty food packets laid out on the worktop. 'We've been having a sort-out.'

'Looks like a good job I brought the eggs.'

Cass ran her eye over their remaining food. 'Actually, it is. It really is. Thank you, Theo. I appreciate it.'

She went to the counter, touched a hand to the mugs that he must have set out himself, opened a cupboard and realised it was the wrong one.

'Here, let me.' Theo stood between her and Ben, put a hand on her arm. 'I'd like to. Why don't you sit down for a bit? I'll bring you a coffee.' As he spoke, the kettle clicked off.

Cass nodded and slipped into the chair next to Ben. She leaned over and kissed his hair. She could smell the dust on it, feel the grease under her lips. What must Theo think?

'We could eat, then go for a walk maybe,' he said.

Ben wriggled, already wearing a broad grin.

They went out into the clean cold air and turned towards the river. Across the field she could see Bert, ambling his way along the path towards them, the low black shape of Captain waddling at his side. He looked like part of the landscape. Cass smiled, raised a hand and waved.

The distant figure paused. The dog came to a stop too, waiting.

It looked as if the old man had seen her, was staring directly at her. Then he tugged on Captain's lead and headed back the way he'd come.

Cass exclaimed.

'He's a funny sort,' said Mr Remick, 'one of the more local locals, if you know what I mean. You shouldn't let it bother you.'

He took her arm and they headed around the mill instead, towards the pond.

Ben slipped his hand into Mr Remick's, laughed and swung on his arm. 'Will you play soldiers later?'

'Of course,' he said, and Cass found she didn't mind the idea. Ordinarily she liked her own company, hers and Ben's, but the teacher's company was comfortable. He fitted.

Ben whooped and ran ahead, kicking chunks of ice into the air. The previous snowfall was frozen solid, as deep as ever.

'He's been so odd lately,' said Cass. 'Last night . . .' But she found she didn't want to tell him about last night. The thought of those grey bodies crawling over her son, lapping at his fingers, their feet on his body, made her feel sick. She stopped.

'Is everything all right? I know he had that thing with Jessica. He seems fine now though.'

'Yes, he is.'

'A great kid.'

'Mm.'

'You know, we always show our worst side to those we love the most.' Remick turned to her and smiled. 'It's the perfect strangers we perform for best. If he's playing up it's because he knows you'll still be there to love him when it's over.'

'You think so?' She paused. 'Do you think he's testing me?'

He sighed. 'We're all being tested, Cass, all of the time. Kids, they push the boundaries, you know?'

'You have rather more of them to deal with than I do.'

'Ah, but it's not the same. They show me their good side – most of the time, anyway.'

'Do you think he'll calm down?'

'He's settling in, making friends. I think so. You, on the other hand . . .' He brushed the hair back from her face. 'You need a little looking after, I think. Why don't I get Sally to babysit? I'll cook for you again.'

'You might have to. We might be on a starvation diet soon.'

'I wouldn't let that happen.'

'Seriously, though, when will the roads be clear? The snowplough hasn't been once. And the phone lines are still down.'

'I suspect it may be some time yet – but you don't have to feel alone, Cass. You have friends here. Really good friends.' He leaned forward and kissed her lightly.

'I'm glad you came today.'

'Good. So am I. Of course I have an ulterior motive.'

'Oh?'

He tilted his head. 'Ben, of course. I want him on the team.'

'Team?'

'He's a great snowman builder. Of course, he may be good at other things too – football, rugby. We haven't had much chance to find out, have we?'

'I think you'll find he prefers video games.'

'Ah – then perhaps we need a video game team. Hey, Ben, time to play!'

Ben spun round. His cheeks were pink, his eyes bright. Cass thought of what he might have been like had Mr Remick not come round, the way he was last night – sullen, pale. Why could she not work this transformation alone? She should just let him go, let him enjoy things – let him be a kid. She watched as the teacher ruffled Ben's hair, raced him back down the lane, sliding and shouting. She remembered the touch of his lips on hers, so light it might barely have happened at all.

SEVENTEEN

On Sunday Ben was up before Cass, filling the apartment with the sound of gunfire. He didn't jump when Cass bent to kiss his head, he didn't even turn, and she could see that his face was pale once more.

She made toast from the last of the bread and watched Ben play while she ate. The plate at his side remained untouched. 'Come on,' she said at last, 'eat up. We're going out.'

They saw Bert as soon as they opened the front door. He stood by the lamp post at the bottom of the lane, Captain motionless at his side. Snow fell all around him, settling on his shoulders, the hood of his coat, the dog's rough black fur. Captain shook himself, sending it flying.

Cass hesitated, then said, 'Look Ben, it's Captain.' He frowned. He didn't show any sign of being afraid, or of wanting to see the dog either. It was impossible to gauge his feelings.

'Wait here,' said Cass. She put up the catch and went

out. *Why here, now?* Yesterday Bert had turned away rather than exchange a hello as they passed.

''ow do,' said Bert, tipping a hand to his hood. He coughed, air spurting out in a cloud of spittle. ''scuse.'

'Are you all right, Bert?' His face, now that Cass was up close, had a faint yellowish tinge.

Captain's sides jerked and he coughed in a rough bark.

Cass and Bert exchanged startled looks.

'Saw you walkin' with that teacher yesterday.' Teacher with a short vowel: *ticher.*

'Yes, that's right. Do you know Theo?'

'Theo. Tha's his name now, is it?'

'Well, of course it's Mr Remick to everyone at school, but—'

Bert turned and spat into the snow. 'An' you're not everyone, I tek it.'

'Bert, I don't think—'

'No bother, I can see I'm poking me nose in. Just wanted to say watch out for the bairn, like. An' yourself.'

'Whatever do you mean?'

He squinted, pushing his face towards hers. 'You'd be best to get t' bairn out for a while,' he said. 'It allus comes in like this, when he wants it.' He nodded at the snow. It was almost featureless again, covering old footprints, softening everything.

'He?'

Bert tutted up at the sky.

'Bert, are you sure you're all right?'

'I'd say come to church,' he said. *Chuch.* 'But it's too

late for that. Priest'll not get here now, not for a while yet, I shouldn't think.'

'No.' Cass paused. 'I heard there's a tree down on the road.'

'A tree?' He tossed his head. 'A tree, is it? Well, it might look like a tree. Same as t' other way might look like the road's cracked and fallen in. Aye, that's what it'll look like, all reet.'

Cass took a step back and glanced at the door. Ben's face was pressed up against the glass, partly obscured by mist. As she watched, his hand pressed into it, clearing a space. 'Bert, I don't think— I mean—'

'You 'ave to go – aye, I don't doubt it. He's started already, 'an't he?'

'Goodbye, Bert.'

The old man's hand shot out and caught Cass' arm. His fingers shook and Cass realised he was freezing. 'Bert, let go of me,' she said gently.

'I'm getting out,' he said, his grip tight, 'tomorrer or the next day, walking o'er tops to Moorfoot. If you want I could phone someone for you. 'appen I'll rent one o' them buggies from one o' the farms. I can 'elp you. I don't suppose the lad'll leave now.'

Cass stared at him, remembered Ben sitting with his back to the witch stones, refusing to move. *I don't suppose the lad'll leave now.*

'If you want me t' phone anyone for you, you know where I am,' Bert said. His eyes went distant, staring up at the white sky. Snowflakes settled on his scalp, on his face. He let go of Cass and yanked at Captain's lead, started dragging the dog towards the lane.

'Bert, wait. I want to know what you mean.'

There was a bang behind her and Ben was walking through the snow towards them. He was wearing that same scowl.

Captain stopped dead, a growl rising in the back of his throat.

'Ben, stay there.' Cass gestured for her son to stop, but he kept on coming.

Captain settled back on his haunches then jerked forward, snapping his lead taut.

Bert looked down at him. 'It's not 'im as needs to be on a lead,' he said.

'How dare you?' Cass stepped in front of Ben. 'How dare you say that? Your dog attacked my son.'

Captain moved back, pushing against Bert's legs, the growl turning into a whine.

'I'm going,' said Bert, dragging him away up the hill. He called back over his shoulder as he went, 'You know where I am.'

Cass stared after him, then dropped to Ben's side. 'Did he scare you? Don't take any notice, Ben, he's just a strange old man, but I don't want you going anywhere near him, do you hear?' She looked into his eyes. They were hard, frozen, shining back the blank sky.

'I don't want to go,' he said, his voice monotone.

'What did you say?'

'I don't want to go.'

'Ben, will you look at me?' Cass found herself wishing for Theo Remick. He would know what to do.

I don't suppose the lad'll leave now, Bert had said.

'I'm not going.' Ben turned and Cass' fingers slipped on his coat. He ran back to the door, fumbled with the entry panel, hit it with one curled fist and then ran round the side of the building.

'Where are you going?' Cass followed, her feet slipping on the ice beneath the snow. She saw a flash of Ben's coat as he rounded the corner; he was heading for the place where the digger stood abandoned. The millpond.

'Ben,' she called, but when she turned the corner there was no sign of him. The embankment that led towards the millpond was a fresh white sheet, nothing to show where they had walked only the day before. The path round the back of the mill was different: snow had drifted deeply against the back of the building, but it was churned with fresh footprints. Ben had circled the mill. Or headed back to the empty apartment and its open windows.

Cass followed, the blood rushing in her ears. Other than the footprints, there was no trace of her son. As she passed the ground-floor apartments she caught glimpses of dark interiors, but nothing moved inside. She saw no sign of rats.

An empty window yawned at Cass' side and she jumped even though she'd been looking for it.

Snow that had fallen inside was grey where it had met the dust. Cass jumped onto the windowsill and swung her feet over; they met the boards with a hollow sound.

The apartment smelled of rot and damp, and something else too: the acrid tang of rats.

It took a moment for Cass' eyes to adjust. There was no sign of grey bodies, and no sign of Ben except wet footprints.

There was something on the floor, though, half-buried in the dust. She knew what it was and bent to retrieve it. The doll was dirtier, the fabric more faded, but she could see where a T-shirt and shorts had been drawn onto the figure. Then she saw the other doll: dirty wool for hair, a face scrawled onto the cloth. She bent and picked it up, wrinkling her nose.

The doll's mouth had been crossed out, over and over again, with fresh black ink, and there was a hole through the body which looked as if it had been chewed by small, sharp teeth. The fabric was darkened at the edges.

There was something inside the hole. Cass poked a finger into the fabric and felt it, dry and smooth and rounded. She couldn't prise it out until she bent the doll back on itself and managed to ease the object free. A blue-grey shape appeared, then shattered, spurting liquid across her hand. Cass threw the thing down and stepped back. She sensed something behind her: Ben, standing there, his eyes shadowed, his gaze impassive.

'I can't get in,' he said. 'Mummy, let me in – I can't go. I *can't*.' His face crumpled and he began to cry.

Cass stared. She wanted to hug him, and yet she couldn't move.

The doll lay on the floor, the shattered object bleeding from it, forming globules in the dust. All she could think was that the rats would come; they would fight over this prize, lap at the fluid, gnaw on the doll until its face and hair and everything else was gone. *An egg*, she thought. *It was an egg.*

Ben's wails grew louder. 'Mummy, let me in,' he cried, 'Mummy, *please*. I can't. I can't.' As he lashed out at her she grabbed his arms, and abruptly Ben stopped crying.

His face twisted in anger and he opened his eyes wide and spat in her face. 'I'm not leaving,' he said.

Cass felt Ben's forehead as she settled him down on the sofa. She wished she had some milk she could warm for him, a little boy's drink, but all she had was water. She sat next to him while he drank, sipping from the glass and pulling a face. 'Sally would—' he started, then shot a glance at her and looked away. 'I want my game,' he said.

Cass bit her lip. Sally would have all the right things, she knew; she would know all the right things to say. Mr Remick, he'd know what to do too. 'How about you have a break from the game,' she suggested. 'How about you draw me a picture?'

Ben narrowed his eyes, but after a moment he nodded, and Cass got out the coloured pencils and paper. She wondered what he would draw – another soldier, perhaps, spurting with blood. The teacher had said Ben hadn't drawn anything else like it, not since the first time, but if her son was in some way disturbed, perhaps Cass would be able to tell from the things he drew.

She went into the kitchen and sorted through their

remaining food, glancing through the open door from time to time. Her son was bent over the paper, his arm wrapped around it, shielding his picture. He kept tossing his head, flicking his fringe back. She should cut it. She should give him good things to drink. Make his tea. Make him smile, make him laugh – make him a normal boy, not one who glared and spat at her. Now his face was pale, but it was pinched in concentration, not in hatred or that horrible blankness. His hand flicked forward and back, a blue pencil gripped tight in his fist. The tip of his tongue poked out and the corners of his mouth creased. He was enjoying himself.

Cass pulled the door closed and looked at the food, wondering what they could eat. There were no potatoes or pasta – but there were dried noodles, and beans. The carton of eggs was on the counter. She flicked open the top, half-expecting a spurt of gelatinous fluid, but only two smooth brown eggs sat there.

Cass found the tin opener. They could have them with beans. She set a pan on the hob and the bubbling sound was familiar, domestic.

'Lunch is ready, love,' she said, nudging the door open with her foot and carrying the plates through. The smell filled the room. Ben looked up, smiling. There was something in his eyes.

'Did you do a good picture?'

He stood, took the paper from the table and held it behind his back. Smiled again, showing his dimples. Cass set down the plates and tousled his hair. 'Good boy. Are you going to show me?'

Ben slipped into the chair next to hers and Cass passed him a knife and fork. Ben didn't take them, just sat, smiling at her, until she put them down. Then he put the paper on the table and smoothed it out.

A soldier stood in the centre of the picture. He wore desert camouflage, swirls of khaki and beige. He had straw-coloured hair and was tall, much taller than the other person in the picture. Cass knew this because Pete – and it had to be Pete – had one arm stretched out at his side and had hold of the other person, a woman, by her long black hair. Her breasts hung outside a dress of brilliant blue. Her feet dangled above the yellow desert floor. She had sienna skin and brown eyes and a wide black opening for a mouth. Cass could see that she was screaming.

The soldier, though, wore a broad smile.

'He sexed her, Mummy,' said Ben. Cass turned to see that Ben was smiling too. 'He sexed her.'

She lashed out, slapping her son across his cheek. His skin reddened at once as she cried out, 'Oh, I'm sorry. I'm sorry!' She pushed the drawing away with one hand, reaching out for her son with the other. 'Ben, I didn't *mean* to—'

He was holding his hand to his cheek and she could see each breath as it was sucked into his mouth and hissed out again. His eyes were screwed up in anger. He grabbed his fork from the table and held it out in his fist.

'Ben.'

He jabbed at her with it and Cass jerked back, knocking into her chair. He did it again, and the tines flashed silver in front of her eyes. He got up and stumbled away, fleeing from the room.

Cass heard his door slam. She picked up the drawing from the floor: her husband's fist, wrapped in the woman's hair, the wide black opening of her mouth. *He sexed her.*

She slumped into her chair and put her hands over her eyes. Her breath wouldn't come. She felt the tears as they began to ooze between her fingers.

EIGHTEEN

The footsteps and scuffles Cass heard coming from the hall didn't sound real. She pictured all of the doors out there, doors with no one behind them, all of them opening at once and neighbours she had never seen stepping out.

Then she heard quick, smothered laughter. She reluctantly got to her feet as she heard a knock, followed by another smothered laugh. She folded Ben's drawing and shoved it into her pocket.

When she opened the door there were four boys standing on the threshold. They didn't meet her eye. One of them stepped forward: Damon.

'Good evening. We wondered if Ben is coming out to play.' His words were too polite, full of sarcasm.

One of the boys laughed and another dug him in the ribs.

Cass heard a sound behind her and knew that Ben was standing at her back. She didn't want to look at him. Her hand went to her pocket.

'We're going to play by the river and not fall in,' said Damon. 'Mum said not to.' His mouth twitched.

Weariness settled on Cass' shoulders and when Ben pushed past her, pulling on his coat, she didn't try to stop him.

'Bye. See you later.' Damon's voice was bright.

Cass didn't answer. She closed the door after her son, went into the lounge and slumped into the sofa. Its curves settled around her. *Pete*, she thought. *Pete.* Yet it wasn't Pete's face she saw, but Theo Remick's, his clear, intelligent eyes, his lips pressing down on hers.

She should have told Ben what time to be back. Damon was only a couple of years older, but he was much more assured than Ben: a natural leader. She couldn't imagine Sally letting her son go out to play without telling him what time to be home. The boys would drop Ben off on the way.

Cass sighed. Things would be different tomorrow. If Ben were feeling happier, more like himself, he could go to Sally's. And she could go to Theo Remick's.

She was asleep on the sofa, her head crooked on her arm, when she heard the door bang. She glanced at the clock. It was well after nine, far later than she would have liked, but Ben was home now. It didn't matter. She was so very, very tired.

Water ran in the bathroom sink; the toilet flushed. Then water ran again, for a long time. Cass should call out to him, see how he was, but somehow she did not.

The bathroom door banged, then his bedroom door.

She should go and see her son, but she lacked the

energy to get up. She didn't even know where he had been. Ben had done that awful drawing, and instead of asking him why, calmly, sensibly, she had lashed out at him. And now she hadn't even seen him come in.

It occurred to her that she didn't even know it was Ben in there at all. It could be one of the other boys huddled beneath his sheets; that hard-eyed Damon, perhaps, playing a trick.

She pulled the drawing from her pocket and a sudden pain stabbed behind her eyes. How could he have done that? It looked like his work – but surely her sweet child couldn't have done it, certainly not alone.

And Pete. Her husband. Surely he couldn't have done it either.

Cass ran a hand over her eyes and went to see her son.

At first Cass could see only a heap of covers, piled high on the bed, a man-sized bulk. She found herself reluctant to step closer, but forced herself to move. There was the curve of Ben's shoulder, the pale hair flopping over his face. His breathing was loud, the deep breath of sleep: just a little boy worn out from playing with his friends.

She should have asked where he'd been, what they'd been doing. She frowned. Carving signs into doors, perhaps. Chasing through empty apartments.

She shook her head. They'd probably just been snow-balling, racing each other, finding makeshift sledges. The builders' yard would be the place for that, and Cass reminded herself to warn Ben away from it. Anything could be there – sheets of corrugated iron, rusted tools, splintering planks of wood embedded with nails. And anything could be lurking underneath: grey rats, huddled together for warmth.

Rats. And Ben, sitting so still while they swarmed over him, eating the food.

He had wanted to be kind, that was all.

And tonight? Had Ben gone looking for the rats tonight?

Cass looked at the floor where Ben habitually dropped his clothes. There was something there; at first it looked like a grey writhing mass, but she blinked and it resolved into nothing but his jeans and a T-shirt. She swept them up and slipped out of the room, closing the door behind her.

As she walked to the bathroom she realised the clothes were too heavy, and something in the bundle was soaked. At first she thought her son might have wet himself, that maybe he'd been upset at the other boys' games. She pictured her pale-faced boy, being dared to do who knew what? Climb trees maybe – or draw pictures, nasty, *awful* pictures. She straightened out his jeans. They were fine; the only dampness was around the ankles where he'd walked through the snow. It was his T-shirt that was wet; the front was a dripping mess. She remembered the tap running in the bathroom: why had he been so long? She smoothed out the fabric, held it up to the light. Behind the water was a darker smudge, some kind of stain. He'd got muddy perhaps. She brought the fabric to her face and sniffed. There was a faint meaty scent, the warm smell of bodies. She screwed it into a tight ball and threw it into the laundry basket. His jeans followed.

Cass wiped her hands on a towel and looked at her reflection in the mirror. Her face was pinched, her hair greasy. The skin around her eyes felt dry. The lines on her forehead were deepening. She hadn't looked like this when she had known Pete. Had Theo Remick seen those lines? She leaned over the sink and splashed water on her face. She felt so tired. She was going to sleep, to clear her mind and think of nothing.

But Cass didn't sleep. As soon as she climbed into bed she felt her brain working, turning things over. She thought about Ben: how could her child have done such a drawing? How could he even have thought of such a thing? She leaned over, grabbed her clothes from where she too had thrown them on the floor and pulled the drawing from her pocket. She didn't look at it, just felt the paper between her fingers as she stared at the ceiling. And she found herself thinking of Pete.

His arms had been so strong. It was one of the things she had loved about him, the way he'd wrap his arm around her waist and pull her to him mock-forcefully. The way he'd pin her down with one hand while he ran the other over her body.

Could Pete have done such a thing? *No.* It was just a drawing. Something imagined, not something seen.

He was Ben's father. The man she loved. *Had* loved.

Cass threw off the covers and swung her legs over the side of the bed. Her skin prickled in the cool night air. She reached under the bed, feeling the edge of the box, pulling it free. She felt the smoothness of ribbon under her fingers and riffled through the letters. Her hands did the choosing, pulling one loose. It rustled, crackled, and Cass started. The sound wasn't coming from the paper. Somewhere inside the walls, rats were moving again.

Cass flicked on the lamp and the shadows fled. She saw her husband's writing, so familiar, so dear to her. When she ran her finger over the page she half expected to feel the words written there, as though they had taken on the character of something carved.

We took turns, it said. Cass squeezed her eyes shut.

We took turns, and the locals laughed. You'd think haggling would come easy to a northerner like me, but it's surprisingly tough. They saw us coming a mile off. We'd line up, forming an orderly queue so they could fleece us.

You'd have loved it, Cass. They all gather round and bicker and wave things in your face. It's a bit worrying, but so full of life, not like our shops, just everyone diving in and all chattering at once.

They had leather shoes and blankets and embroidery, and I tried to find something I could imagine you wearing, but I couldn't.

Then I saw the lapis lazuli. It looked like little chunks of rock, which is of course what it was, but if you know how to treat it, it turns into the most brilliant of colours.

Men fought and died over those rocks. For a while it was the most expensive colour in the world. I bought some for you, Cass. Maybe one day we'll find out how it works.

Lapis. Blue stones, falling from his hands. Cass had thought her husband was trying to tell her something, and all the time her dream had sprung only from this: an old letter, put away and forgotten.

Scritch, scritch.

Cass fell back onto the bed, staring up at the ceiling. She needed to get away. Darnshaw was a black-and-white place. Pete was right: she needed colour around her, life.

She felt around for Ben's drawing and held it up in front of her face. The blue stones of her dream had come from life. Where had this drawing come from? She stared. The khaki-clad soldier, his arm stretched out. The girl, her face a scream, silent now, perhaps for ever. Her dress a clear brilliant blue.

NINETEEN

Cass snapped awake to the blare of the alarm clock and leaned over the side of the bed, scrabbling for it. She touched cardboard, then the smooth plastic of the clock. She switched it off and lay back, tempted to just let herself drift. Then she sighed and pushed herself up. She had to get to the school early today, to try and see Lucy. Five minutes now might mean another eight hours of waiting.

Cass headed for the bathroom, calling out for Ben along the way. She saw his T-shirt sticking out of the laundry basket and pushed it back in.

'Ben.' She threw on her clothes, remembered she would be seeing Mr Remick and pulled a clean jacket over the top.

'Ben, come on,' she shouted, but Ben was already there, standing in the doorway, dressed for school, his rucksack over his shoulder.

'There you are,' Cass said, and smiled. Ben's cheeks

were flushed and she wondered if one was a little redder than the other, where she'd slapped him. She went to her son and put a hand to his cheek, kissed him. 'Come on, love. I'll make us some breakfast.'

Breakfast was a couple of crackers that had survived Ben's raid, soft but passable. Cass spread butter thinly over them. 'We can eat and walk. Come on.'

They trod new paths in the fresh-fallen snow. It was deeper than ever, reaching the top of their boots. The lane was slow-going, but once they reached the road it was easier. The air was cold in Cass' nostrils, sharp and clear, and smelled of nothing at all.

Someone had reached the school before them, leaving a trail of footprints down the path. The car park was a fresh white blanket that no one had disturbed and the sun glittered back from its surface.

'Enjoy school, love.' Cass kissed Ben, forgetting he was getting too old for such things, and squeezed his shoulder before he started down the path. A piercing whistle sounded and a snowball flew from the playing field and glanced off Ben's arm. Damon was in the field, waving. Ben waved back.

Mr Remick appeared at the doors and Cass went to meet him. Ben had seen him too and wheeled round, running towards him as a son might run to his father. Cass half-expected Theo to sweep Ben off his feet and spin him round.

Cass met Theo's eyes, saw the warmth on his face. It made everything seem so simple.

'Hi, Ben,' the teacher said. 'You ready for Sally's tonight?'

Ben grinned enthusiastically. He looked different this morning – happy, carefree. He ran off towards the playing field where Damon waited.

'I hope that's still all right with you, Cass,' Theo said.

Cass nodded, but there was a sound from behind her that she recognised. 'Excuse me,' she said quickly, 'I'll just be a second. There's someone I need to speak to.'

A Land Rover came into sight, its bonnet dipping as it edged onto the slope of the car park. Cass waved at the windscreen and hurried around to the driver's side.

The door swung open and a woman Cass didn't know looked out.

'Oh, I'm sorry,' said Cass, 'I mistook you for someone else.' She backed away, and found that Mr Remick had followed her up the slope.

'Good to see you, Mrs Jackson,' he called out.

Mrs Jackson looked up at him, smiled, and fussed over the child in the passenger seat.

'Is everything all right, Cass?'

Cass met Mr Remick's gaze. His eyes were free of worries. There was no line between his eyes.

'I really need to see Jessica's mum. Have you seen her this morning?'

'No, she hasn't been in yet. Do you want to watch for her from inside? You look cold.'

Cass looked around the car park. No one was going to negotiate it in a hurry, not today. If she watched from the school, she'd easily see Lucy in time to catch her.

Mr Remick led the way into the first classroom and Cass looked out of the window, seeing the white world between brilliantly coloured window paintings. He pulled up a tiny plastic chair and perched on it, his long legs splayed, and she couldn't help but smile.

'You'll fall for my charms yet, Ms Cassidy,' he said.

She turned back to the window and caught her breath. A vehicle was turning in at the gate, but it was a pick-up, a white one.

Remick pushed himself up and stood next to her. 'That's Myra,' he said. 'Her husband left her the truck.'

'Isn't he around any more?'

He shook his head. 'No, she's on her own.' He paused. 'It's not easy for her. You know, I get the feeling things are a little rough on you too at the moment.'

Cass felt his breath on the side of her neck as he leaned in; there came the faint tickle of his stubble and the lightest of kisses. A shiver ran down Cass' body. She forced herself to keep watching the white slope outside.

Myra was walking down the path, one hand on her child's shoulder. As Cass watched, the woman turned her head and looked in through the window. As their eyes met, Myra's lips twitched into a smirk.

Cass tossed her head and shot a look at Mr Remick.

'Really,' he murmured, 'you can make friends here. If you want to.'

They watched the path. A couple of kids skidded down it, followed by a mother who walked her child to the door and left. There were no other cars. Cass shifted, leaning close to the glass.

'I should gather up the troops.' He looked at his watch. 'But—?'

He raised an eyebrow. 'We're a bit depleted now. Still, we have to keep going.'

'But so few?' Cass looked out. Maybe a dozen children had arrived, not even enough for one full class. As she watched, Sally hurried past the window and waved. 'And I haven't seen Lucy. She'll be here, surely.'

'Sorry.' He squeezed her shoulder. 'I'm sure she'll be fine, but there was more snow overnight. The roads were pretty bad as it was.'

'She might still come.'

'Well, why don't you keep watching a while? You can stay in here if you like.'

Cass heard his shoes tapping across the floor and the sound of the door closing. She leaned against the glass, looking at the fingerprints smeared in the window paint: so many little hands. The slope outside remained stubbornly empty. Lucy wasn't coming. But the disk – surely Lucy would have sent the files for her?

It looked like Cass wouldn't find out that day. Chairs shuffled and scraped in the next room, Sally's voice rang out, and Mr Remick laughed. Cass felt a stab of jealousy. Sally was a single woman, spending the whole day with Theo. She remembered the other mothers, laughing about it.

But she would be spending the night with Theo Remick.

Cass swallowed. Had she really thought that? She shook her head. It was dinner, that was all – it was just dinner, and they would talk, get to know each other a little better, and then Cass would leave and pick up her son.

She thought of Pete, the letters under her bed.

He sexed her.

She pushed the thought away and made herself think about her client. Lucy was half an hour late; she clearly wasn't coming. And if Jessica wasn't at school today, Lucy wouldn't be here tonight to collect her either, so Cass wouldn't find out what had happened to the files until tomorrow.

Well, there was one thing she could still do. Just in case Lucy had taken against her, after all.

TWENTY

The post office door was locked, a CLOSED sign turned to the glass. Cass looked up at the row of windows in the building above. It was hard to make out if there were any lights on inside. *The flats*, Bert had said, as though Cass already knew where they were.

At the side of the post office was a narrow black door. It looked unused, the paint peeling. *The flats.* Cass looked for a sign saying who might live there, but saw none. There was no doorbell either.

She knocked on the door and waited and almost immediately a gruff bark came from somewhere inside. A moment later footsteps beat out an irregular rhythm, *bang-bang, bang-bang*, as of someone edging down the stairs.

When he opened the door, Bert's face was red. 'Just coming,' he said. 'Ah, it's you, love.'

He ushered Cass into a narrow hall. Just behind him was a steep staircase with a patterned carpet worn down at the centre of each tread. Bert stood back against the wall, letting Cass go first, and she squeezed past. She looked up to see a single wall light illuminating a ring of yellowed wallpaper.

'Go on in, go on in,' Bert said, pushing the door closed until it latched.

Cass went up and paused on the landing. A sketch portrait of a woman looked down at her from an oval frame. The lady wore a long dress and a shy smile. Bert's wife? Cass had never imagined him as anything but alone, just him and his dog – and now Captain stuck a salt-and-pepper muzzle around a doorframe and regarded her.

'Hello, Captain,' Cass said. She didn't go any closer. 'It's only me.'

''e's harmless.' Bert spoke at her back and Cass jumped. 'Just an old un.'

Captain withdrew as Bert gestured towards the doorway and as Cass went in, the dog eased down onto a faded jacket lying on the floor. There were green chairs adorned with antimacassars, dark wooden furniture, and photographs everywhere: children of various ages, the same woman Cass had seen before.

'Enid,' said Bert, following her gaze. 'Been gone a long time now. And the young uns.'

Cass didn't ask whose 'young uns'. She wondered how often they visited.

Captain let out a loud sigh.

'I know you said—'

'Aye, love. If you want I can phone someone for you, come back with one of they quads or some such thing. Or 'appen I'll get someone to come and get you.'

Cass paused. She looked at him and down at the dog. She bit her lip. 'You know, it's very kind of you. But I don't think you should go.'

'No?' His eyes narrowed. 'Why not?'

'It's just, it's such a long way. It might be too much, and— Well.'

Bert let out a bray of laughter. 'You don't think I'm up to it.' The laugh turned into a wheeze and he slapped his leg as he dropped into a chair, gesturing to Cass to take the one opposite. 'That's it, in't it?'

'It'll be really hard work in the snow. I'm not sure about Captain, that's all. He looks tired.'

Bert grew serious. 'I know, love, an' he is: 'im and me both. But I've been walking they paths in these parts since I were a lad, an' that's saying something.'

'But—'

'I'm no lad any more, I know it. Listen, love, I walk every day, no less, and so does Captain. An' it'll be a tough un, I'm not saying it won't. But I'll tek me time, and once I'm on t' road, it'll be all reet. You'll see.'

'Are you sure?'

'It's nine mile, more or less. I'll be tired at t'other end, but once I'm up top, it's all downhill an' I'll be reet. Now, what I can do for you?' He looked at her. 'I'm going, love, with or without any messages you want to give me, so you might as well come out with it.'

Cass fumbled in her bag and brought out an envelope. 'I really need to get this to someone. If you wouldn't mind posting it in Moorfoot, I'd appreciate it.'

Bert took the padded envelope, looked at the address.

'It's for work. I have to get those files to my client or I could lose him. I don't have any stamps, but I can give you the money.'

'Is that it?'

'Well, yes, but it's—'

'You don't get it,' he said. 'You don't get it at all.'

'What?'

'Is there nothing else?' The accent seemed to fall away, his voice becoming clipped. 'No message I can take for you? No one I can call?'

Cass thought of her father and shifted in her seat. Perhaps she would write to him, but not now; she could do it when this was over, the snow thawed. Then she could go and see him, or maybe he could visit her in Darnshaw.

She thought of her father looking up at the church, awe and something deeper written on his face.

'No, Bert, there's nothing. It would be great if you could do that for me, but I'd understand if you didn't want to go. I'll work it out somehow.'

Bert folded the envelope and stuffed it in his pocket. 'I'll tek it for you, love. I hope it all works out, that's all.'

'It's kind of you.'

'Just one thing,' he said.

Cass waited.

'I'm going, like I say, but he's too old. He'll not make it o'er t' tops.'

It took her a moment to realise he meant Captain.

'I need to leave him at 'ome. I can leave him 'ere, but – well, I wondered if you might tek him.'

Cass' mouth fell open.

'He's not used to being on his own.'

'Bert, I'm really sorry – I know you're helping me, and I'd like to help you in return, but I have to think of Ben. Captain went for him the other day. I just can't take the risk.'

'No, no.' Bert hung his head. 'I'd forgot that. It's not like him, you see. But no, it's all reet. He'll be fine here, will Captain.'

The dog's ears twitched at the mention of his name.

'He'll probably be glad of the rest, wi'out me dragging him all ower.'

'I wish I could.'

'I know, love, no, it's fine. I shouldn't have asked. Just a thought, tha's all. Don't you go minding about it. We'll be fine, me an' Captain.'

They walked back down the stairs in silence, Bert hanging onto the rail. He rattled the door open and looked up at the sky. 'No let-up yet,' he said as fine flakes drifted down. 'No, I'd best be off soon. I can smell it in the air, can't you?'

Cass sniffed and looked about. When she looked back at Bert he was smiling at her.

'Take care o' that lad o' yours,' he said, as he closed the door.

Cass watched the snowflakes falling outside her window. They were thicker now, heavier. She imagined Bert huddled in his coat, bent into the wind, going up the hill one slow step at a time, and Captain, whining at home for his master.

She shouldn't have let him go.

But he was probably well on his way to town, already looking forward to a drink in the nearest pub. He was used to walking, he knew the land. He knew what he was letting himself in for, and anyway, he'd said he had his own business to settle on the other side of the moors.

Cass had to stop worrying about Bert; there was something she needed to do. She hadn't been able to put Ben's drawing out of her mind. It was hard to shake the feeling that her son knew something about his father that she'd never even guessed at, but of course that couldn't be true. The picture had come from Ben's imagination, or maybe something he'd seen in his game or on television.

Pete's letters were in Cass' mind all the same. It was time to sort through them. To try and gain some clue as to the person her husband might have become.

Then to get rid of them, move on.

The bundle looked so small once she held it in the daylight. Such a little thing to show for their years together: a few observations, impressions of people and places she hadn't seen and never would. Cass lifted them to her face. A faint dusty smell rose from them, like something already beginning to decay.

She'd tucked Ben's picture into the box. It wasn't the image that hurt any more, it was his words: *He sexed her.*

Cass pulled open the ribbon and spread the letters on the floor.

I saw a young boy today. He was maybe five or six. He sort of reminded me of Ben, and yet he didn't. Is that

*weird? But there was something in his eyes. Knowledge, I
suppose. Or the total absence of hope.*

*It wasn't till I'd gone past I saw his leg was taken off
at the knee.*

Cass shook her head. It wasn't what she was looking
for.

*When I come home, I'll bring you the blue stones. The
most expensive colour in the world.*

I love you, Cass. I always will.

Cass caught her breath, held the letter to her face and
closed her eyes, waiting for the tears to come. But they
did not. Instead she saw Theo Remick's eyes, clear and
candid, as if everything was straightforward, already
decided between them.

She gathered the letters together and stood. She should
get rid of them all: a statement, if only to herself, that
she was ready to move on.

And yet she turned and threw them back into the box
and kicked it under the bed. What if she needed them
one day? She might need his voice for company.

And Ben might want to read them when he was older.
Of course he would.

Cass poked her foot under the bed, giving the box a
last shove. They could stay there. She would leave them
in the dark until she had forgotten about them.

TWENTY-ONE

Cass pulled a silk top from the wardrobe and held it against her body. Pete had loved that one. He had made her buy it, though she hadn't wanted to spend the money. She put it back. Saw a flash of red at the back. Red. It was a little obvious, but did it matter? She was a grown woman with lines in her forehead and a son to collect. No, it didn't matter. She put it on, seeing the way it made her hair brighter, made her eyes shine.

He sexed her.

Yes, it would do.

She tried not to think of Pete but couldn't help comparing them in her mind. She knew that Theo would never be loud, never be laddish like Pete. Did she miss that? She pressed her lips together. But wasn't Theo Remick the sort of man she'd have chosen for herself, before she met her husband?

Cass shook her head, brushed mascara onto her lashes and slicked gloss over her lips. Remembered the feel of

Remick's lips on her neck. She grabbed her bag and prepared to set out.

The school had already closed. A couple of children lingered, a boy and a girl. They wandered away, their coats bright against the snow.

The corridor was empty. Cass walked down it, her footsteps too loud, her heartbeat too fast. She knocked at Theo's office.

'Here,' he said from behind her. He stood at a classroom door, a gaunt figure. He looked at her with those eyes. She could reach out and touch him if she wanted. And yet he was a stranger, someone she hardly knew.

He reached out, touched her hair and smiled, and didn't say anything, and that was all right because she could see in his face she did know him after all. He was the one who made her smile, someone her son looked up to, became his old self with.

'Well, Ms Cassidy.'

'Well, Mr Remick.'

'I'm half tempted to kiss you right here, but it would be most unprofessional.'

Cass kept her gaze on him and stepped forward. She pressed her body against his, his thin, tall body and kissed his lips. He pulled away, rested his head against her neck, turning the kiss into a warm hug. 'I'm glad you came,' he said. 'There's been no one like you here for a very long time.'

She stirred, wondered about his past, and realised she didn't want to know.

They walked outside together. He locked up, then Cass

took his arm and they started towards the road, sharing the silence. Snow billowed around them, and although the sun had already faded the sky was white except for an orange stain from the streetlights. An icy flake settled on Cass' lips and she opened her mouth, felt the coldness dissolving on her tongue.

Cass drank and the wine threaded into her. Mr Remick had led her straight to the sofa this time. 'Talk to me from here,' he said. 'This one's a surprise.'

She'd forgotten how small the room was, but it was warm and inviting; it didn't have that empty feeling the mill had. Theo lit candles and shadows wavered about his face. Cass sat down and ran her hands over the sofa. The fabric felt clean, new, as though it had never been used. She remembered Bert's faded living room and smiled, tried not to think of him out walking in the cold.

She took another sip of wine. Bert was no doubt tucked up by some warm hearth by now, enjoying a drink of his own.

She felt Theo's hand on her shoulder and jumped, splashing wine across her jacket.

'I didn't mean to startle you. Here, let me take it.'

Cass set down the glass and slipped off her coat.

He looked at her appreciatively. 'You look nice.' Before she could speak he handed her a dish of fat black olives and retreated to the kitchen. They were pungent, salty, bursting on her tongue.

Soon she smelled rich tomatoes, baking cheese. He showed her into the dining room and refilled her glass.

The table was spread with silver, ornate cutlery, and wax dripped from the creamy candles in the gilt candlesticks. They set lights in Theo's eyes, and Cass wondered if they did the same for her. They ate lasagne, hearty and good, with green salad.

She opened her mouth to compliment him, to ask how he came by the fresh salad leaves, but he raised a hand and stopped her. 'Shh,' he said. 'Don't talk.'

For the first time Cass didn't know what to do with the silence between them. She wanted to break it, but Theo shook his head. 'I know what you're going to say: you have to go and collect your son – but you don't need to leave unless you want to, Cass. Sally has offered to let Ben stay. Your son will be fine.' He moved around the table and touched his finger to her lips, stalling her words. 'I realise it was presumptuous of her, but she's more of a friend than you realise, and it gives you a choice. I like you, Cass. I want you to stay with me.'

She stared. His face was serious, his eyes intense. She wanted to say she couldn't; she had to go, and yet she didn't speak. An image of Pete came into her mind, and Ben's drawing. Tears came to her eyes.

He didn't ask why, didn't make any comment. He leaned towards Cass and kissed her cheek. His breath was warm. She could put out a hand and touch his chest – and she did, feeling the softness of his sweater. She closed her eyes, parted her lips.

Theo pulled away. 'Stay with me,' he said.

She nodded and he drew her up. She kissed him, harder this time, and he moved her back against the wall, pressing against her. Cass' hands were on the back of his head, caught in the short softness of his hair. His lips met hers once more, hungry, firing energy through her.

'Come upstairs,' he whispered and caught her hand, leading her out of the room and up a dark stairway. He didn't switch on the light.

The bed looked as old as the house, broad and solid. Theo drew Cass to it and as she fell back she felt his weight on her, his tongue meeting hers. Her blouse was thrown to the floor, a red rag, and now his hands were on her: exploring her back, stroking her neck, supporting her while his tongue caressed her spine. She heard the sound their breath made, rising together without words.

Theo framed her face in his hands while he moved on top of her, found the place their bodies fitted. He eased inside her, paused before pushing his hips against hers. All these things she remembered: him moving against her, the strength of his narrow hips, the sound of his breath against her neck, the wetness of his tongue on her collarbone.

She closed her eyes, and when she opened them, she found Theo watching her. His hands were on her body, stroking her, touching her, *in* her, and suddenly her heart contracted. It turned to pain, as though he had caressed that too, the living, beating muscle at her centre. Cass looked down at his hands. They were resting on her breasts, his fingertips smoothing her nipples. On the surface of her skin.

Then he thrust harder and she cried out because heat blossomed inside her and it felt like everything; an encompassing heat that didn't fade even after he pulled away and lay down at her side, one hand resting on her belly.

The heat was still there. Cass twisted away from him, drawing her legs under her. Closed her eyes. She felt hands pulling her close, holding her. She stayed where she was, keeping her eyes tight shut. Watching the darkness behind the lids.

All these things she remembered, and yet she remembered nothing clearly, nothing in focus. There was a series of impressions and deep physical joy, but nothing more.

TWENTY-TWO

Cass woke in the night and turned to see Theo lying next to her. His face was motionless. She watched for the rise and fall of his breath and couldn't see it. There was still heat, though, radiating from his body. She could feel his heat inside her too, but her skin was cold all over. Her shoulder was gooseflesh. Theo slept on. Cass shivered.

This was the man she'd slept with. She watched him now and tried to regain that sense of togetherness, of being comfortable. The way they'd shared a silence had been easy, good. Now she wanted something to break it, ripple the surface, to give her a reason to get out.

Inside her, the heat burned. Cass wrapped her arms around herself, moving her fingers as though brushing his touch from her skin. She shouldn't have stayed. It was too soon, that was all. When he woke and looked at her it would be all right, it would be different. Cass closed her eyes.

It had never been like this with Pete. He'd slept with his arm under his head, breathing loudly, deeply. Often he snored, a living familiar sound. Not like this silence. Cass knew she couldn't sleep, wouldn't sleep with this motionless man next to her. If he should reach out in the night, touch her . . . Revulsion rippled across her skin.

What was wrong with her? Theo Remick was a decent man, a solid man, someone she could talk to. He made her laugh, made Ben laugh. He was a good man.

Cass shivered and swung her legs over the edge of the bed, the night air cold on her body, and stood without making a sound.

In the early morning she showered, afraid to wake Theo but unable to bear the idea of his hands all over her skin, running over her breasts, legs, shoulders, thighs, the centre of her. The way her heart had clenched as he touched her.

She ran the water cold and stood beneath it as long as she could.

Theo came to her while she sat on the sofa, staring at the floor. He stroked her dripping hair, planted a light kiss on her head, but didn't speak. He went away and a few minutes later brought in a tray piled with toast, eggs and bacon. The smell repulsed her and she turned her face away.

'Cass?'

She looked at him.

'It was good,' he said, and smiled.

'Yes. Good.'

'I felt like we truly connected. Didn't you feel that, Cass?'

She nodded.

'Are you all right? You look pale.'

She glanced at him, looked away again. 'I'm tired. I didn't sleep well.'

'No.'

'I need a shower,' she said, and caught her breath; realised that she'd just had a shower.

'Are you sure you're all right?'

'I need to get Ben.' She stood. She hadn't touched the food.

'You can't – he's with Sally, remember? He's going to school with her. It's a little early to call in, don't you think?'

'Of course. Of course it is.' Cass wanted to feel her son in her arms, bury her face in his hair.

He sexed her.

She shuddered, pushed the thought away.

Theo reached out and touched her shoulder, and Cass jumped. 'Is it something I did?'

She looked up. Light streamed through the curtains, a new day. Ben was at Sally's, and she was here. It had been good; she knew it had been good. 'Theo, I'm sorry. I feel a little strange. Too much wine, maybe.'

'Yes. Maybe.'

'A walk would do me good. Some fresh air. I'll go home. It's fine, honestly. I just need to wake myself up a bit.' She paused. 'It's been a long time. I'm not used to waking up with someone.'

She felt Theo's eyes on her but she couldn't meet his look.

'Cass, I know you lost your husband. If it was too soon, I'm sorry.'

He sexed her. Sexed her.

'No, it wasn't; it's time I moved on. But I just didn't sleep too well.' This time Cass met his eyes.

'You don't have to feel bad. Your life is your own.'

She smiled, too brightly.

'You made the right choice, Cass. You may not see it now, but—'

She stood, still smiling, and a moment later she had grabbed her coat and was walking down the road, pulling it on, wrapping it tightly about her body.

The further she walked from the rectory the more Cass' head cleared. The air was icy on her wet hair and she flicked it away from her neck. She must look ridiculous, hurrying through the streets with dripping hair. What had made her leave like that? Theo Remick had done nothing wrong – and he had been right: it *had* been good.

It had been very good.

All the same, as soon as she reached the mill she would climb into the shower, turn it on full and stand under it for a long time. Her skin still crawled with his touch. It didn't help that she had no reason to feel guilty. Pete had been gone a long time; he would want her to rebuild her life. That had been the whole purpose of coming here.

Cass wished Ben was with her. She would shut the door on the world, keep him from school and stay inside. He could play his wretched video games all day if he wanted. She frowned. It was fortunate that Ben was with Sally.

She shouldn't be so selfish. He was happy in Darnshaw, happy at the school. And she should hurry, make sure she got home before any of the other mothers saw her like this. She could only imagine what Lucy might think.

Thinking of Lucy reminded Cass of her client.

Once inside the apartment she didn't shower after all; there was no time. She dried her hair and put her coat back on, then walked to the top of the lane and watched for Lucy's car, shifting her weight from foot to foot to keep warm. After a time a Land Rover did go past, but it was silver, not black – not her friend's. Where was she? Perhaps Jessica was ill. Perhaps she was afraid to go to school after what had happened with Ben.

Cass waited. If she stood here a while she might even see Bert, back from his trip over the moor. She leaned against the wall.

After a time the silver car headed back in the other direction. A face peered at her out of the window, but still Lucy didn't come.

Cass decided to walk into the village; that way she could still keep an eye on the road but also check on Bert – and see if he'd posted her letter. At least then she'd have some chance of keeping her client. But when she looked up at the hills on every side it felt as though there was no outside world at all; there was only here.

No cars passed as Cass walked down the road. When she reached the post office and banged on Bert's door, there came a faint answering bark. She waited, but there was no further response. Cass shuffled her feet and stared at the peeling black door. She fidgeted, brushed at the old paint, revealing the bare wood. Then she frowned and leaned closer, scraping away more fragments with her nail. There were old marks underneath, running against the grain. Now that she was looking closely she could see it without removing the paint; there was the clear imprint of a line scratched into the door, another one at right angles to it.

A cross, like the one at Foxdene Mill.

Cass drew back. This cross was old, long painted over – but perhaps Bert would know why it was there, or when it had happened. Maybe he would know who had carved it.

She banged on the door, louder this time, but no one came.

Cass waited a moment and tried again, and this time she thought she heard snuffling. 'Captain?'

The noise stopped. Cass bent down and pressed her ear against the door. She heard nothing. 'Captain, are you there? Bert?'

She remembered the irregular thumping she'd heard yesterday as Bert came to the door, the way he had gone down the stairs sideways, holding onto the banister. She glanced up at the steep hillside. She should never have let him go.

'I think he's out, love.' It was Irene, standing at the post office door, rattling some keys.

'But he should have been back. He went out yesterday. Have you seen him since then?'

'No, I don't think so, love. He's probably gone out for his walk this morning.'

'He can't have. Captain's still inside.'

'Is he?'

'I'm sure I heard him.'

Irene fiddled with her keys.

'I'm really worried. He was going to walk over to Moorfoot yesterday. I'm afraid he might not have made it.'

'Was he? That'll explain it. He'll have stayed over, love. Not one to tear hisself away from the pub once he's found it, our Bert.'

'But he wouldn't leave Captain.'

'He'll be fine, love. He'll have left him some food. Don't worry. He's done it before.'

'He has?'

'Oh aye. It's a bit much, there and back in one day. He'll have broken it up.'

'So he'll be back later.'

'I should think so, unless he decides to stop.'

'But Captain—'

'He'll have sorted the dog, don't you worry. Are you sure he didn't take him? It's not like Bert to leave him behind.'

Cass paused. She had thought she'd heard sounds. In the face of Irene's calmness, though, she was no longer certain. 'Could you please tell him I came? I'll pop back later.'

'Of course I will, love.'

Before Cass walked away she turned back and looked up at Bert's windows. The panes of glass reflected back the sky, blank white eyes. She shivered. The air was bitter, colourless and yet heavy, threatening snow. If Bert was out on the moors . . . But he couldn't be. And he'd walked these hills many times before, knew what he was doing.

Of course, if more snow was to fall and Bert was in Moorfoot, he might not be able to get back. Cass bit her lip. If that happened she would take Captain in. She'd find a way of getting the dog out of the flat and look after him even if she had to lock him in her bedroom to keep him away from Ben. She was pretty sure he was all the old man had.

When Cass reached the mill lane she looked down at the mellow stone building and found she didn't want to go inside yet. All she could think about was the cross scratched into the front door, a twin to the one at Bert's flat.

Instead she walked further down the road, passed the turning that led up onto the moor and followed the lane leading through the valley, out of Darnshaw and towards Mossleigh.

White fields flanked the road, the ever-present hills rising beyond, with an occasional barn or farmhouse breaking the vista. The road was coated with snow and unmarred by tracks. Cass had to step off the pavement where it had drifted against the roadside walls. After a time she took out her mobile and checked the signal. Nothing.

She followed a gradual bend and the valley opened out. The river, which had been running parallel with the road, swept round and the road crossed it on a pretty stone bridge. Cass stopped and stared. The snow covering the tarmac was fissured with deep grey scratches like huge claw marks. The road had crumbled, slabs of snow falling into the cracks that had opened up. Ice glistened, translucent where it clung to the dark tarmac.

Beyond that the bridge was still standing. The surface of the snow was rippled and cracked, though, suggesting that the road was fractured beneath. Cass squinted. What looked like tape was tied across the far side of the bridge. The road was closed. It was clearly unsafe, and the river beneath was high and rushing. Cass could hear it from where she stood, a lonely sound.

What was it Bert had said? *It might look like a tree. Same as t' other way might look like the road's cracked and fallen in.*

No wonder Mr Remick's classes had shrunk. No one would be coming from this direction for some considerable time.

Cass kept looking up at the hills on the way back. Steep, white, cold. She hoped Bert wasn't still up there.

TWENTY-THREE

In the end Cass' impatience became too much and she headed back into the village long before she was due to collect Ben. She tried Bert's door again, pressing her ear to the wood and shouting Captain's name, but this time there was no answering snuffle. Cass looked up at the freezing hills. The cold made her eyes sting and she wiped at them with her gloves, smearing dampness across her face.

'There, love,' came a voice. Irene was closing the door to the post office, hurrying towards her, holding something out. 'Don't take on. We'll have a look for him, if you're still worried.'

Cass stared at the object in Irene's hand. It was a key.

'Come on, love. Let's have a look inside, shall we?' Irene slotted the key into the lock and shoved the door hard. It rattled open a crack and she kept pushing it until the gap widened. She headed up the stairs without putting on the light and Cass followed, feeling her way, holding on to the banister.

Irene stopped on the landing. 'There,' she said, 'looks like he did take Captain with him after all. He always comes to see me, that dog.' She led the way into the lounge. Cass followed, checking each high-backed seat, making sure there wasn't a figure slumped there. The room was airless, and the jacket where Captain slept gave off a fusty smell.

The kitchen was small, with fragile-looking units, peeling Formica taped down here and there. A pull-out table was scattered with biscuit crumbs. There was a single folding seat, nothing else: no sign of Captain.

'You see,' said Irene, 'they always stick together, those two.'

She headed back onto the landing, squeezing past Cass in the doorway. There was only one room left to try and Cass found herself reluctant to enter. Irene didn't hesitate. 'Have a look, love. Put your mind at rest.' She beckoned, and now Cass noticed something strange. She shook her head, putting the thought out of her mind; it could wait. She followed Irene into the room.

The bed cover was a crocheted blanket pulled roughly straight. It was pale pink, as were the curtains. The wallpaper bore a pattern of roses. A Bible lay on the dresser. Bert had left clothes strewn on the bed: a beige shirt, brown socks bundled together, a pair of Y-fronts, greyed from too much washing. Cass looked away.

'He got some things together before he went,' said Irene. 'See? He was obviously planning to stay a while. He wants to be careful he doesn't get stuck that side of the moors. Looks like more snow's blowing in.' She sniffed the air as though she could sense it and grimaced. 'He wants to clean up in here a bit. Come on, love. You happy?'

Cass nodded, glad to retreat from these private things. She headed down the stairs ahead of Irene. They felt steeper in the dark. She held on to the rail and went down sideways, as Bert had. Perhaps it hadn't meant he was frail, just careful.

A gruff bark rang out from somewhere behind the wall.

'That's the Turnbulls' dog,' said Irene. 'They're in the next flat. Maybe that's what you heard before, love.'

'I suppose it must have been.' Cass waited while Irene pulled the door closed, expertly forcing it into the jamb. 'I appreciate this, Irene. You must think I'm mad.'

'Of course not,' she said, grasping Cass' wrist and squeezing it. 'Not at all. No, you were being neighbourly, and that's what we like round here. Neighbourly. That's us, you know. So kind of you.' She nodded in Cass' face. 'So kind.'

She let go of Cass' arm, turned and went back into the post office, leaving her standing on the street.

Cass took a deep breath and let it out slowly, watching it fade into the air; rubbed her hands together, making her fingers tingle. She felt warmer, more herself than she had all day. Is that why she'd felt so odd with Theo? Was it worry about Bert, guilt that she'd let him go? And all the time Bert had been safe in town, Captain at his side. The next time Cass saw him she would kiss his wrinkly old cheek.

Cass waved at the post office window as she passed, but it was dark inside and all she could see was her own reflection. Her hair was wispy around her ears, her eyes unfocused. And then she remembered what had struck her as odd in the flat.

When Irene beckoned Cass into Bert's bedroom, there had been a red line crossing the palm of her hand. Just like Damon's. Like that other boy's – James.

TWENTY-FOUR

Cass was at the school before the doors opened. She paused and listened to the singing that came from within: a heavy, slow melody punctuated by clapping. Then came the scraping of chairs.

She didn't know what she was going to say to Theo Remick. Last night already felt like a long time ago, another world. Far more vivid was her memory of running out of his house, hair dripping, not even waiting to pull on her coat. He might not want to see her again after that, and she wouldn't blame him.

An engine growled behind her, changing tone as the driver slowed and eased into the car park. Cass turned in time to see Myra's red hair through a side-window. The woman turned and saw Cass, looked her up and down before turning her attention back to the wheel. Her gaze was like the touch of a cold hand. Brake lights bled over the snow and Myra got out, swinging her hips as she walked past Cass.

Theo Remick appeared in the doorway. He didn't greet

Myra as she approached, he just reached out his hand, not to shake Myra's, though, or to wave to her; he touched her hair, just once, a brief stroke, such as someone might give a dog or a cat.

She went past him and inside without pausing to say anything or brush him off, and his eyes fell on Cass. The corner of his lip twitched. Then he gave a welcoming smile.

Cass turned away, staring at the snow as blood rushed to her cheeks. She felt heat at the core of her, deep inside. It burned.

She heard childish voices and turned to see Ben standing on tiptoe while Theo spoke in his ear. Ben grinned, took a bundle from the teacher and ran towards her. It was like old times, Ben with a big smile on his face, no consciousness of who might be watching or what they might think. And it was Theo Remick who had made him that way.

Ben skidded to a halt and pushed the bundle towards her. 'From him,' he said, jabbing a finger towards the teacher. Cass peered inside the brown paper bag: bread, eggs, bacon. How did he get such things? She smelled warm dough.

She looked up to see Myra snaking her hips past Remick, leaving now, her child in tow. The woman went past Cass without looking at her.

The scent rose from the bag, and Cass imagined Ben eating, a smile on his face. She bent and kissed him. 'Did you have a nice time?'

He nodded. His eyes were too bright, almost feverish. 'We shared again.'

'What did you share?'

'Things.' He frowned. 'A game.' He put one hand in the other, tracing a line on the palm. Cass caught it, turned it over. The palm of his hand was clean and unblemished.

'What game, Ben?'

'Just a game.' He pulled his hand away.

'I'm sorry I didn't pick you up last night,' Cass said. 'I missed you.'

'It's all right, Mummy. Sally said it was supposed to happen.'

'What? She said what was supposed to happen?'

'Not picking me up.'

Cass touched his hair. 'Is she here? I should thank her.'

He shook his head. 'She went.'

Cass turned and looked around for Theo. He was still standing in the doorway, hands behind his back. 'Wait here,' said Cass. 'I'll be back in a minute.'

He smiled as she walked towards him. 'I didn't think you were going to come over.'

'Of course I was.' Cass bit her lip.

'I thought . . . I mean, what we did. It seemed a good way of ending the evening. A special way. It meant a lot to me, Cass. I wouldn't want you to think it didn't.'

'No – I didn't—' She held the bag in front of her. 'Thank you – for these, I mean. That was kind of you.'

'We wouldn't want the boy going hungry, would we?'

Cass looked away, then forced herself to meet his eyes. They were wide-open, candid.

'Theo, I'm sorry I ran off.' She wanted to say more, to offer him something, but found she could not. She remembered how her heart had contracted when he touched her. As though his hands were inside her skin.

'Are you all right, Cass? I mean if it was too soon . . .'

'No.' Cass drew herself up. 'I like you, Theo, but— I don't know. It doesn't feel right.'

'You're ending it?' He raised an eyebrow.

'No— I mean— Theo, I'm sorry, but I think I have to.' She hadn't known she was going to say it.

'If this is about your husband—'

'You know, I don't think it is. I thought it was guilt, but it just doesn't fit, somehow.'

His fingers on her chin, lifting her face.

'I don't think I'm ready.'

'You're ready, Cass.' He smiled. 'You just don't know it.'

His skin was dry and she recoiled from his hand.

'You'll come to me, Cass. When it's time.'

'What?'

'I don't think ill of you. Remember that, Gloria. When the time comes.'

'That's not my name.' Cass couldn't catch her breath. The air was cold in her throat. 'What's wrong with you, Theo? I didn't mean to upset you – if I did, I'm sorry.'

He raised his head, a gleam appearing in his eyes, and a smile spread slowly across his face. He reached out and touched her hair, the same gesture he'd made to Myra.

Cass pulled away, turned from him and hurried back towards her son. Ben was glowering. 'You always spoil everything,' he said.

'What do you mean?'

'You spoiled it.' Ben's face crumpled. 'He won't want to be my daddy now.' His voice rose.

Cass looked back, but Theo had gone back inside. 'Ben, you *have* a daddy. Pete will *always* be your daddy. But he's gone. Mr Remick isn't your daddy; he's only your teacher. You know that.'

'You're a liar,' he said, yanking his arm away. 'You're a lying bitch.'

'Ben!' She had never heard him use that word before – it was wrong, a dirty thing in his mouth. 'Ben, don't say things like that.'

'A lying fucking bitch.'

'Ben, that's enough!'

'You're his whore now. Damon said.'

'What?' It was as though he'd slapped her.

'That's what girls are. That's all, just his fucking whores.'

Cass had a sudden clear vision of the way Myra had looked at her, the way she had looked at Theo, and she swallowed. 'My God, Ben, what's got into you?'

'All of them.' Ben threw his head back and grinned, but there was no humour in it.

'Where did you hear such things?'

'They all say it – all the boys.'

'The boys? Well if you say it again . . . Ben, I never want to hear—'

'Or you'll do what?' His eyes burned. 'What will you do? Run away? You'll never get away from here, not now.'

'What did you say?'

I don't suppose the lad'll leave now.

'We belong here. He said so.'

'Damon. It was Damon, wasn't it?' Cass remembered the boy's cold eyes, the way he looked at her. 'He said it when you went to Sally's, didn't he? And those other boys. Ben, you're not to see them again. They're not good boys.'

'They're not good boys, Ben,' he sing-songed. 'It wasn't at Sally's. Sally doesn't know anything. She's just a dirty whore, like you.'

Cass raised a hand and Ben stared at it. There was no fear in his eyes, only contempt, and she let it fall back to her side. 'What's happened to you?' she whispered.

'I want my daddy.' His lips twitched.

'Oh Ben.' Tears flooded Cass' eyes. 'I'm so sorry. You're hurting so much. All this— I know you're just upset; I know everything seems too much sometimes. Especially now, when everything's new, and we haven't really settled in. But we will, Ben. We'll be happy again. You'll see.'

He stared at her. She reached out and wrapped her arms around him, drew him close. His body was small and frail, but unyielding.

When she pulled back and looked at him, he was staring into space, his eyes unblinking. Cass hugged him close once more, burying her face in his shoulder. 'I love you, Ben,' she said. 'It will be all right. I promise.'

TWENTY-FIVE

Ben sat in front of the screen, staring at the game. The intensity had drained out of him and his body was loose, slumped.

Cass brushed back her hair, thinking of the way Remick had touched it, like something possessed and cast off. *You'll come to me.* She shuddered. And those things Ben had said; she wished she could keep him inside, playing his game, never letting him see those other boys, or Sally or Mr Remick, if that was what made him say such things. Maybe she should keep him away from school tomorrow.

A headache was starting behind her eyes. She frowned. If she did keep him at home tomorrow, there would still be the next day, and the day after that. And Ben liked his teacher.

Cass suddenly wished Bert was there to ask about everything, or Lucy. She should have tried harder to meet some of the other mothers, but she had only really spoken to Lucy, and now she was out of reach. And Bert might have known what the cross on the door meant, the circle of bones on the riverbank, the doll, its body crusting with bloody yolk. Had Bert seen the mark on the mill door? Is that why he had warned her to be careful?

This made her think of the empty apartment. Even now someone might be down there, looking up at the ceiling. Cass shuddered. She watched her son. The curve at the nape of his neck, frosted with pale hair, looked innocent, vulnerable. He was sitting perfectly still.

Cass looked at the door. The key was in the lock. She wouldn't be gone long; she could lock him in, make sure he was safe. 'Ben,' she called, 'I'm going out for ten minutes. I'm just popping downstairs, okay?'

He didn't answer.

'Ben?'

A slight turn of his head, a shrug of a shoulder. It would have to be enough. Cass went into the kitchen and grabbed a torch from the cupboard. When she checked on Ben he hadn't moved. She went out and closed the door softly, locking it behind her. She jumped when the lights flickered on and hurried down the hall towards the stairs.

Her footsteps rang out on the flagstones then were silent on the ground floor's crimson carpet. The door to Apartment 6 was closed. Had she done that? She couldn't remember. She only remembered the feeling of revulsion when she touched the dusty surface of the doll, felt the viscous fluid spill over her.

The same feeling she'd had with Theo Remick.

She put her hand on the door handle. Someone could be in there now, but it didn't feel that way. It felt empty, like the rest of the mill. The way even their apartment felt.

Cass opened the door and saw the skeleton of a home and the gleam of moonlight on the snow outside. She didn't know what she'd expected to find. The place was empty. Dust blanketed the floorboards, scuffed here and there with her own footprints or Ben's and the grey shuffling of rats. There was no sign that anyone else had been here. Even the rats were gone.

Perhaps no one had called them.

Cass blinked, pointed the torch and pushed the switch.

The doll lay where she had thrown it. Half the body was missing, gnawed away, frayed threads like hair poking from the hole in its chest. The boy doll was half-buried in the dust. Cass bent, saw it was coated in rat droppings and straightened without touching it.

She didn't know why she had come. There was nothing here, probably never had been, only kids messing about, and that could have been long past – back when there were builders on the site or even before that.

Yet it felt as though there was something she was supposed to know, something she was supposed to see. Cass went to the window, cold air on her face like wintry breath, and shone the torch out. A cone of light appeared on the snow. Somewhere an owl hooted. Hunting rats maybe. Cass silently wished it luck.

As she turned, the torchlight fell on a pale triangle almost hidden by the dust. Cass bent closer, shining the light onto it. It was a piece of paper. She picked it up, shook the dust from it. One edge was ragged where it had been chewed.

> Cass, got your files. Looks rather better. We launch in a few days. I need changes as per the attached. Do I need to get someone else on this? Call me urgently – maybe we can sort something out.

Cass stared at the printout. It wasn't signed; that's what she thought about as she stood there blinking. The email wasn't signed. All the work she'd done, and her client was so angry he hadn't even typed his name. And she had no way to reach him. Not unless she got out, out of Darnshaw, away from here. Instead she had let everything close in, not just the snow but Remick, everything.

Cass was dimly aware that she was only thinking these things to delay the real questions, the ones gnawing at the edges of her mind. How had the email got here? Had Lucy brought it to her, come to help Cass in spite of what Ben had done to Jess? Or had someone else left it? And, most importantly, if Lucy had come to see Cass, what had happened to her?

The attached, she thought.

She shone the light around until she saw another piece of paper. It had been screwed up and pushed into the wooden studwork that would some day be a wall, a part of someone's home. It was almost hidden behind dangling wiring.

Cass fumbled with it and heard it tear as she pulled it free. She flattened it out. It wasn't the attachment her client had mentioned; it looked like a photocopy of an article from an old newspaper. At the top was a picture of women in caps and children wearing rough smocks. They stood outside Foxdene Mill.

There was nothing to explain why it should be here, and yet Cass could hear Lucy's words as though she stood next to her: *I'd love to see it. I'm something of a history buff, and I never have been inside. Silly really. I drive past it all the time.*

All the time. And Lucy had driven to Foxdene Mill, bringing this with her. Cass held it in front of her face, the torch picking out the smudged headline: MISSING CHILD FOUND AT FOXDENE MILL.

She scanned down the page. 'One of the less savoury aspects of Darnshaw history . . .' It was a modern account then, not contemporary with the picture.

'A child was found, the victim of a ritual killing. A girl of six or seven years old, her throat cut and other marks left upon her body.' Other marks. A cut across the palm of her hand, perhaps? It didn't say.

'Her body was left on the ground floor, hidden by abandoned machinery. It was some time before she was found, and the body had been visited by animal life, causing some difficulty over the identification.' Animal life. Cass looked around her, seeing everywhere the imprints of rat claws in the dust. Her fist clamped tight on the torch. She bent and vomited, clutching the paper to her chest, heaving until her stomach was empty. When she could bring up nothing more she looked around, half-expecting someone to have heard.

The mill had fallen into disuse some years before, at least by the owners. However, signs showed it had become the focus of activity some said to be witchcraft, others demon possession. It is suspected that many of the villagers were aware of this, since superstition abounded about the mill and its environs.

Among the sacrilegious symbols found, some at least appeared to attempt to reclaim the mill, or at least protect it, for Christian crosses were also inscribed upon the door.

Cass' mouth opened and closed. The sour tang of vomit was on her lips. She leaned over and spat, imagined a rat lapping at the spittle and choked back her nausea.

A cross on the door: not sinister graffiti but a sign of protection. In front of her eyes Cass saw a peeling black door, another cross etched into the wood and painted over. Bert, walking past the mill every day. She had thought it was teenagers, but she had only ever seen Bert wandering around the mill.

She shook her head. *Ridiculous.* Bert was too old for graffiti.

The Bible lying on his dresser. The cross carved into his door.

And here, in the mill, a living, breathing child had had her lifeblood spilled. For what? Cass looked down at the floor. It was here; she knew it had been here, she could feel it. She could almost see the spray of golden hair, dulled by dust and time. No one had seen her and no one would have found her – if it weren't for the rats. The child had been alone. That was the thing that burned most of all: they had taken the girl's life and left her alone, in the dark, in this empty place, perhaps even where Cass was standing. She edged back, staring into the shadows, half-expecting a small childlike shape to push itself up and reach out its arms, needing someone to hold her one last time.

And what had Lucy said about children doing the sacrificing? Cass closed her eyes, almost thought she could hear the step of someone coming closer. She started, and thought of Ben, alone upstairs. How long had she been down here? Her son was *alone*. He might be looking for her, might be frightened.

The night outside had grown darker, the room narrowed to a beam of light on a smudged piece of paper. When Cass looked at the window, snow flurried through the air. Coldness oozed into the mill and lay close against her skin.

TWENTY-SIX

Cass woke, opening her eyes wide. The darkness in the room had a strange quality. She couldn't work out what it was. She got up and padded across to the window.

Snow danced in the air, pushed this way and that by the wind. It fell thickly, fat flakes against the blackness, and settled, new softness covering the crisp white. It was burying everything, smothering everything.

Cass caught her breath. A figure stood on the slope outside. Flakes fell and melted upon arms and face and chest, which was bared; dark smudges underlined each rib. She knew this body, had run her hands over it, clutched it to her. Cried out his name in the night: Theodore Remick.

As she watched, he raised his hands to the sky, threw back his head and swallowed it in, the snow, the night air, everything. His eyes were a white gleam.

He turned to Cass' window; his mouth opened and she recognised his grin, the flash of teeth. She caught her breath and spun away; covered her face with her hands.

When she looked out again, Remick had gone. Cass looked for his tracks in the snow, but there was nothing. Her mind registered only confusion, and an odd thing that Bert had said to her: *It allus comes in like this, when he wants it.*

At the time she'd thought he meant God. It had just sounded like something an old person might say, something her father might have said, but now she wasn't so sure. She wasn't so sure of anything.

In time Cass slept once more. She wasn't sure if the things she saw were dreams.

TWENTY-SEVEN

The next morning Cass wrapped Ben's coat around his body and held his collar while she knelt in front of him. 'Ben,' she said, 'we have to talk about something.'

His eyes were clearer than yesterday. He seemed less upset, less angry. He looked at her, her little boy. Cass paused. Was he really all right? She couldn't be sure of anything any more. Last night she thought she'd seen Theo Remick outside her window, half-naked in the snow. It hadn't been real, of course, but it hadn't quite felt like a dream either.

Without thinking she took Ben's hand in hers and turned it over. The skin was clear, smooth, not a mark on it.

'Ben, do you know how the other boys cut their hands?'

He shrugged.

'Some of them have a mark, don't they. Do you know how they came by it?'

Nothing.

'Did they do it on purpose?'

He pulled his hand away.

'Okay, Ben, listen to me: there's something very important I have to say. Do you remember when we went for a walk, just the two of us, out of the village?'

He shuffled his feet.

'Well, we need to go again. I think it would be the best thing for us to leave here for a while. Do you understand?'

He started to shake his head.

'Ben, we need to stay together.'

Ben whipped around, turning away.

'We can go right over the moors.'

'*You* can.'

'We need to go together.'

Ben didn't turn. His shoulders were a wall. Cass remembered the way he'd sat with his back to the witch stones, refusing to move. He had been too heavy for her to carry.

I don't suppose the lad'll leave now.

Cass sighed. 'All right, Ben. But I have to go, love. I have to make some calls for work, and maybe see some people. I won't be gone for long.'

He was motionless.

'If I set off as soon as I've dropped you at school, I should be back in time to pick you up. I'll ask Sally to look after you, just in case I'm late.'

She pushed the thought of Damon out of her mind. Ben would only be with the older boy for a short time; what more harm could it do? She took a breath. 'And Ben, I know you like Mr Remick, but for now it might be a good idea to keep away from him. I'm going to ask Sally to keep an eye on you at school too.'

He scowled. 'I like him.'

'I know you do. And he likes you too, Ben, but I'm not so sure he likes me any more.'

You'll come to me, Remick had said.

'I want him to be my daddy. Like the other children.'

'Sweetie, we'll talk some more about this later, okay? But Mr Remick isn't those boys' daddy.'

'He is. Damon says.'

'Well, sometimes, people make things up. Perhaps you shouldn't listen to what Damon says.'

He met her eye. 'I can't help it if you leave me with Mrs Spencer.'

Cass' mouth opened, but she couldn't think of anything to say. Of course Ben looked up to his friend; if Damon had latched on to Remick, Ben would want to copy him. But she only had to leave Ben with Damon for one more night. After that . . .

She ruffled Ben's hair, planted a kiss on his cheek.

'Come on then. Sorry I might be late tonight. But I need to go, okay? I'll miss you.'

Ben's expression didn't change, not when she kissed him, not when she spoke. She put on her own coat and grabbed the rucksack she'd packed and left ready by the door. Lucy's printout was tucked into its pocket. She wasn't sure yet who she would show it to or what she might say; first she would find Bert; then she'd know what to do.

Ben stared at her, waiting. She opened the door, ushered him out and locked it again behind them.

TWENTY-EIGHT

Cass had dreaded dropping Ben off at school, but as it turned out she managed to speak to Sally without seeing Remick. Sally had arrived at the same time as Cass, waved her whole arm in the air and shouted 'Yoo-hoo!' as she came down the road. Damon followed with a gang of other boys. When she saw them all laughing together, Cass knew she was never going to stay in Darnshaw. These were the friends her son wanted to mix with, and she didn't want to see her boy become like them, with their pale faces and sly expressions.

She didn't think this but *felt* it, in the same way her skin had recoiled from Remick: it was not a mental but a physical knowledge, *soul* knowledge.

She forced a smile as Sally approached. 'Sally,' she said, 'nice to see you. Listen, I know I've trespassed on your goodwill lately, but I wondered—'

'Not at all, not at all.' Sally beamed at Ben. 'Such a nice boy. Quite one of the gang.'

Not for long.

'I need to go over to Moorfoot today.'

'No problem, I hope?'

'Not at all, not at all.' Cass echoed Sally's words without thinking. 'It's something for work – a bit of a drag, to be honest. I need to phone a few people, then I'm coming straight back.'

For now. For as long as it takes for the snow to melt and to pack our things.

Cass found herself grinning, her eyes staring fixedly at Ben's head. She stirred. 'I shouldn't be late, but with the snow and everything . . .'

'I can take him. It'd be a pleasure,' said Sally at once.

'That's so kind. I really appreciate it.'

'He could stay the night – save you coming to collect him.'

'No, that's fine. I might even make it for the end of school. But if I don't, I'll come to your place as soon as I do get back. And Sally—'

'Yes?'

'He's been a bit out of sorts lately. Not ill, just— I don't know. Not himself. Have you noticed anything?'

'No, no, but I don't know him as well as you, of course.'

'I'm sure it's nothing. But would you mind keeping an eye on him today?'

'Of course. No trouble.'

'Thank you.' Cass put out a hand and touched Sally's shoulder. 'You really are kind.'

'What are neighbours for? But you know, you shouldn't go in this weather. It's a bad idea, Cassandra. The drifts can be eight, nine feet deep up there. Better to stay here.

I'm sure we can help with your problem, whatever it is.'

'I'll be fine.' Cass said it firmly. 'It won't take long.' How many times had she said that? As though she were trying to convince herself. She bent and kissed Ben's head, rested her hand on his hair. 'Bye, Ben. I'll see you soon.'

He slipped out from under Cass' hand and ran to Damon.

'See you later, then,' she called.

He waved over his shoulder without turning and was gone, and her heart ached for him.

The road to the moor was empty. The sound of Cass' feet crunching through snow was loud in her ears and there was no other sound: no distant whine of traffic, no bird-song. It seemed odd not to have Ben's footsteps at her side, wrong, as if she were even now abandoning him to strangers. But he'd be fine; he'd have a much better time than Cass. Already the cold was biting through her coat and making her shiver. Each step was an effort. It'd be easier once she reached the top; then it would be down-hill all the way into Moorfoot, and she could buy hot food, find Bert. He'd surely know of an easier way back. She wouldn't have to walk like this, with each step sinking into freezing snow.

She turned into the Broaths' farm. This time no dog barked. There was steam, though, emerging from the vent on the wall. She didn't stop. The rough track threatened to turn her ankles but she was careful, putting her weight slowly onto each step. Her trousers weren't waterproof and a dark ring formed around the top of her boots.

The snow got deeper. It made Cass' eyes ache to look at all that whiteness. The sky was a deep, innocent blue scuffed with little white clouds. Beautiful.

The snow was above her knees now. As Cass headed up the hill she took a step and finding nothing firm beneath her, sank up to her thigh. She was soaked at once, and it was punishingly cold. As she floundered it reminded her of being on holiday with Pete, trying to wade through deep surf, him laughing while the sea pulled at her thighs. It was like that, but cold; deep bone-cold. Her cheeks stung, her ears stung. Clumps of snow covered her trousers. She brushed at them. The snow smeared, then melted, gluing the fabric to her skin. The sky was mocking, clouds melting away. Soon it would be a single clean blue arc: a summer sky, a desert sky. The sun was a white hole that gave no heat, only dazzled, glinting off hills and fields.

Cass went on, each inhalation hurting the back of her throat. The slope seemed steeper than it had before, the snow deeper. She dragged her legs from the holes they made and pushed forward, sank again, leaving behind her a wide broken trail, as though something had crawled along on its belly.

That made her think of Captain. How could the old dog possibly have made it across the moor? Bert must have been crazy to take him. And yet for all the strange things he'd said to her she couldn't think of the old man as crazy. She needed to talk to him: he knew things, even if he did get carried away with his ideas sometimes. He could tell her things.

Things about Theodore Remick.

Ben was at school with the teacher. She tried not to think about that. Ben would never have made it this far, especially if he'd been determined not to. She hadn't had a choice. Anyway, he would be fine; it was Cass who was in trouble.

Pete would never have let himself get into this situation. It was Cass who'd messed up; she was the one who had chosen to come to Darnshaw, chasing some dream, some idyll she hadn't even recognised. Stupid. *Stupid.*

She stared at the snow, glowered at it, dared it to give way. It felt a little more solid now. Maybe there was a path somewhere beneath her feet. But the snow was terrible, a terrible thing that didn't want her to leave, sucked at her, wasn't going to let her go.

Just one step. Then another. One at a time.

When she reached the witch stones she would stop. She'd drink a little soup from the flask in her rucksack. There was bread too. Remick's bread. She grimaced.

Cass looked up, her eyes stinging, and now she saw the witch stones, stark against the snow. At first the perspective made no sense: the stones looked like holes – black holes, leading somewhere dark – and then she saw a white circle in the centre of one and her vision cleared. They were only stones, standing against the snow and the sky, stones to keep the witches out.

Better to keep them in, she thought. She imagined Sally in a tall black hat, stirring something in a monstrous cauldron. She almost laughed out loud. Yes, Sally the witch. She could just see that.

Cass unzipped her coat and let the cold air in. She felt

hot suddenly, welcomed the cooling draught. The stones were closer. They made the sky appear more distant, impossibly far away. When Cass reached the first one her legs were trembling. She put out a hand and touched the rough black surface with her glove.

Cass allowed her knees to give way. She sat at the base of the stone and leaned back, closed her eyes, felt the cold air pinch her cheeks. The rucksack dug into her spine. She opened her eyes to see the valley, Darnshaw's white roofs almost indistinguishable from the fields. Only the church stood free and clear and black. Cass was above it now, and it felt like freedom.

She looked around at the witch stones, at the hillside on which she rested. Not a hundred yards away a white shape looked back.

There was a snowman on the hill, white against white. It was lumpy and misshapen, sinking in on itself, troglodytic. The only reason she had seen it was the blue striped scarf tied about its neck. It had no eyes, and yet it seemed to stare.

Cass' breath froze in her throat. She rubbed her face, making her eyes sting, but when she looked up, the white shape was still there and now she could see another was sitting next to it, and beyond that, another, this one sunk so far in on itself it had almost collapsed. It looked a little like a hunched old man.

She took a deep breath, and another. Her heart punched out a too-quick rhythm. 'Don't,' she whispered. '*Don't.*'

It was worse once the words were out into the air: like an accusation.

Cass pushed herself up. The stone rasped on her coat and made her jump. The world was still, empty, except for the white figures. She couldn't stay here and look at them. Had to go on, find some other place to rest.

Or she could go closer.

She didn't want to approach them. She recognised the scarf. The last time she'd seen it, Remick was wrapping it around the neck of the snowman her son had built. Now it was here. Of course anyone could have taken it. Or it could be someone else's; it might just look like his. And it was only a snowman.

Remick, standing bare-chested in the snow, welcoming it. Urging it to fall.

Cass walked towards the snowmen. Her limbs felt uncertain, though the ground felt solid beneath her feet. They were built in a half-circle, looking towards the stones. Cass stood in front of the first of them. She looked over her shoulder, though there had been no sight nor sound of anyone else for hours, and the witch stones looked back.

The figure wearing Remick's scarf did have a face, after all: three hollows were gouged out: two empty eyes and a screaming mouth. Cass reached out and touched it. The snow was hard, packed tight. She looked at the others.

She took a deep breath and prodded at the snowman's head. It rocked a little on the body, but it didn't fall. Then she spread her fingers and prised away the snow, and chunks fell away, revealing what lay beneath, and Cass' mouth opened, silent but screaming. Her lungs continued to seize the air, dragged it in and pushed it out, but she could not move—

Then her hand reached out, but stopped short of touching the thing that lay beneath the snow: pink, peeling flesh, ragged and torn.

Cass' breath came in gasps. She looked at the other figures, back to the one in front of her. Her mind asked, *How many?* and she found she couldn't answer; she could not comprehend the shapes. She could only see the thing in front of her face.

The witch stones. Someone might be hiding there. Someone had done this; they might be waiting for her at the witch stones. They could be watching her even now.

Cass spun around. The stones were tall, black shapes, implacable. Someone could have been hiding behind them, but somehow Cass knew they were not. There was nothing watching but the stones themselves.

She pulled the glove from her hand, balled the fabric in her fingers and used it to knock more snow from the figure in front of her. What she could see was a scalp, with white hair clinging to it – no, grey hair. The skin was grey too, but in parts it was pink and in others white.

The breath in Cass' throat made a low whistling. The scalp was tender, defenceless, taken by the snow. There was nothing to protect it. Cass reached out and caught herself as she was about to stroke it. She recognised it, of course she did: the last time she had seen it, it had been standing under a dim light in a narrow hallway and she had refused to look after its dog. That was the last thing it had asked her, and she had refused. Now here it was, that scalp, exposed and laid bare.

Cass let out a long, deep breath and it sounded like a sob.

The old man had given up. He had fallen to his knees here, and the snow had taken him. It had covered him like rust or mould, taken him to itself, its heart. He had made it this far and no more; such a little distance. Poor, poor Bert.

Cass squeezed her eyes closed, but no tears came. It was too late for tears. He had asked for her help and she had refused him. He had died here alone.

Then someone came along and pressed snow against him and made hollows for a face and wrapped a nice warm scarf around his neck.

Cass made an inarticulate sound, looked about, but found the hillside empty. Saddleworth Moor: where bodies were buried and lost, and people go and don't come back.

You'll come to me, Remick had said. Somehow that gave her comfort now. *You'll come to me.*

The scarf was Remick's. She knew it was his; he had wrapped it around the neck of her son's snowman and laughed with him. *Daddy. I want him to be my daddy.*

What kind of a man was she? Did she even know? She only knew her flesh crawled at the memory of his touch. And this man, this man was looking after her child.

Sally. Ben was with Sally. And someone had taken the scarf. Anyone could have taken it.

'Bert,' Cass whispered, 'I'm so sorry.'

She knew she shouldn't touch, but she reached out and swept more snow away. She needed to see the old man's face. There were the lines that creased his forehead, the round bulge of a nose, broken veins still written on his skin. And here was something hard, under her fingers. She drew back. Something black was jutting from his face. She cleared the snow from it and found a stone, thrust into the socket where his eye should be. And another. Stones for eyes, and his mouth – she started to uncover his mouth and her finger slipped inside. She bent and peered closer: a cylindrical rod was poking out. She pinched it between her fingers and pulled, but it was jammed against his teeth. She tried easing it, and at last it shifted and came free: a short metal post, a crossbar and a curve. A cross of confusion.

'Christ.' Cass threw it down, the blasphemous shape sinking into the snow. 'Bert, I'm sorry.' She shouldn't have let the old man leave. She had known it at the time. But she had done nothing.

She turned to the figure next to Bert, not looking at the smaller one that had collapsed. She went to the other and put out her hand and, feeling as though she were in a dream, pushed. Snow fell from the figure like heavy snowflakes, making a sound as it fell: *ploomf*. A nice sound, like the end of winter.

Cass shook her head. Her mind was coming loose.

She pushed again and more snow broke and fell and hair emerged. It was dark, still shiny. Cass knew that hair. She fell onto the snow and her knees sank in and she put her arms around the figure and pulled it towards her. She wailed, and the sound was both close and a long way away, but she couldn't stop it, didn't try. She stroked the hair, hugged tighter. Lumps of impacted snow fell away and Cass saw a yellow jumper covered with little bobbles, the sort of jumper a little girl might like to play with until Mummy got tired of it and told her to stop. More hair. Cass stroked and it came away in her fingers. She made an inarticulate sound and shook her hand but still the hair clung and Cass retched and twisted and vomited sourness onto the snow.

'Oh God,' she said, then quieter, 'Oh *God.*' It was Lucy – *had* been Lucy, this thing under the snow. Cass brushed smears from her friend's grey, ruined face. Lucy had come to help her – she had tried to help, and now she had stones for eyes; *oh God, she had stones for eyes.* Cass cleared her friend's face. Her only friend, perhaps. Lucy's mouth had no metal inside; her mouth was broken. Fragments of teeth surrounded a black rock that had been thrust into it. Her lips stretched around it in a scream. Saliva had dripped and frozen in smooth icicles. Cass brushed at them and they snapped, dragging at the skin beneath, skin that Lucy would have cleansed and toned and moisturised to stay looking young, and now here she was grey and broken, and Cass raised her head to the sky and shook it, denying this thing.

The sky was silent, changeless.

Cass turned to look at the small figure by her friend's side, let herself fall back onto the snow and wrapped her arms around herself. 'No,' she said, 'not Jess, no. *Not Jess.*'

She looked back at what had been Lucy. The black stones were an abomination in her face. Cass owed it to her to see what might have happened to her daughter. She couldn't do this; couldn't *not* do this. She crawled to the small shape and brushed at it with bare hands, wishing the snow would fall from it at once so that she would see and know and not have to go on with this possibility coursing through her veins like poison. She waited for Jessica's hair to appear, the stones that were her eyes, the scream that was her mouth.

She eased the snow away, little by little, gently. It was more respectful that way.

Black fur beneath her fingers.

Cass cried out and started to claw at the snow, prising it away in chunks, revealing Captain's jaws, his sharp white teeth. His tongue protruded. His fur was dense and matted. As she pushed at his frozen body she felt something smooth and rounded and whipped her hands away. Small pink fragments clung to her fingers and melted on her skin. She wiped them on the snow.

Captain's belly had been torn out. The edges were rough and his twining intestines spilled out of him, solid clumps and knots and ropes that vanished into the snow under Cass' feet. She was standing on them. She shuffled backwards and looked at the dog's face, the way the ridges of his lips were drawn back over his teeth.

He was alive. When they did this to him the dog had been *alive.* She didn't know how she knew that, but she did.

'I'm sorry,' she whispered, turning to take in the three of them.

She stumbled away, and something caught her foot under the layers of snow and she went down. There was something else under there. Cass turned to meet Lucy's eyes and saw only stones staring back. She had to know.

She dug into the snow beneath her feet, burrowing down with her chapped red hands. They were so numb she could barely feel them, but this time when she pushed down she met resistance, and her fingers found something that wasn't snow.

A sound echoed around her, a groaning, wailing sound; then it was gone. Cass bit her lip, looked at the witch stones—

It was the wind, that was all, exploring their black shapes.

She looked back at her hands, still buried, and scooped more snow out of the hole.

There were fingers under her own – not small, delicate fingers but fat, white, bloated things that looked like maggots. Cass peered in and gagged. One of them was pinched in the middle, making her think of a string of sausages. The flesh had split there, forming dark crevices. The finger had swollen around a plain gold ring.

Despite the swelling, Cass could see signs of age, so not a child's hands; this was an older woman. Her hands were pressed together as though she were praying . . . as if pleading for mercy.

They had stayed that way, even while they buried her.

Cass sat back on her heels, her mind blank. She knew of no one else missing from the village, and all she could think of was that someone new had come: Theodore Remick.

We've been praying for someone like him.

Mr Remick, with his air of authority, sitting behind the desk with the little sign, picking it up and dropping it into a drawer. MRS CAMBREY. Making it disappear, just like that. Mrs Cambrey, whose disappearance had cleared the way for Mr Remick.

They had killed her before he even came, before the snow came. Someone had killed her and brought her up here. Cass bowed her head and wept for this woman she had never known. Then she sat back on her heels. 'It wasn't him,' she whispered to the sky. 'It was never him.'

She remembered driving over the moors in the fog, unable to see left or right until a face came stumbling out of the whiteness and into her path. She mouthed the name: *Sally*.

Sally, who was looking after Ben. Sally, whom she had asked to take special care of her son.

Ben had seen it better than Cass. *I don't like it*, he'd said. *The lady smelled. She smelled bad and I hate it here.*

'Oh God,' Cass cried, staggering back, her feet pedalling at the snow. She had to get back to Darnshaw. She scrambled to her feet and heard that strange groaning sound again; looked around. It hadn't been in her mind after all. It was coming from beneath her.

She stepped forward, and underfoot it creaked, long and slow, a straining, complaining noise.

'Oh, God,' she whispered, '*no . . .*'

She looked all around and realised the snow was flat, stretching away in an even white layer.

She heard Bert's voice as though he stood at her elbow: *'Watch out for the lake. It'll be iced ower. Up by the stones. You might not see it.'*

She stared down at the snow. She wasn't standing on the ground at all. She was standing upon a frozen lake.

Mrs Cambrey's fingers had been bloated, swollen by the water until the ice caught and held her.

Cass took another step and heard a crack. Her knees almost gave. She crouched, trying to keep her centre of gravity low, and took another. The wind blew, chill in her face, taunting her. The breeze was from another world, from the long walk up the hillside before she had come here and seen the things she had seen. She felt the figures at her back, their blank stares. She couldn't turn.

As the wind lifted a swathe of powdered snow and carried it across the flat surface there came a long, pained moan from beneath.

One more step. Just one.

Ahead was a ridge, then the slope began again. The witch stones were waiting, and beyond that was the moor. When she was a few strides away Cass threw herself forward, forgetting to keep low, to spread her weight. She ran, and flung herself onto the bank, crawling forward through the drifts. She was soaked, but she was off the lake.

She looked back and saw the snow figures leering, their pink flesh obscene scars against the ice. She looked at them for a long time.

When she finally stood up again she realised that she could keep going: cross the moor and never come back. She could send someone for her son, for them all; she could tell the police, send help – they would have to help her after this, bring helicopters, even, and at that she imagined flying in with them, landing in the park, and everyone coming out of their homes and staring.

But she knew she could not.

Ben was in Darnshaw, and Sally was with him. She had to get to her son.

Cass scrambled down the hillside, out of control, her feet twisting, never stopping to see if the hurt would flare into something worse. When she fell she pushed herself back to her feet and pressed on. Cold numbed her face and she couldn't feel anything any more, only the time passing, both slower and faster than she would have liked. She didn't look back.

Ben. She imagined him small and pale, spitting into her face, and his words of hate: *You're his whore.*

Cass stumbled to a halt.

They were trying to take him from her.

That was it: the visits to Sally's, the circle of boys with their blank, cold eyes, sitting in a half-circle and staring up at her. *We shared.*

What did they share? Did they tell him things, *lies*, about her, about Pete? She closed her eyes.

I want him back. How's he going to find us now? He won't know where to look.

What had they *said* to him?

It didn't matter. Whatever they'd said, she could undo it, once they were away from here. Once she had him safe. Cass made her legs take another step, and another, before her muscles loosened up and she was once again careering down the hillside.

TWENTY-NINE

The school was locked. Cass stared at the door, rattled the handle, kicked it until it creaked on its hinges. Then she stood back – and that was when she saw the notice taped to the glass: CLOSED, it said, HEATING BROKEN. That was all, no message for her, nothing to say where Ben had gone. Her throat hurt. Her heart hurt. Cass sagged and leaned against the door, put her cheek to the cold glass.

When she turned she noticed the quiet that had spread like a tangible thing through the schoolyard and into the lane. There was no one here.

She had asked Sally to watch Ben.

Cass hurried back to the road and through the village. For the first time she noticed places where the snow had thinned, revealing dark shadows of the tarmac beneath. The snow was melting. At last the snow was melting, but it was too late; Sally had her son – Sally, who had maybe killed Lucy, Bert, Mrs Cambrey.

But Sally hadn't touched Jess – or had she? Cass swallowed, hard chips of ice tearing her throat, and went on.

WILLOWBANK CRESCENT. The sign was half-swathed in snow. Ordinary houses, built of brick, not stone, with their doors painted red or green or white. A bird trilled as though to underline the normality of the day. Cass stopped at the gate. The day *was* normal; she only had to look at the place. It was Cass who was out of touch with reality. She had had some sort of turn, had seen things that couldn't be there.

But this woman had her son. Cass reminded herself of the way Ben had reacted when he first met Sally: *The lady smelled. She smelled bad and I hate it here.*

Cass threw open the gate. Sally's curtains were drawn – why was that? It was still bright daylight.

Cass knocked on the door, paused only a moment and hammered again. She tried to call her son's name – *Ben* – but it came out as a whisper. Her stomach roiled.

The door clicked and scraped and opened. Sally peered out, her eyes pouchy, hair damp. Her skin was shiny with face-cream. 'You're back,' she said. 'I didn't expect you so soon. They're in the lounge.' Her face withdrew; the door closed and opened again, wider this time. Sally clutched a dressing gown around herself. 'I was just having a shower. Ben's fine, he's with Damon. Are you all right? You look like you've seen a—'

Cass pushed past, calling her son's name.

The lounge was dark. A curious half-light played on the seated figures.

'Ben?'

Faces turned towards her. She couldn't see which one of them was her son.

'Cassandra, are you all right?'

'I'm taking him.' Cass looked around the circle and expressionless eyes looked back. Then she saw Ben's pale hair. His hands were folded around something in his lap. Cass strode to the window, pulling back the curtains, letting in the view of the ordinary street.

'I must say—'

'I've seen them. I know what you did.'

'I don't know what—'

'Ben.' Cass bent and grabbed his arm, hauling him to his feet. Ben's eyes were shadowed. He dropped the thing he held. Cass looked down and saw a games controller. There was movement in the corner of her eye. Damon, shifting on his haunches, picking up the console and cradling it.

'We're going, Ben. Now.'

Ben still didn't speak. Cass' fingers dug into his arm; she knew she was doing it but couldn't stop, and he didn't pull away. She looked down at him. His eyes were blank.

'Ben,' she repeated.

Slowly he turned to face her and his mouth twisted, with hatred, not anger or fear. His face was dead-white.

'I think he might prefer to stay here,' said Sally, 'until you calm down, perhaps. Has something happened? Are you ill, Cassandra?'

'Don't call me that. I saw what you did to her.' Cass remembered Lucy's broken features, the rock forced into her flesh. She fought back a choking sound.

'Ben, I think your mother's ill,' said Sally. 'Remember, you can come here any time. We're your family.'

Cass froze.

'We *share*, remember? We share everything. We don't hide from our family, do we? We don't stop them coming to us when they need us most.'

Cass looked down at him to see a tear tracking down her son's cheek. Cass' grip on his arm was the only solid thing in the room.

'Don't you speak to my son,' she said, and marched him out.

'She's gone a little crazy.' Sally followed them just as though she was showing a guest from the house, but her voice was too loud. 'She's gone a bit mad, Ben. Don't forget, you can always come to me.'

Ben hung back, a reluctant weight, and Cass' fingers clutched harder. Behind her she heard the *tap-crunch* of footsteps, but she ignored them and dragged Ben along, fumbled with the gate, pushed him through it. When she looked back there were four of them, Sally and three boys; their dark eyes were fixed on her.

'A bit crazy.' Sally's voice was laced with amusement. 'Come back soon, Ben. We'll miss you. Come back soon.'

Cass' eyes went from one stony, unblinking face to the next, and they all met her look.

From the corner of her eye she caught sight of something moving in the window above their heads. It was a wide window with a white frame. A hand pressed against a pane and was gone.

Cass' breath was trapped in the back of her throat. She tried to swallow. Ben squirmed in her grip, but she didn't let him go as she took a step back towards the house. 'You've got Jessica,' she said.

Sally flicked damp hair over her shoulder, raised her hands to smooth it down. Her expression was solemn as she met Cass' eyes. 'You're the maddest bitch I've ever known,' she said.

Damon's mouth twitched. He folded his arms. Another boy grinned and nudged his friend.

'I'm going to get her back,' Cass said. 'You're not going to hurt her. I'll see to it.'

Damon spluttered derisively, raised his hand in a mock wave, displaying the red line bisecting his palm. The boys were laughing openly now, and another waved, showing a matching line across his hand.

Cass took hold of Ben's shoulder. 'Come on. We're going.' She pushed him ahead of her and he took automaton steps down the road, not hanging back, not going on ahead. Her hand fell from his shoulder, but he didn't slow down or stop. Her fingers were shaking and her knees felt weak, and the feeling was spreading throughout her body. She began to shiver. She leaned against a wall and called, 'Ben, wait for me. Wait a minute.'

His footsteps ceased, but he didn't turn.

'Ben, please. Come—' Her voice faltered. She couldn't explain, couldn't tell him what she had seen on the moor.

He dragged himself back, scraping his shoes on the pavement, but he did not step into Cass' outstretched arms. She realised he hadn't spoken since they left Sally's house.

'Sweetheart, please,' she whispered, and he came to

her then, burying his face in her chest. She wrapped her arms around him and held him there, feeling his shoulders shake. 'It's all right, sweetheart. I'm here,' she murmured. 'I'll look after you.'

He pulled back suddenly, the crown of his head bumping her chin, and Cass' teeth knocked together. He held out his hand: *Stop*.

'Ben, Sally and Damon are not your family. I'm your family, not them. They did something bad, so we need to go and tell someone, as soon as we can.' Cass had a sudden hope that maybe the telephones were back on, that she could call someone.

Ben shook his head.

'It's okay, love. I won't let anybody hurt you.'

He didn't move, just stood there holding out his hand, and she saw it, the thing he was trying to show her: a red line bisecting his palm.

Cass reached out and took his hand, opened her mouth, but no words came out.

Ben looked away. His chest heaved.

'What is it, Ben? What did they do?'

He was trying to speak.

Cass rubbed his fingers, warming them.

'The book,' he said at last, 'the book. It's the book.'

'What do you mean, love?'

Ben looked up and the sky was in his eyes, cold and white. 'It's to write with,' he said. 'It was so I could write in the big book.' And then he turned and ran, and the sound of his feet was loud in the empty street.

Cass caught up with him. His eyes were big with tears.

'Ben, what do you mean? What book?' All she could think of was her father, leaning over her, inspecting her dress to see if she was good enough, and behind him the church, looming tall.

Ben pulled away and marched wordlessly towards the lane that led to the mill.

The cross etched into the door had been obscured by deep scratches that furred the wood with splinters. Ben stood before the door and she saw his pale, pinched face reflected in the glass.

She punched in the code and pushed Ben before her into the dark interior. The light did not come on, but she didn't stop to investigate. Ben was her priority, and he was cold and hungry and upset. For now he needed to be at home, then tomorrow – early – they would escape. Ben would make it this time; she'd carry him if she had to. She'd tell the police, and everything would be all right.

Ben allowed her to bathe him; he didn't resist and he didn't help. There were no other marks on him, just that livid cut in his hand. It made her think of blood pacts, of boys cutting their hands and pressing them together. Blood brothers. *Family.* That's what Sally had called them: her family. Cass brought his palm to her lips and kissed it, but Ben didn't smile.

'Ben, what did you share?' she asked.

He looked up. His eyes were flat.

'You said you shared, when you were at Sally's. What did you share?' She stroked his hair and waited.

'We ate the stuff,' he said.

'What stuff?'

He shook his head.

'What did it look like?'

'It was just stuff. Like bread, only it was black. And we had the drink. It tasted funny. I didn't like it.' He pulled a face.

'What did that look like?'

He shrugged his skinny shoulders again, hugged his legs. 'We played games,' he said. 'I liked the games.'

'I know you do. Let's get you out and then you can play now – anything you like.'

Cass dried him, led him to the television and put the controller in his hands. His cut hand didn't seem to pain him as his fingers moved rapidly over the buttons, but he didn't react to any of it, didn't laugh or sigh or crow over the deaths on the screen. Only his fingers had life in them.

'Ben?'

He stopped. Cass knelt by him, turned his face towards her. His eyes made her catch her breath. They were dark, rimmed with shadows: *soulless*. She forced herself to speak. 'It's time for bed, sweetheart.'

Cass thought she would lie awake, but instead she found herself slipping in and out of sleep. She floated on the surface, yet the dream pulled her under. Her dress wasn't good enough. Her father looked down at her and his face was angry. She wasn't sure what she had to do to make herself better. *This is love*, he kept saying, but when she looked into his eyes there was no love in them.

The book was lying open on the altar, a dusty black leather volume with yellowing parchment pages. Cass went over and looked at it. The writing was grey-brown, then dark brown, then rust-brown. The latest entries were brighter, reddish. Some of the ink had pooled as from an imperfect nib and dried into little crusts. She could smell the book. It smelled of age, dust, dry stone. There was spice there too: cinnamon, cloves, sharp pepper.

Written in the book was a list of names. Sally's was there, signed with a flourish, with Damon's printed beneath it. Cass could picture him forming the letters, tongue resting on his lip. There was Myra's. Cass read on and she knew it was a dream then because she willed herself to stop, but still her eyes kept tracking down; she had no choice. She followed the names towards the blank space at the bottom of the page, left for others to sign – for *her* name. He would never have it. She would never cut a line across her palm and write her name on this blasphemous page. And yet she couldn't stop herself reading the last name, almost the last, and then a bright streak of light cut across her vision as sun lit the windows, turning everything to day.

She looked up, expecting some vision, Christ, maybe, but it was only Pete, smiling down at her. The light faded and her husband held out his hands and they were heaped with stones the colour of sky. He spoke, but she couldn't hear the words. He held out the stones for her to take, but she couldn't hold them and they fell to the ground, and the ground took them. Pete frowned: he was telling her the thing she had to know, the thing she was supposed to see. She reached out, caught a stone. It shone in her hand and became the sky.

At last she heard his voice: *Now you see*, he said. *Now you see.*

Cass woke, clawing the covers from her throat, wiping stinging sweat from her face. She opened her hand, closed tight in a fist, looked for the stone, and remembered it was only a dream after all.

Now you see. She put her hands to her face. Whatever Pete wanted her to know, it was no use; she couldn't understand. She wasn't good enough. 'I *don't* see,' she whispered. 'Pete, I'm sorry, I don't see at all.'

Someone knocked on the apartment door.

Cass was motionless. All she could think of was Lucy, coming to see her, a printout held in one hand: *I brought you this.* No – it could be Sally, coming to whisper her poison in her son's ear, or the boys, knocking with their tainted palms.

It could be Remick. Theodore Remick, come to see how she was, holding out his offering of bread.

All at once she felt his hands running over her, the warmth of his breath on her night-cold skin, heat blossoming inside. Somehow she did not flinch from it. She closed her eyes, crossed her arms over her breasts, heard him whisper, *You'll come to me.*

Cass' lips parted; she suddenly wanted to feel his lips on her, wanted it more than anything–

She drew her lip between her teeth and bit down. The pain brought her back.

There was no one at the door. She had been dreaming,

that was all. There was no Pete; there were no blue stones. Cass closed her eyes, wondering if she had fallen asleep up by the witch stones, whether she had really seen the white figures looking back at her.

You're the maddest bitch I've ever known.

Maybe Sally was right.

The knocking came again, an ordinary domestic sound, but this time it didn't come from the door; it came from the wall at her back. Cass got out of bed and looked into the dark. There was nothing, no one there.

Ben might have heard something; he might be frightened.

Cass took a deep breath and went to check on her son. As she reached the hall the knocking came again, louder this time, coming from the door and from the wall and from the ceiling.

She looked up, saw nothing – of course she saw nothing; it was only the children, Damon and his friends. They had got into the mill somehow, crept into the flat next to hers and the one above and the one below, and they were waiting for her to show she was afraid. Well, she wasn't.

She felt her pulse beating in her throat.

She went into Ben's room. He was sitting up in bed, his eyes wide and his mouth hanging open, a string of drool hanging from it.

There was banging on the ceiling, the walls, the floor.

Cass went and put her arms around him. 'Shh,' she said, although he hadn't spoken. 'It's just children messing about. Naughty children, Ben. We won't have to put up with them for long.'

'They've come for me,' he said.

'No, no, they haven't. It's a game, that's all: a silly game they're playing.'

His skin was clammy against her arms. He squirmed and pulled away from her. 'It's not a game.'

'It doesn't matter, Ben. Whatever it is, we're leaving tomorrow, you and me. Do you understand that?'

He shook his head.

'Yes, Ben. We're going away from here. We're not coming back.'

'It doesn't matter. He got me.'

'What do you mean?'

'He's in here.'

'In here?' Cass glanced towards the door.

Ben raised a finger and pointed to his chest. 'Here – he's in here. He told me.'

'Who is, Ben?'

'Daddy.' He paused. 'He's my daddy now – they said so. They gave me the bread and the stuff and I wrote in the book.'

Cass had a sudden image of her father: *This is love.* 'You mean like in church?'

Ben scowled.

'What did they make you do?'

In answer he held out his hand, the dark line vicious against his pale skin.

'You wrote your name in a book.'

He nodded.

'What book, Ben? Where was it?'

'Damon said it was okay,' he said. 'He said it was okay 'cos it was in the church. But it doesn't feel okay.'

She remembered her dream, the image of herself in a white dress, trying to please Daddy, trying to be good enough. 'The name book.'

'It means you're family,' he whispered. 'I wanted to be in the family, Mummy. I want my daddy.'

She pulled him close.

'They said I could be in the family, only it has to hurt if you want to be in. That's why they do your hand and you write in that.'

'You wrote in *blood*?' Cass thought of the dream, the letters almost black at the top, then dark brown, then rust. 'Who did that to your hand? Was it Damon?' It struck her that it could have just been the children, hearing old stories, playing silly games. Sally might not have even known about it.

But what had she said to Ben? *We're your family.*

He's in here, Ben had said. Cass looked around, half-expecting to hear the knocking again, remembered the way it had sounded as if it was coming out of the walls. She shivered. 'Who did they say is inside you, Ben?'

She felt she already knew. She sensed the weight of her father's hand, pressing down. *Let him into your heart, Gloria. Leave no room for another.*

But Ben was so young. How could she have let this happen?

'Your soul,' she whispered.

'That's what they asked for,' said Ben. 'Is it wrong, Mummy? Did I do wrong?' When he looked up, she saw a trace of the little boy he had been – the little boy he still was. She bent and kissed his head. He was innocent; he couldn't have known what he was doing. It was a crazy sham, nothing more than some religious mumbo-jumbo.

You're the maddest bitch I've ever known.

Cass closed her eyes. It was her; she must be going insane. She felt Ben pulling on her arm again, but it was Lucy's face she saw: blank stone eyes, staring out across an empty hillside. She shivered.

'Mummy?'

Cass kissed her son. She stroked his arm and held him and rested her cheek against his head until he slept.

THIRTY

Cass peered into the mirror, staring into her own eyes. She had already woken Ben, but left him to doze a little longer. She couldn't bear the way he'd sat up and looked at her, his eyes glassy, without interest or light or fear, like there was nothing inside him.

I don't suppose the lad'll leave now.

Bert had been wrong about Ben, and yet he had been right too. It didn't matter how far away she took her son, a part of him would stay in Darnshaw with Sally and Damon and the pack of boys. His eyes would always be blank. A vital part of him was gone and she would never get it back.

Unless she did something . . .

A rush of heat burned her chest, her throat. She *would* do something – but first she had to see the book for herself. She had to know it was real.

She roused Ben again, looking into his face as he sat up, hoping it would brighten, that his eyes would shine, but they were still blank, *soulless*. She turned her head away, rubbed her eyes, then said with a smile, 'Come on, love. We've an errand to run, and then we're going far away from here.'

She helped him up. Ben was limp in her hands, but he stood. He didn't ask why he wasn't going to school. He didn't say anything.

'Ben, do you remember before we came here? You didn't want to move. Do you remember that?'

He rested a hand on her shoulder and leaned while she pulled on his trousers.

'Ben, do you—?'

He interrupted, blurting out, 'I was never anywhere,' he said. 'I wasn't anywhere, and you were always here.'

'Ben?' She tilted his face up.

'You were here,' he said and pushed her away.

'I wasn't here, Ben. We lived at Aldershot, remember? With—' It felt cruel to make him remember, but she pressed on, 'with Daddy.'

'I have a daddy. He's here. He's always been here. With you.'

'Well, I was here for a while, Ben, when I was a little girl. But that was with my own daddy. Then I went away and had you, and that made me very happy.'

Ben's face twisted, and it looked as though he was blinking back tears. 'It made him happy too,' he said, and no matter how Cass pressed him, he wouldn't say anything else.

In the lane everything was dripping. Their feet punched through brittle snow and Cass heard water trickling beneath it. She looked up at the grey sky. It was definitely warmer than yesterday.

The road had twin tracks running down it now. It wasn't raining, but as Cass guided Ben down the road fat droplets pattered on their heads: icicles disintegrating. Everything was melting.

Cass remembered her dream: Remick standing outside, his chest bared, raising his arms to greet the snow as it fell.

The church tower loured, a black hole in the sky, and she remembered how she had feared it, standing there as her father inspected her dress, the way he had led her to the altar. Now she felt nothing. In the morning light she couldn't believe the book was real, any of it: the figures on the moor, Sally's threats. Nothing in her life seemed real, nothing since the moment they told her that her husband wasn't coming back.

She looked down at Ben, caressed his hair. His eyes were more shadowed than ever.

His footsteps faltered as she led the way past the rectory. She glanced sidelong at the windows and glimpsed only her own reflection. Would Remick be at home? He could be looking out at them even now. Cass shivered as Ben stopped, his eyes fixed on the church spire.

'Come on, love.' She reached out her hand. 'I can't leave you here. I just need to look at something, that's all.'

He swallowed, his eyes becoming hard, but after a moment he slipped his hand into hers. Cass felt the coldness of his skin, found herself tracing the line across his palm with one finger.

Ben hung back as Cass twisted the iron handle on the church door, but as she pushed it open he ducked under her arm and rushed into the darkness of the church. She shoved the door and it scraped on stone as it thudded back.

She went inside, and found herself surrounded by brilliant colours: reds, yellows, blues, and dust motes dancing in the dazzling light. She blinked and started walking, her shoes loud on the stone. She opened her mouth to call Ben's name, then made out the pale arc of his hair.

He sat in the first pew, looking at the crucifix on the altar: Christ with contorted face, protruding ribs. Cass looked at her son's rapt expression. She had tried to shield him from such images, not like her, a little girl in a white dress marched down the aisle, the messages repeated and repeated in her ears:

Pray to be delivered from sin. Turn away from evil. His voice will whisper in your ear, call you to the world. You must not listen.

'You got dedicated,' Ben said. He pointed at the place just in front of where he sat, the place where Cass had knelt and bowed her head, her father's hand pressing her down, opening her mouth and feeling the dry paper on her tongue and the tang of sour wine. *This is love.*

It hadn't tasted like love.

Cass blinked.

'I was confirmed.' Her voice was dry and cracked. 'I was confirmed, Ben, not—'

He didn't look at her and she did not go on. *Dedicated*, he'd said, and she had been about to correct him, except that he was right: she had been dedicated. That was the word her father had used. *I dedicate this child to the Lord.*

The weight of her father's hand, pressing down. The weight of his words. The sour taste of wine on her tongue.

Gloria, I named thee. You will glorify the Lord's name.

She had left that name behind a long time ago, and yet here she was, back in Darnshaw, seeking the memory of her father, perhaps, just as Ben had been seeking a father.

'How did you know that, Ben? Were you dedicated?'

He closed his fingers over his damaged palm, opened them again and rubbed his hand against his cheek. His eyes never left the window. Colours streaked his face: yellow, red.

Cass stepped towards the altar. There was no book, only the same white cloth she'd seen before, covering the centre of the slab, not hiding the abattoir groove carved into the edge.

Lucy had said something about children and a sacrifice – not *being* sacrificed, but *doing* the killing, the knife in their small hands—

Cass turned back to Ben.

He wasn't there. She blinked. The coloured light played across the pew where he had been sitting. There was movement in the shadows, a shuffling sound, and Cass could see Ben, crushed against a tall figure. She knew the shape, had felt those hands on her body. Ben wasn't being held; his arms were wrapped around Remick in a hug. And as she watched, Remick raised his hand and rested it on her son's head.

'He's come home now,' Remick said.

'Ben, come here.'

He didn't move.

'Do you really think he wants to go with you, Cass? He's quite comfortable here. He's happy.'

'*Ben.*'

Remick smiled and stepped forward, and his hand twisted Ben's head so that he was facing her.

She could see the silver lines of tears on her son's face.

'He needs stability, Cass. Security. Peace.'

He needs *me.*'

'Really, Cass? Do you think so?'

'Ben, come here.' Cass shouted this time, and the sound reverberated from the walls.

'You can take him, Cass, but you can never have him back.'

She held out her hand and Ben left Remick's side and reached for her.

'Ben, show her who you are,' said Remick. 'Show her who you belong to.'

Ben stared down at the floor and he opened his hand. The cut on his palm was a vivid slash.

'That's right. He belongs to me now, Gloria. It doesn't matter where you go. A part of him – the important part, you'll find – will always be here with me.'

Remick's lips continued to move but she couldn't hear him. She closed her eyes and saw her husband, mouthing words, trying to tell her something. He was holding out his hands. She opened her eyes and Remick stepped back towards the window. Blue light fell across his face. He smiled. 'You understand now, don't you, Cass? Now you see.'

Cass squeezed Ben's shoulder, indicating he should stay where he was. She walked towards Remick.

'Welcome back, my dear,' he said, and opened his arms. But she brushed past him, stood beneath the window and looked up.

The pietà. Christ on the Virgin's knee, dead in her arms. His face was empty, the eyes black smudges. A fallen god. The Virgin's cloak was the colour of the sky. The same colour as the stones her husband had been holding.

And then Cass looked at the Virgin's face and her mouth dried up. It was a narrow, almost hollow face, a little too long, a little too defined. The skin on the cheeks looked mottled. The eyes were dark and triumphant.

It was a man's face, not a woman's. 'You,' she whispered. She felt Remick's touch on her shoulder and at the same time she could feel his hands on her face, her arms, her breasts, feeling their way down her spine, her chest, touching her heart.

'I was always here,' he said, 'before time was measured; before the first stone was laid. I was here, watching for those who would take my name.'

'But–' Cass looked up at the window, the god held in Remick's arms.

His voice was at her ear. 'It's good, isn't it? Just think, all that time, all those worshippers looking up and singing his praises, and all along it was me, holding the dead Christ. It's a nice touch, don't you think? And funny, when you think about it: they see me every day and yet know me not.'

'You're—' *Just a man*, Cass was going to say, but she felt his breath on her neck, his lips caressing her face, working their way down. She closed her eyes, saw Pete holding out the blue stones, letting them fall to the ground one by one. They were the exact blue of the Virgin's gown. He had been trying to show her, make her see, but she had been blind to everything.

Remick laughed. 'Lapis lazuli,' he said, 'the stone of the desert, isn't that ironic? The most expensive colour in the world, and it's right here in Darnshaw: the colour of sky and the heart of a flame both. *Both*.' His voice became wistful. 'A connection to two worlds, Cass. His and mine.'

He nestled close, rested his chin on her shoulder. 'You know something, Cass? The finest lapis contains sulphur too. Isn't that delicious? It contains sulphur and iron pyrite – fool's gold.' His laugh brayed in her ear.

'Such a thing your husband chose for you: fool's gold.'

'How do you—?'

'I showed you, Cass. They call me the Father of Lies, but I only ever showed you the truth.' He held out his hand and she saw blue stones turning to dust in his palms.

And Cass understood. 'He wasn't there – Pete was never there. It was you in my dreams.'

Remick smiled. He licked his lips with the tip of his tongue.

Cass looked at her son.

'Oh, he's better off, Cass. Besides, the other lot have

been doing it for centuries. "Give me the child for seven years, and I will give you the man." That's their boast, isn't it? I do the same thing and they get all indignant.'

'Leave Ben alone.'

'As you like – but he's already marked as my own. It's very fetching, don't you think?' Remick went to Ben, picked up his arm and straightened his fingers so that Cass could see the mark. 'It's somewhat melodramatic, all that writing-in-blood business, but it seals it in their minds; that's the important thing. And I have always liked the smell, I must confess.' He turned back to Cass, his eyes gleaming. 'Do you want to see it, Gloria? Put your hands on the book? Of course you do.'

He danced away towards the lectern and reached up for the book that rested upon it. *It was there all the time,* thought Cass, *in plain view. Like the window.*

Remick's face grew cloudy. 'You don't think I'd hide, do you? Here it is.' The book was cased in dusty leather and it smelled of animal hide and time. Remick whistled between his teeth as he ran a narrow finger down the open page. He turned the book so that Cass could see, but the words swam in front of her eyes. She scanned down, saw Damon's name written there, deep brown. Sally. Myra. She did not want to see, and yet she could not stop her eyes following their course down the page.

Remick closed the book with a snap.

'All there,' he said, 'all signed, sealed and dedicated.' His eyes went to the spot where Cass had once knelt.

The church spun around her. Her father's hand, resting in her hair: had it even been that way? In her mind's eye she saw her own palm held out, small and white, and a knife raised above it. An open book waiting on the altar. She shook her head. That's not how it was. Her father had been a good man who did his best. Gloria, he had called her.

'Quite so.' Remick's voice was in her hair. 'He possessed your every thought, did he not? He took you from me. He thought he could protect you, give you to the other. Well, I will tell you this, Cass: you can only ever give your-self.'

Cass reached out for the book, felt the decaying cover beneath her fingers before he took it away.

'You can't take it back.'

Cass forced herself to stand tall. 'You're deluded,' she said, 'insane. Nothing more.'

'Am I?' He looked at the window. 'A simple sign, isn't it, Cass? Anyone who cared to come here could see it. This church was built long before you were born. I'm doing well for my age, aren't I?' He grinned. 'Still plenty of life in me, didn't you find?'

Cass looked back at the window. It was a coincidence, that was all; whoever made the window couldn't have meant—

She looked into the Virgin's face and Remick's eyes looked back at her.

'You see,' Remick breathed, 'you *do* believe.'

She remembered the touch of his face pressed against her own, his kisses on her skin.

Remick smiled and Cass felt her nerves prickle. She shuddered. *I knew*, she thought. *My body always knew.*

She met his eyes, caring, loving eyes, and they were full of amusement. She shook her head. 'You can't have him,' she said. 'You can't have my son.'

He smiled, set the book back on the lectern.

'I'll burn it.'

He laughed. 'Will you, Cass? We'll see. Of course, it's written on his skin too, is it not? In his heart, his eyes—'

'No.'

'Perhaps it's best for you to go, Cass. Your destiny is written on you too. Gloria: for the glory of God. Well, now you can take your son and go. Glorify him.'

Cass stared. 'They'll come for you,' she said. 'I'll tell them everything. I found the bodies – Bert, Lucy.' *Jess.* Jess was still in the house with Sally.

'Cassandra.' He smiled. 'How ironic, that you should have her name. Do you know who she was, Cass? She had the gift of prophecy, and yet she was doomed never to be heard. Funny you should choose it for yourself.'

'My name is Cassidy.'

'If you like.'

'You can't have him.' Cass felt tears spring to her eyes. 'You have to let him go.'

'*Have* to, *have* to—'

'Please.'

'Ah, begging – I like that. I like it.'

Cass stared. After a moment she dropped to her knees. The stone was cold, unyielding.

Remick smiled.

'Please. Whatever you did to him – took from him – let him go.'

'You're begging me?'

'I'm begging you.'

Remick's eyes shone. He threw back his head and laughed. 'Oh, Cass, please – really?' He paused, became serious. 'There is one thing and one thing only I want, and you know exactly what that one thing is.'

He fell silent, but his lips continued to move. Cass heard the words quite clearly: *I have tasted you.*

Cass opened her lips. '*Me?*' She felt his hands on her body once again, shivered. The thought was in her mind: *You already had me.*

'Oh, not your body, Cass, sweet as that was – although I wonder what your father would have said? No, I don't need that; that was a foretaste only. A flavour.' He kept his eyes on her.

She shook her head.

'Your love? No, your heart is turning cold, Cass; I don't want it. That's not what it is at all. You know the game, you were taught the rules as a little girl: that part of you that was signed over, sealed, dedicated to *Him*: That's sweet, Cass, the sweet, sweet soul of a forbidden flower. *Give it to me.*' His eyes were suddenly greedy. He licked his lips, and a drop of saliva remained visible. '*Give it to me.*' He couldn't stop the words falling from his mouth. 'Sign it over – one little thing, one moment, and it's done. I'll let him go, expunge his name, and it will be as though it had never been written.'

She backed away, shaking her head.

'Look at him, Cass: so young and yet so troubled. See the shadow in his eyes? That's no shadow; you know what that is, Cass? The absence of light. It's quenched, Cass. Extinguished. *Gone.* And it'll be gone for ever, for all eternity, unless you say yes. That's all it takes, Cass. One little word.' He tilted his head, changed his tone. 'It was *good*, Cass, wasn't it? You and me – everything you wanted.'

Except the way her flesh had recoiled from him.

'I can give it to you.' He smiled, and it was *Theo's* smile, warm, full of comfort. It soothed her. Cass looked away. Her son stood in the light that streamed from the windows and yet his eyes were in shadow, would always be in shadow.

And she was his mother.

Remick reached out, tracing a shape in the air, and she felt his touch, strong, warm, the comfort only a man's arms could bring. *Safety.* He breathed into her hair, her neck. She moaned.

'It was *good*, Cass.' His fingertips caressed her body, so light on her arms, the inside of her wrists, her hips, touching her secret places, lighting sparks inside her, easing into her . . . filling her. His fingers were cool against her heat.

'No.' She opened her eyes. His were blue. Blue.

'Come to me,' he said, and held out his arms.

Cass shook her head. Such warmth, such light, it soothed her heart, her soul. She looked down and was troubled by Ben's eyes. There was something she had to do for him – she had to help him. One simple thing—

'I'll give you your life back, Cass.'

Suddenly it all came back to her, everything she had lost.

'Cassandra. *Gloria.* Come.'

His arms were open and his eyes were warm, welcoming, so full of love, full of promise, everything he could restore. Cass stepped forward before she knew she was going to move. It was such a simple thing, after all, to step forward and let him take this weight from her, the hand that still pressed down upon her head. How it would feel to rest in his arms and let the burden be lifted. He drew her close, smoothed her hair, eased her head down against his shoulder. She let him take it all.

Remick walked with her towards the altar, his arms still wrapped around her, and Cass rested within his warmth, felt light touch her face. Her palm was innocent of marks, a helpless thing as she held it out, and he took it in his, laid it flat on his own hand. He held out a blade. The knife was long and curved and he smiled, drawing back his lips, baring his teeth.

She didn't look at her hand as he cut, though the pain was sharp, surprising. She felt it sever something deep inside her, but still she didn't cry out. It was already over, and the empty space it left behind was good, safe. It belonged to him.

Her eyes were fixed on Remick's – they were beautiful; had she seen that before? – and Cass felt him closing her fingers on something: a pen. He pushed the book towards her.

She bent to the page, caught its bloody cinnamon scent. It only took a moment to sign her name. It was her true name and she gave it to him, a gift. The thing he wanted.

When she straightened he kissed her forehead. 'Go,' he whispered. 'Go in peace, my child.'

She blinked. Ben was standing close by and she reached out a hand to him. His eyes were dark hollows. He did not smile, nor speak; he just looked at her, unblinking.

'You're supposed to free him,' she said, and her head cleared as she spoke. 'So free him.'

Remick had turned his back. He snapped the book closed, set it back on the lectern, slipped the pen into some hidden pocket. He wiped the knife on the white cloth adorning the altar and secreted it beneath his coat. He did not speak.

'Expunge his name, like you said.' Cass pointed. She waited for him to respond, but he did not.

'I said *do it*. Keep your promise. Set him free.'

'He is free.' Remick brushed dust from his coat, the movements rapid, businesslike.

'But you said— You said you'd put it right. If I just—'

'If you *just*—'

'Yes.'

'I don't think you understand, Cass. There appears to be some mistake.'

Her throat constricted. She had no air. 'No. You said. You *promised*.'

'I did. And I keep my promises, despite what they might say.'

'You *said* you'd *free* him.'

Remick straightened, turned to face her. 'I told you. He is free.'

'But the book—'

'The book,' he mocked. 'Don't you know anything, Cass? I thought you knew better than that.'

'But his name—'

'He's a child.'

'But you— His hand—'

'Yes, yes. He's a child, for heaven's sake. Do you not *listen*? A child: an innocent, in the eyes of the Lord, anyway. He's done nothing binding, nothing I can hold him to. Don't you understand?' He smiled. 'Oh Cass. You see now, don't you? At last.'

'He's—'

'Innocent, yes. Free, if you like. For now at least.'

'But he signed—'

'Nothing binding. As I said.'

She was silent.

'Take him and go.'

'But—'

'I have nothing to hold him. Take him and go.'

Ben still stared straight ahead, his eyes charcoal smudges.

'Of course, he'll probably find his way back to me; it'll be his own choice. It's true what I said: *his own choice*. There's the beauty of it. And he thinks of me as his father already, don't you, Ben?'

'But the others. Damon, the other boys—'

'Oh, Damon's mine; he's old enough to understand, barely. The others – who knows? But my stamp is on them.' He grinned, wolfish. 'They'll come back. Don't you feel it, Cass?'

'But not Ben. You said—'

'I said I'd free him. I didn't say he'd *stay* free. Of course, that's where you come in. You are his mother, aren't you? You can guide him. Do you think you can do that? Are you a fit mother, Cass?'

She looked down at the blood that was drying on her palm.

'I thought not. Well, time will tell, won't it?'

'But the way he was – he *hit* me. He said such things to me.'

'Not really surprising, Cass, the way you uprooted him – the way you stopped his daddy coming home. Really, Cass.'

'He said—'

'Children are so easy to manipulate; did I not mention that? And with *me* for his teacher . . .' Remick turned to Ben and smiled. 'Hugs are for sissies, aren't they, Ben? As for your drawings, you follow instruction so well. The one of your husband and the lady – really, Ben, you should join the family. You *belong*. You still can – when you're old enough, of course.'

Ben looked away.

'You told him he *sexed* her. That my husband . . . that woman—'

Remick snorted. 'Words – just *words*, Cass. Ben thought that meant *rescued*, didn't you, son?' He smiled. 'Of course, I wouldn't have put it past your husband: he's got a very literal mind, hasn't he, Pete? He's not the type to worry about the spiritual. About guilt.'

Ben shuffled his feet.

'Quite right, Ben. Time to be off.' Remick turned his

eyes on Cass and they were blue no longer. They were steel. 'Thank you,' he said, 'for your business.'

'But what about—?'

'You? What about you?' He nodded towards Ben. 'Your son didn't know what he was doing. He's as free as a bird. That was our arrangement, wasn't it?'

'But—'

'There are no buts, Cass; there's no taking back. Your son didn't understand, but *you* did, didn't you? You knew exactly what you were doing.' He paused, a slow smile spreading across his face. 'Dear, sweet Cass. Welcome to the family.'

THIRTY-ONE

The sound of water dripping was everywhere: from the roofs of houses, from the church spire, from the trees. It filled Cass' ears. When she walked down to the road that wound through the village she saw it was almost clear of snow; only icy cobweb veils remained. She turned to check that Ben was following. He was. Her chest was filled with freezing air. She wondered if it would thaw, come the spring.

THIRTY-TWO

Cass threw herself down on the sofa and Ben went to his room. She looked at the wall. It was silent now, no scratching or knocking; the only sound came from outside, water pattering onto the ground. It meant time was passing. She should be taking Ben out of here, getting him away, but there no longer seemed to be any point.

She thought of the bodies on the moor. They had been left there for her, a sign. Remick wouldn't be caught, *couldn't* be caught. The world had no authority over him.

She didn't need to look out of the window to see the moors were still covered in snow. It would keep its grip up there a while yet, even as Darnshaw thawed. But the roads across the hills might be clear. She could load up the car and drive away. She should pack, ask Ben to get his things ready. But somehow it was easier to sit and listen to the water drip.

But Ben was at her side, and he was hungry. He pulled at her arm until she stood up. There was bread in the cupboard, although she couldn't remember how it came to be there. She buttered some, put it on a plate. Ben pulled a face and she nudged it towards him. He took it and went back into his room.

Cass looked out of the window and the moor looked back. There was the sound of an engine somewhere that seemed at once near and distant, amplified by the topography of the valley. Something big, a 4x4 maybe.

If she could get the car up the lane from the mill she could leave. But the thought of packing, turning the key to start the engine, steering it through the curves of the road – it was all too much.

She couldn't remember when she'd last tried the telephone – but who could she speak to now? No one would understand. They wouldn't *know*.

Cass realised the pit of her stomach was burning. She went into the kitchen, folded a piece of bread and stuffed it into her mouth, chewed the dry, cloying stuff. *This is love.*

She leaned over and choked it up, fingering chewed pieces from her mouth.

When Cass closed her eyes, Remick was there. She could feel the heat of his breath. She was naked before him, and that was all right. She was not ashamed. He ran the back of his hand down her arm, proprietorial.

She heard knocking at the door and buried her face in his shoulder. He was there for her, he would always be there for her, someone to turn to when she couldn't go on, a rock in time of need. She heard the sound again but she didn't look; it only hurt when she looked. She would stay in this place with Remick's arms around her, a guarantee that everything would be all right.

A door opened and closed.

Remick's hands were on her thighs, pushing them open. She screwed up her face, keeping her eyes closed.

'Cass?'

The deep voice was familiar, and Cass knew she should recognise it, but somehow she could not.

'Cass, are you all right?' A hand on her arm, solid, heavy. Not like Remick's. She brushed it away. Her head fell back and she opened her eyes.

The shape loomed over her, outlined by the light from the hall. Somehow she knew it. It looked at her, up and down, and did not say anything. She knew her clothes must be crumpled, her eyes rimmed with dark, still half-asleep.

The figure bent down, peering, finding her not good enough. She had *never* been good enough.

'Mummy?'

Cass blinked. Ben stood beside her bed, pulling on her sleeve. She caught his arm, felt the frail bones beneath the skin: Ben was safe. She drew him to her and put her arms around him. His hair was greasy under her lips. She should take him away from here, make sure Remick's eyes never fell on him again.

'Cass.'

She looked up and saw something that didn't make any sense: the face was her father's. It was his voice too, though different, mellowed by time. He had creases around his eyes that hadn't been there before, and heavy folds scored his cheeks. Old. He was old, that was it. Cass pulled Ben to her and looked up at her father, waited for him to list all the things that were wrong with her.

One thing. One simple thing.

'Has something happened?' He knelt at her side and rubbed her arm. 'Please tell me you haven't been like this since Peter—'

Cass blinked. She couldn't understand what he was saying. It was her dress, maybe. That was it. She was supposed to go to church, but she had mud on her dress. She clutched Ben tighter, heard Remick's whisper in her ear: *I'll give you your life back.*

Her father spoke. 'It's good news, love. I thought— I thought you'd be more over it by now. I never thought he was good for you, you know that, but seeing you like this . . .' He smiled, and the lines scoring his cheeks formed two arcs.

He could help her. The leap of hope was dull, but it was there: her father was a man of God. Cass kept her eyes on him. He could take this all away. They would leave here together; he could take them both with him, and they need never see Darnshaw again.

'He's back, love. He came back.'

Cass didn't know who her father meant. Remick? Remick never went away. He had always been here.

Her father stroked her forehead with the back of his hand and it reminded her of the teacher, his gesture of ownership, and she shuddered and looked away. Was this really her father? It could be Remick, one of his tricks. She clutched Ben close and her son gasped. Her father tugged at her hand, but she brushed him off. He wasn't going to take her son away from her. *Never.*

'He's alive, Glor— *Cass.* I came here to tell you – he's been back a while, but we had to wait on the other side of the moors until we could get across to you. He can't wait to see you, Cass. I thought it best if he stayed in the car, though. I didn't want it to be too much of a shock.'

He felt her forehead again, this time gauging her temperature. 'Cass, can you hear me? Can you understand what I'm saying? You look ill. I – I was going to come anyway, you know. This place – I never thought it was good for us. I would have come as soon as I heard some-thing from you, but this wouldn't wait for that.

'Everything will be all right again, Cass.'

His words didn't make sense. Was she supposed to be happy? She knew Remick was alive – he would always be alive, long after her life was over. She licked her lips. They tasted like dust.

'He tricked me,' she whispered.

'No, Cass, no, he didn't – not on purpose. There was an attack and he was taken prisoner. Then they thought he was someone else, and he couldn't speak, not for a long time. But he's back now. He's come back to you, love. He – he's scarred, sweetheart; you should expect that. But he's here.'

She blinked. 'Pete?'

'Of course. Peter – Pete. Who did you think?' Her father smiled, squeezed her arm. 'He's here, Cass. He's outside.'

She tried to get up and follow him to the door but in the end she leaned back against the wall and let him go.

Her father nodded as though he understood. He held out his hand to Ben. 'Do you want to come and see your daddy?' he asked.

Ben shrank back against Cass, shaking his head, and Cass' father glanced at her. He looked half-puzzled, half-disapproving. Cass heard his footsteps retreating down the hall. He wouldn't come back, surely he wouldn't come back. The idea was disconnected, somewhere beyond her reach. *I'll give you your life back.* That was the thing she clung to, that played over and over in her head. *I'll give you your life back.* And the thing Remick hadn't said: *As soon as it's no good to you any more. As soon as you no longer want it.*

It was Ben who opened the door to reveal Cass' father, and someone standing behind him, a little taller, a little broader.

Her father stepped aside.

Pete was thinner than before. His cheeks, once softly rounded, were hollow. The skin was roughened, possibly burned.

Cass' mouth twitched.

Pete smiled at her, lifted his hand, let it fall back to his side. There was a light in his eyes and Cass was putting it out; she could see that. She didn't know what she could do to stop it. It was like seeing someone she had known a long time ago, a childhood friend, perhaps, all the more odd because of how they'd changed. The marks of years on their faces. Pete's eyes were paler than she remembered. Desert-pale. Burned by a brilliant sun.

'Cass.' He tried a smile. 'It's me.' His voice was a croak,

not the way she remembered it. Ben stepped out from her side and Pete fell to his knees and threw his arms around his son. He held him tight, whispering words into his hair, and Ben let out a sudden exclamation and hugged him back. They both started to cry.

Pete straightened and put his arms around Cass. His frame was broad, tall, not the right shape. She didn't want him touching her.

'It's so good to see you, Cass,' he said. He waited, expecting something from her she could not give. 'I tried to get to you,' he said, his voice breaking. 'I thought I'd never get home.'

'Cass.' It was her father's voice. She felt the wall at her back, all wrong somehow. 'Cass,' he said again, urgency in his voice. She could choose, she knew. She could meet his eyes and face this, or go into the dark. She closed her eyes. The dark was waiting and it rose to meet her.

THIRTY-THREE

Remick came to Cass while she slept. His arms were open, but not in welcome; it was as if he were presenting her with a gift. He smiled. His eyes were darker than she remembered. He opened his mouth to speak, but she didn't hear the words because it was stuffed with blue stones. As he spoke they fell, one by one, to the ground. Cass reached out but they slipped through her fingers. She understood them now: half of this world, half of another, and every single one of them a lie. Fool's gold. They wouldn't be caught. *He* wouldn't be caught.

She opened her eyes and pale blue eyes looked back. She took a deep breath. 'Pete.'

He smiled, and his hand curled around hers. 'You're back. I was worried there for a while.'

'*You* were worried?'

He laughed, and it made her remember. It was a sound from the good times, before either of them disappeared. It made Cass think of the day she'd spent with Remick, when she had been new and he called to see them and they had walked together through the snow like a family.

She closed her eyes. She could smell the book, tainted, like meat hung too long, and then came the sensation of the teacher's hands on her body. She opened them again and looked at Pete. His eyes were almost transparent, and she felt she could see right into him.

'I missed you,' she said. 'I missed you so much.'

'Sorry I'm a bit late.'

She slapped his arm, smiled back. It felt good.

'Of course, if you will run away to the back of beyond . . .'

Her smiled faded. She looked around and realised she couldn't see Ben anywhere. She pushed herself up. 'Where's—?'

'Ben's fine. Your dad took him for a walk. He's been really good, actually, much better than he used to be. Anyway, Ben looked like he needed some air. Cass, have you been okay? How long have you been cooped up inside?'

She shook her head.

'Maybe you need some air yourself. You said some pretty weird things in your sleep.'

She frowned.

'It sounded like you were having some kind of flashback.'

'I did?'

'Something from when you were a kid – stuff about hell and damnation.' He looked at the door. 'It must be your dad's influence. Cass, are you okay, really?'

It was in his eyes, the real question: how could she not be okay when he'd come back to her? What might possibly stop her being happy about that? An image flickered before Cass' eyes: Remick's hand resting on her breasts. She shuddered.

'Shouldn't Ben be in school?'

She shook her head. 'It's closed. The heating's broken. There's no need for him to go back, is there? I mean we're leaving, aren't we?'

She could go back to Aldershot, resume her old life, surrounded by other women, people she could be friends with; people she could trust. She need never see Remick again, except perhaps in her dreams.

'If you like, Cass – if that's what you want.'

'Yes.' She forced a smile, and realised her husband looked just the same, really; apart from the weight he'd lost, the scarring on his cheek, it was the same Pete. She could have her life back, forget about Darnshaw. It would be an episode of madness, of delusion, none of it real. She would escape over the moors and everything would fade behind her, swallowed by the fog.

She took Pete's hand. 'It is what I want. I can't wait.'

The door opened and closed and Ben ran in, smiling in a way she hadn't seen in a long time. It lit up his eyes. He opened his arms and threw them around his dad. Cass rubbed her son's hair, pulled them both closer, laughing. She felt a hand on her arm, looked up and in an instant she was a child again, with a dark shape looming over her, staring at her dress.

Her father spoke. 'I need to talk to you, Cass.'

Not good enough, she thought.

Her father's agitation showed in the quickness of his look, darting from Cass' eyes to her hair to her crumpled clothing. He closed the kitchen door behind them.

She opened her mouth, but he spoke first. 'How did Ben get that mark on his hand?'

She found she couldn't meet his gaze and stared at the linoleum. It was scuffed with footprints. How long had it been that way?

'Tell me, Cass.' His voice was gentle.

'He—' Cass thought of the boys, sitting together in a circle, children making a blood pact, becoming brothers. 'He was messing about with his friends. It's nothing.'

'Don't lie to me, Cass. I've seen it before. I know what it is.'

So why ask? There was a hollow place inside her chest and she wanted to curl up and climb into it, never come out.

'Where is he, Cass?'

She looked up.

'I should never have let you come back here. I knew, as soon as I heard. I knew you'd be in danger, but I told myself it was all over. He tried it when you were a child – did you know that? He tried to teach you things, but he *lost*, Cass. He lost. I got you both out.'

'*What?*'

'Cass, you have to understand – I thought I did the right thing, leaving you both, making your mother get out of Darnshaw. When I went into the church, I dedicated you to the Lord – do you remember that? I thought I was protecting you. I thought it was enough.'

Cass blinked. What did this have to do with leaving them behind? He had abandoned them – he didn't want them any longer because she wasn't good enough.

'I knew I'd have to face him again – how could I not? I vowed to fight him in all his forms, Cass. I thought if I went my own way, left you two out of it, you'd be safe.' Spittle flew from her father's mouth. 'I was wrong – such a bloody fool. Cass, I should have armed you better – I tried, I did try . . .

'What has he done, Cass?'

She tried to speak, found herself choking out the words. 'He took *everything*,' she said. 'I thought he was my friend. Daddy, please—'

'Aye, that would be right. He is the Father of Lies, Cass – did you listen to nothing I taught you? But Ben – he's nothing but a child, an innocent. He can't understand what he did.'

'No, no, he's free. Remick said so.'

'Remick, is it, now?' He paused. 'Right, we'll go, get you out of here, the pair of you. I'll come back on my own, once you're safe.'

She shook her head once more and he looked into her eyes and after a moment he got it. 'Cass – *Gloria*. No—'

She didn't need to answer. His face paled and he stepped back, leaned against the table, stayed that way for a long time. Then he bent to Cass and kissed her forehead. He strode from the room and she heard the front door bang behind him.

*   *   *

Ben came chasing into the kitchen, followed by Pete, who bent and caught the child, his bass laugh mingling with Ben's giggle. He looked up at Cass and his smile faded. 'Where's your dad? Cass, what's going on? I thought we were leaving.'

'He— There's something he had to do.' Cass' face twisted.

'What's up, love? There's something not right, isn't there? Are you going to tell me?' Pete bent and whispered to Ben, who ran from the room to set up his video game.

'There's somebody he needs to see. He had trouble with him when he used to live here, and now he's back.'

Pete stared. 'It's hard to see how anyone's caused trouble for him when he's not been here ten minutes . . . unless it's you that's in some sort of trouble. Cass?'

'It's complicated – you wouldn't understand, Pete. It's more my father's sort of thing.'

'What, a religious thing?' He snorted.

Cass stared at the floor.

Pete dragged out a chair, but he didn't sit. He stood with his hands resting on the back of it. 'So you come here to the middle of nowhere, and what – have some sort of conversion? Is that it?'

She shook her head.

'Then what does this have to do with your father? Who's he gone to see? Is it a man, Cass, is that what it is? Have you met someone?' He looked at her, his frank blue eyes preparing to feel pain.

'Sort of. Pete, I – I guess that's part of it. But it's more than that. He's not really a man, Pete, or not just a man. He – he's evil, that's all, and he made me do something.'

'What? Did he force himself on you?' Pete straightened. There was an expression in his eyes that was something like anger, but also something else, a little like hope. She couldn't bear to look at it.

'No, Pete, he didn't force me to do anything, but he did manipulate me. Pete, he took everything from me. He took my soul.'

Pete let out a snort and pushed the chair away and it rocked, almost fell. 'What? Cass, you're getting as mad as your father. You know that doesn't make any sense. You never believed in any of this stuff. I know things must have been hard, but—'

'It's true.'

'Did you sleep with him, is that it? And now you can't face up to it? Is that what this is about?'

She shook her head, but not in denial. 'Pete, that's not it. I mean, I did sleep with him, and I'm sorry: I thought you were gone. But Dad – he's trying to save my *soul*.'

Her husband looked away, staring around at the kitchen as though trying to memorise it. 'Where is this guy?' he asked quietly.

'He . . .' Cass realised she wasn't sure. 'The church, I think.'

'So he's like Satan, and he's in the church. Right? Right.'

'Pete, Dad's trying to help me. Please believe me. I was stupid, but I tried to do the right thing. It's just he had Ben, and—'

'He *what*?'

'He was Ben's teacher, or pretending to be. I don't know, it all sounds completely insane.'

'He had my son?' Pete's voice was quieter, more dangerous.

'Sort of. He—'

But Pete was already turning, heading for the door. 'I'll handle this,' he said and ran out, shutting the door in her face. Cass went after him, almost tripping over Ben as she rushed into the hall. Ben looked up at her, fright in his eyes, and she bent and hugged him. When she opened the front door and looked out, Pete had already gone.

Cass rested her hands on her boy's hunched shoulders. 'Sweetheart,' she said, 'there's something I need you to do.' She told him, and she told him again once she'd pulled on her shoes and grabbed the keys. 'Don't answer the door,' she repeated, 'not for anyone. Not for *anyone*.'

With that she kissed him and slipped out, listening for the *click* of the latch before heading away.

THIRTY-FOUR

Cass raced up the lane after her father and her husband, and only when she reached the top did she realise she could probably have taken the car; she simply hadn't thought of it. Stupid. *Not good enough.* She was starting to see her life through Pete's eyes and she didn't like the things she saw: the way she'd let Remick get a grip on her son.

We're your family, Sally had said to Ben, and when Cass thought of it her fists clenched.

Remick was just a man after all, she told herself: an odd, insular man with odder ideas who had carried a few bored locals along with him. She remembered Myra's smirk outside the school. It was clear that Cass wasn't the first he'd taken to his bed. Well, Cass was a fool, and that was all there was to it. She ran up the hill to the church, which towered over her head, blocking out the light.

The scrape of wood on flagstones was loud; she could feel the vibration through her fingers. She heard raised voices from inside. It was Pete. She caught '—can't do that.'

Her father was standing behind the altar, his arms raised as though delivering an impassioned sermon. Pete stood to one side, his head thrown back in contempt. There was no sign of Remick.

Cass' footsteps echoed from the walls as she walked down the aisle, like a bride in some twisted ceremony. A book lay open on the altar.

Her father held something over the book. Light flared in his hand – a burning match.

'You can't do that,' Pete said.

Cass wasn't sure he was aware of her until he flicked a glance in her direction. 'He's lost it, Cass,' he said. 'He'll burn the place down.'

She felt a stab of gratitude that he had spoken to her, but she couldn't answer. She knew what lay upon the table; she wondered if her father had seen her name written there, her name and Ben's.

Her father held the match to the book. It lit his face from below, distorting his features. Nothing happened – then a page caught, and a flame darted up. It hissed, faltered, grew stronger. A fragment of charred parchment floated up like some dark antithesis of snow. It settled in her father's hair and he knocked at it, leaving a charcoal smear on his forehead. Marking him.

Pete snorted.

Cass stepped forward, her eyes greedy to see it burn. The flame swelled, feeding on the fat pages. It hissed again and there was a smell like burning meat. The heart of the flame was blue.

After a while it began to die. The book had been reduced to a sooty mass. Only fragments remained.

'It's done, Cass,' her father said. 'You're free now.'

She stared into his eyes, hoping it could be true, and heard an echo of Remick's voice: *It's written on his skin too, is it not? In his heart. His eyes— Your destiny is written on you too.*

Remick was nothing but a madman; saying the words didn't make them true. Cass forced a smile, tried to make her heart lift.

'Come here,' her father said. He indicated a place before the altar.

Cass stepped forward and knelt where her father pointed. He placed a heavy hand on her head. She squeezed her eyes shut.

'I dedicate this child to the Lord.' His voice rang from the walls. 'Gloria, I name thee. Glorify his name, Gloria. Glorify him.' He pressed down on her head with each word. She bowed beneath the weight. It occurred to her that her father might be mad too; that everyone here had the same sickness growing inside them.

'Go in peace,' he said, and suddenly the pressure was gone.

Cass looked around, blinking.

Pete refused to meet her eyes. He would never see her the same way again, she knew that. She bit her lip. It didn't matter; she was free now, her father had said so. Her gaze blurred and she saw the colours behind her husband as though for the first time: brilliant colours in a monochrome world. A smile played on her lips and her eyes focused on the lapis blue of the Virgin's cloak, Remick's eyes looking back at her. She started, felt her father's hands pulling her to her feet. He was saying something about Ben, how it was over and she could ask him to come inside now. She looked at him.

The door slammed and Pete was striding back down the aisle, his face grim. He stopped in front of her. 'He's not outside,' he said. 'Where's Ben, Cass? Don't tell me you left him. Tell me you didn't leave him on his own.'

THIRTY-FIVE

They crowded around the door and Cass had to push her father aside before she could insert the key into the lock. She shoved the door open and for a moment she thought Ben was there, playing his computer games. She blinked and the lounge was empty.

'Ben,' Pete called, pushing past her. Her father followed. Cass didn't go in. She could already feel the emptiness in the apartment, an echoing, silent space. Ben wasn't there. Something cold nestled in her stomach. She backed away, listening to her father's voice, and Pete's. She could still hear them as she ran towards the stairs.

She went down and the light in the ground-floor hall flickered on, spilling over the carpet. The door to the apartment beneath hers was open, but she knew which way Ben had gone before she reached it. There was mud on the carpet, a child's footprints – not Ben's, though – larger than his.

The dust was trodden into a filthy paste that clung to her shoes. Scuffed footprints led to the window. It reminded her of the aisle in the church. She knelt. The doll was still there, stained with albumen. The boy doll was gone, taken, along with her son.

She looked about her. The place was already rotting. It had a pungent, almost fungal odour. She thought she heard an echo of young voices, children's voices. Laughter reverberated around the walls, and it was cold and cruel.

Sally's. If the boys had come for Ben, they would have taken him to Sally's.

She pushed herself up, her hands shaking. She turned to go and her foot struck something on the floor, something that hadn't been there before: black stones, rough things that stared up at her. She bent and touched them, snatched her fingers away. The stones had something red-brown and flaking on them. She knew she had seen them before, pressed into an old man's face.

It was a sign, a message. They hadn't taken her son to Sally's after all. She looked out of the window, seeing the white slopes rising all around. The moor. They had taken him to the frozen lake, the place where they left their dead.

THIRTY-SIX

Pete was silent as they followed the road out of Darnshaw. His face was pale, his mouth set into a hard line. Cass knew what he was thinking. How could she have left Ben alone? How could she have mixed with people who had done this? And most of all, how could she have seen the things she claimed up on the moor? She had been acting crazy herself, after all.

Maybe he was right. They would reach the witch stones and find only an empty white space, the wind breathing snow over everything. Of course they would find nothing. It was far more likely that Ben had gone to Sally's. He trusted her and her sly, silent son. Cass pressed her hands to her eyes. She had to find Ben. He would be there. He *had* to be there.

Her father was in the driver's seat, his jaw set, his eyes aglow. He believed he was going to find his grandson on the moor. He had to be right.

Cass pointed to the place and they pulled in close to the stile. She was out of the car in an instant, pulling the driver's door open and helping her father down. Pete was already looking over the wall. His breath came in clouds. The thaw hadn't even begun up here. The moor clung to the cold with reaching fingers of grass and heather.

There were tracks ahead of them, leading up through the snow. Cass' heart beat faster. She told herself they could be her own tracks, hers and Ben's; but surely there had been fresh snowfall since they'd last been on the moor?

As they started out Cass' father slipped and almost fell; he gestured for her to go on. Pete didn't look at her, just paused until Cass started off again.

As long as her son was safe, it didn't matter what anybody thought; not her father, not even her husband. Ben was all that mattered now.

Her father had burned the book, taken Cass back, and now Remick had taken her son. But she couldn't allow herself to think too much about Ben. The fear would get into her throat and limbs and chest and she would just stop; her mind would cease functioning. She thought of Sally and scowled. *Better.*

She looked up to the place where white hillside met pale sky. On the very tip of the rise was a black shape. Cass thought of the witch stones, but then it moved, disappearing over the hill: someone was watching them. Her heart beat faster. She wasn't insane. Ben was here, she could *feel* it. She looked at Pete to see if he'd noticed, but he had gone to some other place; she could see it in the set of his mouth, the far-off look in his eyes. He was probably thinking of his mad wife. His missing son.

*   *   *

The children were waiting for them by the witch stones, the boys from Ben's school, staring down with unblinking eyes. Damon stood with the rest.

A figure stepped forward. It was Remick. He smiled, holding out his hands in welcome.

Cass did not move. 'Where is he?' she asked.

'All in good time. Please, come.' Remick opened his arms wider, the expansive host, encompassing Pete and her father. 'Pete, isn't it? I've been looking forward to meeting you.' He extended a hand for Pete to shake. 'No? Never mind, you'll come round. I'm a lovely chap, really. You'll learn to love me.' His eyes flashed with humour.

'You,' said Pete.

'Me, indeed. Come.'

'It's you.' Pete stood motionless, his expression dazed.

Remick raised an eyebrow. 'I think we've established that.'

'You were in the bunker with us – you said we should sit tight, and then all hell broke loose.' Pete's eyes were distant.

'What a funny idea. Well, if you say so. Are you coming? Or had you forgotten I already have a guest waiting?'

Pete shook his head, rubbed his arm across his eyes. 'Where's my boy? What the hell gives you the right—?' He glanced at Cass.

'Your dear lady wife, of course. She trusted me implicitly with your son. I've rather enjoyed keeping an eye on your family while you were away.'

Pete started towards Remick, his eyes narrowed.

Cass' father reached out and grabbed his arm.

Remick smiled. 'Cass?' he said, holding out his hand. His palm was clean, unmarked. Cass looked down at her own, the red mark she bore. He beckoned.

'Her name's Gloria,' said her father. He stepped in front of her.

'Indeed,' Remick said. 'Is that the name she takes for herself, do you think? Well, no matter. Please, this way. Everybody's waiting. Now we can begin.'

Cass rushed past him towards the witch stones where the children were standing, their eyes fixed on her, but she paid them no heed. She didn't care what happened to them; she only cared about her son. She wanted to wrap him in her arms and take him far away from here, never to have to look into Remick's eyes again. She saw Sally, and beside her, holding her hand, was Ben.

'Ben,' Cass cried and ran to him—

She stared down in disbelief at the staring wide eyes of a young girl. What she'd taken for Ben's pale hair was the furred rim of a hood pulled down over Jessica's face. Strings of dark brown hair poked out.

Cass' mouth worked. She had forgotten— Of course she had to find Ben, but how could she have forgotten her friend's child? The little girl's eyes were wide with fright. Cass looked out across the snow and she wondered if even now Lucy's sightless eyes were looking back at her daughter. The white mounds were still there but they had been covered again, fresh snow packed into their cavities and over their hair, banishing the signs and scent of decay.

'I wouldn't get too attached,' called Remick.

Cass ignored him. A small shape emerged from the witch stones behind Jess. Ben's face was pinched, his eyes too bright. He held something in his hands.

'She's a problem for us, you see.'

Cass bent to her son, pulling him close, but he did not acknowledge her. 'We're going home, Ben,' Cass said firmly. Her eyes flicked to Jessica. She couldn't leave the girl here with Remick – who knew what he'd do to her? He would have already filled her ears with lies.

Her father moved to stand near her, between them and Remick, but it was Pete's voice that carried across the still air. 'It was *you*,' he repeated, his voice still disbelieving. 'You were there – only you said your name was Jackson. You liked sitting in the dark at night. You said you'd take the watch so you could see the sky come down.'

Remick spoke. 'I think you should step away from the boy, Cass, for your own safety.'

She turned her head, but she did not take her arms from Ben.

'As I said, young Jessica, sweet as she is, is something of a problem. A loose end, so to speak. Of course people are looking for her. Ever in their thoughts, hmm, Cass? I can't be bothered with keeping them out for ever. And I'm sure she'd prefer to be with her mummy.'

Cass started, but Jessica didn't move, other than a slight twitch of her mouth as if she was going to cry.

'Ben, however, is proving quite the disciple. It's all about free choice, you see, Cass. We are none of us anything if we are not free. There's the beauty, is it not? You've felt it, Cass. There is no freedom like that of throwing everything you have – everything you *are* – into the arms of another.'

Cass closed her eyes, felt Remick's breath on her skin and jerked away.

Remick smiled. 'So beautiful. Ben knows it, don't you, son? And there is something he has promised to do. Show her, Ben. Show Mummy what you came here to do.'

Ben shifted, stared at the ground.

'Ben.' Remick's voice was a command; it thrilled through Cass, jolting down and dissipating into the ground like electricity. Everyone around her jumped.

Remick spoke again, more softly, his voice comforting, but there was a hint of steel in it too. 'Remember what I said, Ben.'

Sally spun around and caught hold of Jessica's shoulders, her hands digging into the child's coat.

'It's time, Ben,' said Remick. 'I thirst. I hunger.'

Ben opened his hands and revealed the thing he held. It shone white, then dull grey and back to white as he twisted it. Cass reached out, but now Sally moved, grabbing her arm, blocking Cass with her body.

Ben stared down at the knife, his eyes dead.

'Ben, don't you *dare*. Put that down.' Cass planted her feet apart, tried to push Sally aside, but Remick's hand was on her shoulder. He didn't force her but she stopped anyway. He stroked her as though she were a pet.

'It's all right,' he said, and his voice was like a release. 'This is what must be. You're one of us now, Cass. Don't fight us.' He leaned in so that his breath warmed her neck. 'We love you. We know who you are, Cass. You're not a good mother, but we'll never take him from you. We'll never blame you. All we will do is support and help and love you, make you better than you are.'

Sally turned and her smile was beatific. She beamed her joy at Cass.

Remick's voice was low as he gestured at Pete. 'He'll take Ben from you. Why do you think I protected you from him, Cass? He'll break you, *destroy* you.' His voice deepened, became more like her father's. 'You fall short in his eyes. Don't let him hurt you, Cass. He never was any good for you. I am good for you – for you both.' He reached out and his fingertips brushed Ben's jacket. 'It's time.'

Ben raised the knife in one hand, holding it as he might a pen. He glanced at Remick, adjusted his grip, curled one hand around the other.

'Good boy. Good, Ben.'

Sally snatched Jessica up in her arms and carried her to the flat stone on the ground. The sacrificial stone. Jessica cried out, but she did not struggle; there was no point and she was exhausted, helpless.

'That's enough,' said Cass' father, but Remick held up a hand and her father stopped dead in his tracks, as though he had no choice.

'Cass,' he said calmly, 'I need you to hold Jessica down.'

Cass shook her head, horrified, but she stepped forward anyway – she couldn't help it. She was trapped in her body, watching what she was doing as though from a distance.

She heard Remick let out a hiss. 'I prefer free will, Cass, but I don't *need* it. Now, *hold her down*.'

Cass tried to turn, to look at her father and Pete, but she could not, and nor could she call out. Her muscles were moving, expanding and contracting, and she took a step towards the stone. *He could hold Jess down,* she thought, *probably is holding her down. He doesn't need me.*

Oh, but Ben does. She didn't think Remick had spoken out loud, but she heard the words in her ear. *And I so want you to do this for me, dear Cassandra.*

Cass found herself moving around the stone so that she faced Remick. To his side she could see her father, frozen in the attitude of stepping forward. Pete stood motionless too, still wearing that dazed expression; only his eyes moved to follow Cass as she crouched and put her hands on Jessica.

She thought of the girl's mother, half-buried in the snow and watching from her icy prison. She pushed the thought away and instead Captain came into her mind, the way the fleshy ridge of his lips had pulled away from his teeth. He had been *alive.* He had been in pain when they had spilled his bowels onto the ground.

She closed her eyes, and they opened again of their own volition.

Watch, Remick said in her ear. *Feel it. Taste it.*

For a moment it was him she tasted: the salt tang of his sweat on her tongue, the slipperiness of his skin.

She held Jessica down, feeling the girl's fragile bones through her padded coat, her skin and flesh; she could almost sense the hot blood racing through her veins and the rush of her heart as it pumped faster, as though it could outrun what was happening. Cass' teeth set in a grimace, almost a smile. Her head rose until she was looking at her son. She gestured to him, a curt nod. *Now.*

Ben shifted his grip on the knife, held it tight to his chest. He looked to his mother to tell him what to do. She tried to shake her head and found she could not.

'Well?' said Remick. Cass turned to him but he wasn't looking at her. He was watching Cass' father.

'All right,' her father said. 'Stop. Just stop.'

Cass found she could move her arms. She snatched them away from Jess and put out a hand to stop her son, though he hadn't moved, hadn't come any closer.

Remick reached into his jacket and took out a black object that fell open in his hands. It was a book. Cass recognised it, of course, though it was smaller than before. The cover was fine leather, the pages yellow. A book. *The* book – the one she had seen her father burn. She thought she saw fine specks of soot fly from the pages as he leafed through it, flicking each page over with contempt. 'Here,' he said, 'here's where you need to sign. Then I'll release your daughter.'

'And Ben.'

Remick rolled his eyes. 'If I've told you once! Ben is free already. Free will, isn't that so, Ben?' He winked. 'It will be his choice, one day, when he's ready. Of course, if I free your daughter, she can look after him, try to turn him.' He looked back at Cass' father, stroking his chin, his fingers rasping against the stubble. 'I dare say you could trust her. You do trust her, don't you?' His eyes flicked sidelong to Cass, and she looked away.

Remick tutted, as though irritated with himself,

rummaged in his coat and pulled out a long, slender pen. It had a cruel, sharp nib. 'Bring the knife, Ben. It appears it has another purpose after all.'

Ben did as he was told, and when Remick reached out his hand, he put the knife into it, then drew back.

Cass shook her head but her father reached out anyway and snatched the knife. He turned his back on them all and took a few steps away. He stared out over the rooftops of Darnshaw. They were dark now, the snow melted. His head swivelled towards the nearby white mounds.

From somewhere far distant Cass heard a dull, pained sound. She opened her mouth to say something, but somehow she didn't say it, just watched as her father turned towards them once more, a half-smile playing about his lips. He didn't look at Cass. 'Take care of him,' he said, and held out his hand.

Cass realised she could hear Remick breathing, his breath hissing in and out. Vapour rose into the sky. The pale arc above them looked impossibly distant and impossibly near; she could reach out and touch it. The hillside swayed beneath her. She closed her eyes. She couldn't speak. It was Remick, working his influence through the air between them and into her mind. Her hand – the one that bore Remick's sign – was clenched, the nails pressing into the skin. She remembered her father looking down into her face.

What had he said to her? *I should have armed you, Cass. I tried. I did try.*

And he had. He had done his best.

You do trust her, don't you?

'It's all a matter of faith.' Remick's voice rang out, and Cass opened her eyes. His eyes were flashing, mocking her father, whose head was bent now, staring at the knife in one hand, the open palm of the other.

'Come now: you do have faith, don't you?' Remick's voice lowered, became ugly. 'I've been watching you,' he said, 'ever since you forced her to bend her knees and gave her to *Him*. You think you can *dedicate* a life, do you? You think you could keep her from me?'

Her father's eyes flicked to Cass.

'I'm all about choice,' Remick said, and threw back his head and laughed. 'So make yours. Don't keep us all waiting.'

They stood in a circle – the boys, Sally, Cass, Ben, now standing with his father, with the sentinel stones and the white, buried figures – and watched.

'You're all free,' Remick called out, and his voice echoed back from the hillside. 'The only shackles are those you place on your own wrists. Be free. Follow me.' His eyes were clear and honest and his face shone with moisture. Cass realised he was crying. 'I love you,' he said, 'your beautiful freedom. You have no idea how much.'

Pete stepped forward, shaking his head as though waking from a dream, and Ben caught hold of his legs to hold him, and Pete's hand dropped to the boy's hair. Jessica sat up from the stone, her hood slipping and hair falling across her face. There was no sound, only the white silence.

Cass' father lifted the knife, rested the blade against his palm. He watched it intently, as though it might move of its own accord. His shoulders heaved. He looked up at Remick and the light in his eyes went out.

Remick smiled, and tears poured down his face. 'Welcome,' he whispered, 'old friend.'

A blur shot past Cass and she jerked back and slipped, went down. Pete charged at Remick, and the slighter man never saw him coming; he fell, Pete on top of him, his fingers spread wide as though to catch at the blue sky. The book landed on the snow and Cass' father blinked, his eyes clearing. He looked down at the knife in his hand and at Pete, who was crouched on top of Remick and punching hard.

Cass heard something, a long, slow creak, and she caught her breath and pushed herself to her feet. Remick drew back his own hand and punched Pete under the chin, and although the blow didn't look hard, Pete's head snapped back.

'*Pete—!*' Cass called. She didn't know if she was warning him or trying to stop him.

Her father started towards them, slipped and fell to his knees. This time the ice didn't groan, but gave a sharp splintering sound.

Remick raised an arm and pushed Pete off. He started to get to his feet, and his reaching hand found one of the snow-covered figures. He clawed at it, revealing a grey scalp with strands of hair still clinging.

Remick straightened, the smile returning to his lips as he wiped his hand on his coat and turned to Pete, who was transfixed, staring down at the body in the snow.

Remick's lips formed a word; he raised his hand, but

before he could speak, Cass' father crashed into him from the side and Remick flew into another of the mounds, which shattered, scattering pink-grey ropes of flesh.

The ice creaked again, a loud, pained sound that seemed to come from all around them. There was another distinct sharp crack.

Remick looked at Cass. His lips drew back, a secret smile just for her, and he bent, seized something from the snow – a frozen piece of intestine – and held it to his lips and licked it. There was ecstasy in his eyes.

Cass' father appeared behind Remick, the knife in his hand, then Pete was on them and they all went down together.

The ice shook and this time Cass *felt* it, a convulsive shudder. She saw her father stand, his legs spread, hands held out. Somehow he'd kept hold of the knife. He wasn't looking for Remick, though; he was looking around his feet, at the ice. The next instant they were all gone.

Cass watched her father as the ice swallowed him: he did not look afraid. He looked back at her with eyes that saw everything.

Sally's shriek pierced the air and Cass ran towards the hole in the ice. She felt like she was drowning, her lungs filling with snow. She had to reach her father; he had been about to save her, to give up everything he held precious to free her.

She threw herself down and slid towards the jagged hole, her hands grabbing for purchase on the slippery surface as she slid towards the water. She dug deeper, her nails tearing against the ice, and came to an abrupt

stop. Her hair hung down over the dark water and something rose to meet her; she cried out as she saw it was
her own reflection, slowly forming in the pool as the
surface calmed.

She stared into it, reaching out without touching it.
They were all in her mind: her father, Pete, Remick, and
she didn't know who she was reaching for, only that they
were gone, and that somewhere behind her, her son was
crying.

The ice vibrated under her as though someone had
struck it with their hand.

The surface erupted and a pale shape burst from it,
like destruction, like birth. Ice-water raked Cass' face, but
this time she did not pull back. There was something
dead in the water; she recognised the bloated shape of
Mrs Cambrey, her praying hands. Her eyes bulged at Cass.

Other shapes rose to the surface, their limbs stiffened
by ice and time. They surged and the water roiled as
something pushed them aside, something with hands
that flailed and clawed. A head broke the surface; Cass
couldn't see whose. It would be Remick, she knew it was
Remick, and warmth spread unbidden through her
stomach.

It was not Remick. Water streamed from the figure,
revealing pale hair plastered over a strongly formed skull,
broad hands reaching for her: a soldier's hands. It was
her husband. Pete's arms were wreathed with blue and
grey and hindered by damp tendrils. Cass reached out
and felt sodden wool beneath her fingers. It clung to him,
tangling his limbs. Cass clawed at it, almost lost it; then

she had it. As she started pulling, hard, she felt herself slip closer to the water.

Pete's hand came up, waving in front of her face, and he grabbed at the ice. Cass slithered towards him but still she kept pulling, fighting the urge to let his weight take her down too, deep down to where she wouldn't have to *remember*, wouldn't have to *think*.

Then his leg hooked onto the ice and Pete climbed out, his body shaking violently.

Cass looked down. She was holding Remick's scarf. Her fingers closed tightly over it. She heard Ben cry out, and turned to see Sally bent over her son, holding him fast, whispering in his ear. She held Jess with her other hand. Damon stood watching.

Cass pushed herself to her feet and threw the scarf back into the water. It hung on the surface as the dark seeped into it before it sank from sight.

Cass strode towards Sally. As she drew close she realised the woman's face was drained, her eyes unfocused with shock, but she did not pause until she had her hand on her son. 'Let him go,' she ordered. 'Let them both go.'

Sally's mouth twitched and her gaze flicked down to Cass' feet and up again.

Cass put her hand on Sally's, the one holding Ben. 'I said *let go*.'

Sally's lips twisted into a contemptuous smile. 'You were never worthy,' she said. 'I told him you were never worthy.'

Cass' eyes narrowed. 'He chose me over you, you bitch.'

She said it low, under her breath. 'Now take your hand off my son before I make you.'

Sally's smile never faltered as she pulled Ben back to her. Cass heard her child's breath catch in his throat and she let go of him and caught Sally round the neck. She felt cartilage under her hands and she gripped tight until Sally jerked away, her breath rasping; but still she held onto Ben.

Jessica pulled away, and Damon stepped towards them.

Sally bent low over Ben, shielding him with her shoulder as Cass grabbed hold of her again: a loving family sharing an embrace. Ben gave a muffled cry and Sally muttered something; Cass heard, 'He's mine.'

Cass let go of Sally's sleeve and instead grabbed her hair; Sally's head whipped round. Cass gathered herself, threw her head forward and down and felt Sally's nose smash against her skull. Pain shot through the top of her head, migraine-bright, and she slipped and almost went down. Hair blinded her and she tossed it back to find herself still standing and Ben, free now, clinging to her.

Sally was on the ground, her bloody nose and lips bright against the snow. She wiped at it, smearing it across her face. She started to push herself up, saw Cass' expression and stopped.

Cass turned to Damon. The boy's eyes were inscrutable. He was ignoring Jess now, instead moving to stand behind her son, and as she watched he reached into his pocket and drew out a switchblade. The knife shot out with a metallic *snick* that carried across the hillside.

She felt a hand on her shoulder and Pete was there,

bent over and breathing hard. Then he straightened. 'Do you want to try that on a trained soldier, kid?' His voice was laced with amusement, but his eyes were steel.

They waited. Wind soughed across the ice.

Pete let out a low snort and took his eyes from Damon. He shielded them and glanced at his watch. 'Come on, son,' he said. 'Time we were gone.' His shoulders shook, but it was from cold, not fear. His voice never faltered.

In a second Ben had slipped his hand into Cass'. She squeezed it.

Damon let the hand holding the knife fall to his side. His arm twitched, the point of the blade plucking at his trousers. He too looked away. He saw his mother lying on the ground, her face blood-smeared, and the contempt he had for her was clear in his eyes.

For a fleeting second Cass felt pity for her; then it was gone. 'Come on, Jess,' she said, holding out a hand. 'Quickly, Ben. We need to get warm. We're going home.'

'No,' said Pete, and now his voice quavered and his teeth chattered. 'We'll go to the mill first, Cass, get your things, and *then* we'll go home.'

THIRTY-SEVEN

They stopped only once after Pete had showered, staying a long time under the hot water, and they had packed their things and loaded them into her father's 4x4. They talked about Jessica; they couldn't take her home, but when Cass asked the child if she wanted to go with them, she looked alarmed and said, 'Auntie Winthrop – I want Auntie Winthrop,' and she pointed towards the road.

Winthrop – the village butchers. Remick told her the Winthrops were *a waste of time*, and Cass remembered the look on his face as he'd said it – so that meant they were safe.

The shop was closed, but Jessica directed them to one of the cottages near the school, and her aunt welcomed Jess inside, exclaiming not in relief but surprise. Cass realised she hadn't known Jessica was missing – didn't realise Lucy was missing either – and she felt a pang for her friend.

Mrs Winthrop looked up at Cass, her eyes full of confusion.

'I think she's hungry,' Cass said, 'and cold, too.'

And with that the child was bustled inside.

Cass walked away. Later there would be questions, the police, certainly. Jessica might tell them about the witch stones and the people who fell in the water and the boy with the knife, but she probably wouldn't be coherent. Cass inwardly kicked herself for hoping she wouldn't be. As long as Jessica and Ben were safe, it didn't matter what came after. She hoped the girl hadn't seen the bodies that had risen from the black water, nor recognised the mutilated thing that had once been her mother.

THIRTY-EIGHT

Pete drove them away, nosing the car carefully around the bends that wound up the hillside. Cass looked back to see Darnshaw dropping behind them, too slowly. She opened her mouth to offer directions and found herself remembering another journey on another day, Sally prompting her to turn here and watch for this corner. She bit the words back.

She didn't see when they passed the Broaths' farm and the stile leading onto the hillside path; she didn't look up again until they were on the road that crossed the moor, high above the village.

He'll take Ben from you.

It was as though Remick was whispering the words in her ear.

You're gone, Cass thought, and yet her skin had that shrinking, creeping feeling she had felt after he had touched her, after he had slipped his tongue into her, explored her, *possessed* her. She looked down and the scar across her palm throbbed. She opened and closed her hand. The red line appeared, was hidden, appeared once more.

'You all right, love?'

Fuck you: you're gone, and your book with you.

She could still hear Remick's voice at her ear, feel his name written on her heart.

Ben stirred and she heard his sigh from the back, the soft thumping as he drummed his heels against his seat.

I don't suppose the lad'll leave now.

Cass straightened. She could see the witch stones inside her mind, there to keep bad spirits out – or keep them in; she was no longer sure which. She only knew she had tried to go past them twice. *Twice.* She had sat with the stones at her back, leaning against them with the sun in her eyes, and she hadn't got out of Darnshaw. But now she was leaving, and there was nothing to stop her.

He'll take Ben from you.

No, she was leaving with her husband, taking her son. This was where she belonged. Here, in this car, heading down the road and away—

'Are you sure you're all right?'

She opened her eyes and found Pete looking at her. He had stopped the car at the side of the road, and Cass didn't need to look to know where they were. Her hand went to the car door and she pulled the handle and then she was out in the clean air, looking down at the witch stones.

It seemed so long since she'd last been in this place.

She felt sure this was where Sally had stumbled out of the fog, waving for help, not far from where the road itself had tried to repel them from what lay ahead in Darnshaw.

The thaw had set in. On the moor she could see patches of tawny bracken and the green-black of wet heather. From this vantage point Cass could see it clearly for the first time. Her skin had that feeling she'd once known, after Remick touched her. The fires that ran along her nerves, the chill as he reached inside and touched her heart. She shuddered. The scar across her palm throbbed. She closed it into a fist and clenched it so tight she expected blood to squeeze out and drip onto the wet grass.

You're gone, and your book with you.

The witch stones had lost their presence. Now they blended into the hillside beside a lake that was clearly outlined by lingering ice, a flat white area with a hole in it as grey as the sky. Cass wondered if it would keep its secrets. Her father was down there, in the cold dark. She wondered if his eyes were open.

She felt Pete's hand on her shoulder.

He was always bad for you.

She shook him off.

'Cass?' His voice came from a long way away.

Her father had been right. Her father was always right. He had been about to save her, to offer himself in her place, and Pete had stopped him.

'Cass?'

She turned her hand over, looked once more at the

palm. The scar was already paler than it had been, merging with the lines and whorls in her skin. 'I don't know if he's gone,' she said. 'I don't feel like he is.'

Pete put his hand on the back of her neck. 'I'm so sorry, Cass. Your father was a good man. I'm sorry he's gone. It'll get easier, in time.'

Cass turned to face him and tried to hide the contempt in her eyes. Had he really thought she was talking about her father? He didn't understand – he could never understand, not without the years of words in his ears, the imprecations, the lessons, Bible readings, Sundays spent with his back resting against a hard pew.

The heavy hand pressing down on her forehead, all of her life.

'Do you think I'm free?' she asked, and her voice was loud. 'Do you think my soul is free, Pete?'

It was only half meant as a question, but he licked his lips and answered, 'He's dead, Cass. Him and his book, they're gone. Whatever it is you think you did, whatever you *gave* him, it doesn't matter.'

Whatever you gave him. There was an undertone in Pete's voice when he said that, and Cass knew what he was referring to. The pain in her husband's eyes was jealousy. He was already starting to remember all the wrong things for all the wrong reasons.

He'll take Ben from you.

Her father had been right: Pete was bad for her. Her father had always been right, except about one thing. Cass turned her palm, watching the scar twist, remembering her father leaning over her filthy dress, weighing her in the balance. She always believed she had fallen short in his eyes, and the truth was that she should have. But he had trusted her then. He had thought she would be strong enough.

'Come on,' she said, touching Pete's arm. 'Let's go.'

He's dead. It doesn't matter now.

Pete gunned the engine, eased them back onto the road. Soon they would be in another town, another place. Ben would have other friends to play with. He would forget. Maybe he should forget.

Or maybe Cass should make him remember, so that should Remick ever come back, her son would be ready. She glanced at Pete. His jaw was set, though he still had that sadness in his eyes. And she had put it there.

But she couldn't think about him; she could only think about herself and Ben.

Pete turned to meet her gaze and his eyes clouded. Cass forced herself to smile. He mustn't know what she was thinking. He might try to change her, try to stop her.

He'll take Ben from you.

No. No, he would not.

Cass knew that he could not; whatever happened, they were going to be a family again. She smoothed her top down over her stomach, moving the seatbelt a little to the side, and thought about her and Pete, and Ben in the back, and their luggage, all being pulled together over the moors, the way they had come. She thought about the thing that rested on top of her clothes in the holdall she had carefully placed on top of their bags. The thing she had found on their return to Foxdene Mill.

Pete had been in the shower, trying to warm up. Ben had been packing his things. So Cass was alone when she entered her bedroom and saw it lying on her bed. She went to it without switching on the light and picked it up.

It was a doll, but not chewed and filthy and marked as the other had been; this was a new doll, made of pale cotton, with clean yellow wool for hair. Its eyes were buttons, the same clear blue as the sky. The loose-fitting dress was patterned with the buds of little flowers; it fastened with clips at the shoulders and finished at the knees. In the middle it pushed outwards in a rounded bulge.

Cass ran her fingertip over the mound, felt the warmth that nestled there. She did not need to lift the dress to see the blue-grey egg within.

This time she had not thrown it away or smashed it. Instead she filled a bag with her softest, warmest clothes and set the doll on top. She watched it while they packed the car and carried it herself, a precious load, packed it on top of everything else so that it would have a safe journey.

It was hers, and no one could take it away from her; not Pete, not Remick.

Cass had no doubt that one day Remick would come back to her, his lips, so cruel yet so sweet, stretched in a smile. His hands, which knew her every curve, spread in welcome, fingers that knew how she liked to be touched. Her skin warmed at the thought of him. She was no longer repulsed: she *belonged* to him, and in that there was freedom, of a kind.

Cass shook herself, sat up straighter; smiled when Pete glanced at her, his eyes so hurt and so stupid.

She could fight Remick. This child was a gift, something to bargain with, to buy back her soul, if she could. Remick would come to find Cass, only to discover Gloria waiting for him.

Weariness overcame her. *A child is not a bargaining tool*, she thought. *A father is not a sacrifice. And you can only ever offer yourself.* She belonged to him. She knew it now, could feel it rising within her, and knew she could never go back. Her body still craved him, would never respond as it once had to the stranger who sat beside her.

Remick had asked Pete if he could trust Cass to take care of her son. And he could, just not in the way he thought, or that Cass' father had before him. No one could be looked after for ever; there would come a time when everyone had to make their own choice.

Cass would just have to help Ben to make the right one, to make sure that he was ready when the head of the family came home. Because he would come home, one day.

And they would be together.

In the meantime there was his gift. Cass smoothed a hand over her stomach, as though she could already feel it stretching and changing to accommodate the one within; her skin growing round and pale like a smooth, unblemished egg.

Cass rested her head back, smiled, and with one hand still on the warmth of her belly, turned her head and watched the moorland slip by.

ACKNOWLEDGEMENTS

Heartfelt thanks to Jo Fletcher, to Nicola Budd and the whole team at Jo Fletcher Books and Quercus, for making this book a reality.

Also, special thanks to the team at *Black Static* magazine: Andy Cox, Peter Tennant, and Roy Gray – for making the introduction to Jo.

I would also like to thank everyone who has helped me along the way, by publishing my short stories or otherwise encouraging me onward (with apologies to anyone I've left out!) – in particular David McWilliam and Glyn Morgan of Twisted Tales Events, Simon Marshall-Jones of Spectral Press, Michael Kelly, Claire Massey, Stephen Theaker, Allyson Bird, Joel Lane, Marie O'Regan, Paul Kane, Simon Bestwick, Gary McMahon, Stephen Volk, Rob Shearman, Ellen Datlow, Steve Upham, David Tallerman, John Benson, Stephen Clark, Sharon Ring, Gary Fry, Graham Joyce and Stephen Firth. Thanks also to web guru Wayne McManus.

Last but not least, I would like to thank my Mum, Dad, Ian, and of course Fergus – for everything.

Exclusive Bonus Content

RICHARD AND JUDY

Galaxy

BOOK CLUB

2012

EXCLUSIVE TO
WHSmith

RICHARD AND JUDY
ASK ALISON LITTLEWOOD

1) We loved the claustrophobic, isolated little community you create. Do you know Saddleworth Moor? Was it the landscape that inspired you to write this very spooky story?

The landscape was definitely a major inspiration for *A Cold Season*. I spent several years travelling between West Yorkshire and Saddleworth for my job, and a good part of the drive was the narrow, isolated road that runs across the moors between Holmfirth and Greenfield. Cass starts out her journey in dense fog, and I've done that so many times . . . it's a strange experience, as the car feels like an island amid all the whiteness. It's like nothing else is there – it's eerie, and I often wondered what would happen if I broke down halfway across.

The villages in A Cold Season are fictional, but I definitely imagine Darnshaw as being at one end of that road and Moorfoot at the other. If there's a real place it's closest to in terms of positioning and layout it would be Greenfield village, but with the actual places within it – the houses, church, school and so on – all invented. Sadly the witch stones are invented too – though it would be nice, wouldn't it!

Foxdene Mill is in part also based on somewhere I used to live, which wasn't in Saddleworth but not all that far away. We were among the first people to move in, with building work still on-going, and those things found their way into the book too.

When I look back on that time in Saddleworth I think I always had a sense that I was a long way from home, which,

I suppose, I was! It was emphasised by the way the steep hills seemed to rise all around the area – it naturally lent itself to a feeling of being cut off, but getting in or out in the snow became a whole other adventure. There were steep, narrow roads whichever way I headed out, and there was more than one occasion where I thought I'd have to give up and go back. The winter just before I started writing the novel was particularly bad (though very beautiful!) with ten-foot drifts by the side of some of the roads. Trying to manage it without a car and a small child in tow, as Cass did . . . that would be something else entirely!

2) Although this is never explicitly stated, there are definite suggestions throughout the book that this strange Satanic cult in Darnshaw has vampiric elements. For example the drink Ben has at Sally's, which he tells his mother is disgusting, and the fact that Damon says he will only drink Ribena. Do you see this as part of Mr Remick's evil little cult?

Funnily enough I do see it as part of the cult, but only clearly in retrospect. I was hardly conscious of those parts of it while I was writing – but yes, they do put in a regular appearance. Ben quite often mentions 'sharing', and comes home with a stain on his top that he claims to be Ribena but quite probably isn't. It's all a part of fixing things in his mind – of making him part of the 'family'. The fact that he's a child unable to make his own informed choices and that these things are done when he's away from the protection of his mother make it more insidious.

There's a sense that the blood elements (and the sexual ones, come to that) are a way of binding the deal with the body as well as the mind. Mr Remick likes to possess those around him as thoroughly as he is able. And of course he is rather fond of a sacrifice – not just in its own right, but as a way of destroying the innocence of the one doing the sacrificing.

There are parallels, too, with Christian rites of communion – the body and the blood. Remick would particularly enjoy his warped version for that reason too.

3) Who do you enjoy reading? Stephen King? Any other inspirations?

I do love Stephen King's work – his books are amazing. They draw you straight in, and his characters are so believable you feel every nuance of fear alongside them. And he isn't perhaps best known for his use of language, but some of his work contains the most amazing metaphors – wonderful. His book about the craft – *On Writing* – also helped give me the impetus to start writing myself!

I also adore Neil Gaiman's novels. His stories are rich and strange and beautiful, and you can't say fairer than that. There's a sense of layers and layers of belief and magic and *possibility* underneath everything.

Joe Hill's books are always creepy and gripping, and *Horns* is incredibly inventive. Graham Joyce is fantastic – his characterisation is second to none. I love *The Tooth Fairy* and *The Silent Land*. John Ajvide Lindqvist is another whose characters are never less than 100 per cent believable and when violence and horror breaks through the surface it seems all the more shocking. I haven't read *Wolf Hall* yet, but I've admired everything I've read by Hilary Mantel – she's a clever, clever writer.

For sheer fun, it's great when you sit down and read a book that gives you a sense of the author having an absolute blast. Rob Shearman's short stories always feel like that. In a completely different way, Derek Landy's *Skulduggery* books are like that too – they're a real treat to read. There are bits where I can practically picture the author grinning and rubbing his hands together with glee!

I didn't grow up reading just one genre – I loved books from being a young child, when I adored Hans Christian Andersen's fairy tales, and read everything I could get my hands on. I loved *Oscar and Lucinda* by Peter Carey – heartbreaking. And Rohinton Mistry's *A Fine Balance* made me feel like I'd been looking through a little window into real people's lives rather than reading a book. It's incredible (and I do love a book that can make me cry).

My ultimate favourite book is *The Road* by Cormac McCarthy – it's astoundingly well written.

4) There are definite echoes of *The Wicker Man* in your novel. The sexual nature of the cult, and the outsider whom they try to seduce, and then must destroy because they fail. Is this intentional?

Film was an influence when I was writing the novel, but I didn't specifically have *The Wicker Man* in mind – not consciously, anyway! When I was deciding on the storyline there seemed to have been a whole wave of scary films featuring children, such as *The Children* and *The Orphan*. There's something particularly terrifying when children, who are supposed to be innocent, start to seem deliberately evil and *knowing* . . . brrr. I found that really creepy, and I wanted to include things in the novel that I personally found frightening.

I can see the similarities with *The Wicker Man*, though, particularly with Cass being the outsider in an isolated community. The inability to get out and not knowing who to trust became key elements in the story – it provides the opportunity for those around her to manipulate her. She just doesn't know whom to turn to for help, and having a traumatised child thrown into the mix makes both mother and child even more vulnerable.

We have a tendency to think that help is always going to be within reach – when nature takes over, though, it's frightening how quickly the options can be removed. That sense of isolation is essential in *A Cold Season* too – another thing I find scary that found its way into the book!

5) What do you think will happen to Cass, Ben, and Pete? Will Remick (Satan) come back to claim Cass? Has her soul been completely corrupted forever?

You know, I'm not sure . . . maybe I should write the book, and find out! One thing I am certain about is that Remick isn't gone for good – I'm definitely with Cass on that. If he's been defeated at this point it's because, in part, he allowed himself to be – because it was the right time to bow out and see what everybody does next. He's been around for a long time – I imagine he'll be off to cause trouble somewhere else for a while, but he always does seem to be drawn back to Darnshaw!

The question of what will happen to Cass is a tough one, because there's a danger that her love for her family could lead her to try and corrupt them, to keep them together. The priority she set out with at the start of the story, to look after Ben, is the one she still clings to at the end. Up until now it's been taken and twisted and made part of her downfall, and of course it's still twisted . . . but who knows? It might become the thing that saves her. She's ultimately selfless, with her main drive being her love for Ben, which gives me some hope that she'll find a way through.

She's going to struggle with Pete's level-headedness, though – he's not one for belief in the supernatural, and there are hints that eventually he's going to try and take Ben from his wife. I wouldn't like to be in his shoes if he tries it. Cass may have started out feeling like a little girl lost, but the more she's been pushed, the more determination she's developed. There's more of that in her yet, I think.

And Ben . . . well, he has his own decision to make, one day. And he's been lied to and cheated and used – he's a confused child, but when he's older and straightens things out in his mind, I'm not sure he's going to be so easy to manipulate. I have the distinct feeling there's a fine young man in the making, there. When Cass was younger she had a very religious upbringing, and that didn't really stick, either . . .

A BRIEF CHAT WITH ALISON LITTLEWOOD

I've always loved reading, and was a very bookish child – I remember being taken to the library every week and turned loose on a new adventure! Since then I've read a lot of books in a lot of genres, but some of the earliest influences still run deepest. I loved fairy tales when I was little – I can still remember crying over Hans Christian Andersen's *The Little Mermaid*. That influence still lingers in my love of the folkloric in fiction, and stories with an echo of the dark in them – because some fairy tales are very, very dark indeed.

Those things are the reason I love Neil Gaiman's work, too. His use of mythology deepens his stories and gives a sense of the rich and strange lurking beneath the everyday. His novels *Neverwhere*, *Anansi Boys* and *American Gods* are superb. I like that his heroes are ordinary people thrown into extraordinary situations and that the action is rooted in this world, albeit versions of it that are slightly askew – I love the sense that the magical and fantastical can happen, but tend to find it more powerful when it's firmly rooted in reality.

I suppose that's also one of the reasons why I wanted to write a novel that was set in a place I knew, or at least a fictional version of it. Books like *Song of Kali* by Dan Simmons or *Harbour* by John Ajvide Lindqvist are very different, but each has shown me that a specific sense of place can be a powerful thing (and I love reading books that take me somewhere new).

Finally, I do love books that can grip me and not let go until they're good and ready. Stephen King's novels have that in spades – it always amazes me that he can write books that pretty much have only a single character most of the way through, like *Gerald's Game* or *The Girl Who Loved Tom Gordon*, but they never lapse for a minute – it's impossible to put them down. That's an incredibly clever thing to do.

Download our FREE podcast

Find out why we love 'A Cold Season' and listen to Alison Littlewood's inspiration behind her book.

Download a free QR reader app to your smart phone, scan this code and listen to the podcast to discover more about 'A Cold Season'. Or visit http://lstn.at/acoldseason

Available from 7 January 2012

Read the first chapter of your next Richard and Judy Book Club 2012 title for free*

Get the chapter sent to your mobile phone by texting the keyword to the number below the featured title.

Text DEAR to 60300

Text WINTER to 60300

Text JOJO to 60300

Text GIRL to 60300

Text SUN to 60300

Text SLEEP to 60300

Text PARIS to 60300

RICHARD AND JUDY *Galaxy* BOOK CLUB 2012 EXCLUSIVE TO WHSmith